THE GOLDSMITH'S CONSPIRACY

GLASS AND STEELE, #13

C.J. ARCHER

WWW.CJARCHER.COM

CHAPTER 1

LONDON, SPRING 1891

I'd been worried about having Aunt Letitia's friend and her niece for dinner ever since sending out the invitation a few days ago. After all, Lady Sloane was the widow of an earl, the daughter of a marquess, and a friend to Matt's rather snobbish aunt. If they were anything alike, Lady Sloane would spend the entire evening with her nose wrinkled and her lips pinched as banter ricocheted around the room like bullets.

But I needn't have been concerned. Willie, Duke and Cyclops didn't rile one another like they usually did; they were all on their best behavior. In Cyclops's case, I suspected it was due to the presence of Catherine Mason, his fiancée. Willie was too intrigued by Lady Sloane's niece to pay Duke any attention, which explained why he resorted to an observational role. It helped enormously that Lady Sloane took our eclectic group in her stride. She wasn't a snob at all. Indeed, she was rather captivated by Gabe Seaford, our doctor friend, who'd joined us with his fiancée, Miss O'Dwyer. By the time the fourth course was served, she'd agreed to a tour of the Belgrave Hospital for Children where he worked. From the pleased look on Gabe's face, I suspected he planned to ask her to contribute to the hospital's refurbishment fund. Matt had already agreed to donate a substantial sum earlier.

With conversations flowing easily, I wasn't called upon to fill any awkward silences, something for which I was thankful. I wasn't very good at idle chatter. Without any particular responsibility as a hostess, I was able to freely observe my guests, which proved a fascinating study. Lady Sloane's niece, Lady Helen, had quickly become enamored with Lord Farnsworth and Willie. She'd been seated beside Lord Farnsworth because they were both unwed nobility of marriageable age and the entire purpose of the dinner was to introduce them.

Aunt Letitia had insisted Willie sit on Lady Helen's other side, even though that meant having two women next to each other, something which I thought Aunt Letitia would abhor. But now, watching the two of them together, I considered it a master stroke in seating arrangements. Lady Helen and Willie might be from different worlds, but they were cut from the same cloth.

"You're so fortunate to have traveled, Miss Johnson," Lady Helen gushed. "The furthest I've been is Paris. My aunt promised to take me mountaineering in the Alps last summer, but our plans fell through."

"You could go this year instead," Willie said.

"Every time I mention it, she changes the topic." Lady Helen stabbed her fork into the gratin potato with vigor while glaring across the table at her aunt, seated opposite.

Lady Helen was a tall woman of about twenty with broad shoulders that were emphasized by the wide neckline of her bodice and clouds of blush-pink tulle attached to the tops of the sleeves. The spray of freckles across an equine nose stopped her from being conventionally pretty, but there was something compelling about her that I couldn't quite put my finger on. Clearly both Lord Farnsworth and Willie thought so too, because they seemed enthralled.

"You are quite the adventuress," Lord Farnsworth declared.

"Unfortunately not, my lord," Lady Helen said. "But I

would like to be. Visiting exotic lands, meeting new people and seeing things that few ladies ever see, that is my dream."

"You don't wish to settle down with a husband?"

"One day, yes, but not yet."

"Excellent, excellent." He picked up his wine glass, tossed her a cavalier smile, and sipped. I suspected he liked the sound of settling down "one day." He wasn't ready yet either, so he'd recently told me.

Lady Helen's gaze slid to her aunt, who'd been surreptitiously watching the interaction between her niece and Lord Farnsworth. So had Aunt Letitia. The two friends seemed keen for the couple to make a match.

On paper they were well suited. Both were wealthy and titled. But I suspected that was where the similarity ended. Lord Farnsworth was all froth and one had to dig very deep to unearth the substance. Sometimes I wasn't sure there was any substance to unearth. Lady Helen, however, seemed to be overflowing with it. She was certainly interesting.

"Do you like horses?" Lord Farnsworth asked her.

"Oh yes, I ride all the time at home."

"What about the races?"

"I've been to Ascot, of course, but I prefer to ride horses myself than watch others from the sidelines. It's so invigorating. Liberating too. I'm allowed to ride around the estate without a chaperone. Speaking of riding, have either of you ridden a bicycle?"

Lord Farnsworth snorted a laugh but tried to cover it up with a cough when he realized she was serious.

"I reckon it would be fun," Willie said.

"It is. There's a man in the nearby village who owns one. I convinced him to let me ride it, twice. I fell off the first time, but in my defense, I was quite unprepared. I wore the wrong clothes."

Willie gave a knowing nod. "Skirts got in the way?"

"They did. I borrowed a pair of my brother's riding breeches for my second turn. I didn't fall off once, not even when I steered the vehicle onto Trenton's Hill—which I did by design, you understand. Level ground is so dull, I find."

Willie raised her glass in salute. "Here's to hills and bumps."

Lady Helen indicated Willie's clothing. Dressed in trousers, stiff shirt, waistcoat, bowtie and jacket, Willie's attire had raised eyebrows when our guests arrived, but I was grateful she'd chosen to wear evening clothes and not her usual cowboy buckskins. "Men's clothes are so much more comfortable than ours, don't you find, Miss Johnson?"

"Aye, and more practical. Last time I wore a dress, I got kidnapped."

Lord Farnsworth scoffed. "There was no connection between the abduction and you wearing a dress."

"There was. If I'd been wearing trousers they would have thought me a man and not bothered. Most folk make the mistake of thinking women won't fight back."

Duke pointed his knife at her, proving he was listening in. "*You* didn't fight back hard enough or they wouldn't have successfully kidnapped you."

"I was caught by surprise," she told Lady Helen. "But I shot at them first chance I got and escaped."

Lady Helen's eyes widened. "How thrilling. Do you own a gun?"

Willie straightened and squared her shoulders. "Yes, ma'am, I do. My Colt revolver's a nice piece. Want to see it?"

"Yes, please, but perhaps not tonight." She cast a warning glance at her aunt.

"Tomorrow," Lord Farnsworth declared. "Call on us here. Have your maid chaperone you. We can easily circumvent her, can't we, Willie?"

"Aye, we can." Willie winked at Lady Helen.

Lady Helen smiled. "I think I'm going to become firm friends with both of you."

Lord Farnsworth returned her smile somewhat shyly. "I do hope so."

When the ladies retreated to the drawing room after

dinner, Willie joined us instead of remaining behind to smoke and drink with the gentlemen as she usually did. She and Lady Helen fell into conversation about the American west, while Miss O'Dwyer, Aunt Letitia and Lady Sloane chatted on the sofa. It gave me an opportunity to speak quietly to Catherine.

"How are the wedding plans coming along?" I asked.

"Very well indeed. My mother is throwing herself into making my dress with great enthusiasm." She smiled into her glass of sherry. "It makes a nice change to her earlier reticence."

Ever since Cyclops had saved Catherine's rambunctious younger brother from getting into trouble with some wayward youths, Mr. and Mrs. Mason had taken a liking to him. They now saw him as someone capable of protecting their only daughter rather than someone who would make her life more difficult. Their acceptance meant the world to Cyclops, but I knew Catherine would have run off with him if her parents had never come around. She had an adventurous streak too, although it wasn't quite as wild as Willie's and Lady Helen's.

"Did he tell you we're going to move into the residence above the shop?" she asked.

The shop and rooms above it had once been my home, before my father died. I'd almost lost it when my former fiancé inherited it instead of me, but his illegal actions had seen ownership revert to me. The rental income now went to my grandfather for the remainder of his life.

"Does your brother mind you both living with him?" I asked.

"It was his idea. It'll only be temporary, until we find something more permanent of our own."

"You are very welcome to stay here. This has been Cyclops's home for a while now so it's only natural it should be yours too."

She gave me a warm smile. "That's kind of you, but it's rather crowded here, and I think I prefer to be mistress of my own house. Isn't Nate moving into the police station residence until we're married, though?"

"He was going to, but we talked him out of it today. Didn't he tell you?"

"Not yet, but I've hardly spoken to him since I arrived. It doesn't surprise me he decided against the idea. Why would he want to move in with bachelor policemen when he can live in comfort here and have excellent meals?" She nudged my elbow. "He's going to miss Mrs. Potter's cooking when we're married."

"She'll give you some of his favorite recipes."

She closed her hand over mine. "Thank you for talking him out of moving into the policemen's quarters, India. I was worried it would mean he'd be given more night shifts, and with the way the city is at the moment..." She heaved a sigh.

The situation was volatile of late, and I'd been worried about Cyclops too. As a police constable, he was at the forefront whenever law enforcement was called to a fight between the artless and magicians. Most of the disturbances were started by members of the various craft guilds, spurred on by Mr. Abercrombie, the former master of the Watchmaker's Guild, but sometimes the magicians were to blame. A small number taunted their artless counterparts with accusations of inferior craftsmanship, drawing them into retaliation.

I rarely went out anymore, and when I did, Matt insisted on coming with me. Shopping had lost its appeal and walks in the park had become an exercise in keeping to myself. While few artless or magicians knew my face, many had come to know my name. Once they heard it, I was either followed or hounded. Magicians wanted me to extend their magic, and the artless wanted me to encourage other magicians to retreat back into hiding. Both sides saw me as some sort of leader when I was far from it.

When the men rejoined us, the noise level rose a little, but I didn't mind. Indeed, I welcomed their company. My mood dampened a little toward the end of the evening, however, when Gabe Seaford joined me for a quiet conversation out of the earshot of others. He looked troubled, and when Gabe was troubled, so was I.

It could be said that he was the most important person in our lives. Without him, Matt would not be alive. He'd saved Matt by speaking the healing spell into his watch while I spoke the extension spell to ensure the medical magic lasted longer. We didn't know how long the healing magic would last this time, but we knew when it faded again that Matt needed Gabe's magic or he'd die. I was determined to stay within a day's journey of Gabe until we were comfortably in our old age.

"I think I ought to tell you that I've been to see Mr. Steele a number of times in the last few weeks," he said as he settled beside me on the sofa.

"Do you mean in your capacity as a doctor?" I asked.

He nodded.

I clicked my tongue. "Chronos should see a general practitioner if he's feeling unwell, not you. You're far too busy at the hospital to be bothered with house calls."

"I don't mind. We talk about magic, which I don't have the opportunity to do very often. I've learned a great deal about it through him."

Gabe had not known he was a doctor magician until he met us last year. Having never known the father from whom he'd inherited his rare gift, he'd had to use instinct when it came to reciting his life-saving spell.

"I'm sure that's why he enjoys your company too," I said. "Chronos lives and breathes magic, and he'll take any opportunity to talk about it."

Gabe's warm eyes dulled and he looked down at his hands resting in his lap.

"Something's the matter, isn't it? Of course it is or you wouldn't be visiting him." My heart tripped over itself as I searched Gabe's face for answers.

"He's ill."

"How ill?"

"It's impossible to say. His stomach complaint isn't improving—"

"Stomach complaint? I thought it was indigestion."

He shook his head. "I'm afraid I don't know what it is. Another physician he saw also doesn't know."

I swallowed heavily. "Will it… Will it kill him?"

"I don't think so. Not yet, anyway. I think the greater problem is that he's feeling his age lately. He seems melancholy. Would you agree?"

"No. I mean, yes, I suppose." I shook my head to clear it. "The truth is, I haven't noticed much change in him, but now I'm wondering if he's hiding his true feelings from me to stop me worrying."

"It's possible."

"How melancholy is he?"

"Hard to say. He simply doesn't seem like his usual spirited self to me, but I don't know him as well as you do."

Sometimes I wasn't sure I knew Chronos particularly well either. He had entered my life a mere year ago, and our relationship had been on shaky ground since the beginning. Having abandoned my grandmother and father, he'd disappeared overseas for years and been presumed dead. His reappearance had come as a shock, and his lack of remorse for his actions had angered me. I wasn't sure I'd made my peace with him yet.

Perhaps it was time I did.

I smiled at Gabe. "Thank you for telling me. You are a dear friend." I glanced at Miss O'Dwyer, now chatting to Matt, Cyclops, Catherine and Duke. "Have you set a date yet?"

His face softened as he watched the pretty woman laughing at something Cyclops said. "Late summer. I can't wait to present her with the ring I'm having made. I'm collecting it in two days. I hope she likes it."

"I'm sure she will because you gave it to her. She seems delightful and has such a happy countenance. I think you two will do very well together." My smile faded as something occurred to me. "Does Miss O'Dwyer have family in Ireland still?"

"They live in County Cork, but she moved here two years ago. She's an excellent nurse."

I hardly heard him after he mentioned her family were still in Ireland. I shouldn't pry into his private affairs, but I had to know. What happened to Gabe affected Matt in a very important way. "She may wish to return there some day, perhaps to raise a family."

Gabe knew what I was fishing for in my cumbersome way. "We won't be moving out of England, India. I have no plans to leave London, in fact. Not while the hospital needs me. It needs her, too, and she loves working there as much as I do." He clasped my hand. "You don't have to worry." His grip tightened, and he wouldn't meet my gaze.

"What is it?" I hedged.

"We talked about this once, but I want to make sure we still have an understanding. What I've done for Matt can't happen for anyone else. I spoke the spell into his watch to save him that day because the medical magic was already in it."

"Someone else played God, you mean."

He nodded. "The decision had already been made by my father to keep Matt alive using magic. I was simply honoring that, and I will continue to do so if required. But I won't do it for someone else, no matter how important they are to you or me." His lips stretched in a flat, humorless smile. "I'm afraid if I start, I might never stop."

"I understand, and I won't ask it of you. Thank you, Gabe. Gratitude doesn't seem like enough to repay you for what you've done, but…thank you."

*　*　*

I WAS SEATED at my dressing table, hairbrush in hand, when there was a light knock on the bedroom door. Matt opened it, and in shuffled Aunt Letitia dressed in a jade-green dressing gown embroidered with gold dragons. She carried a chocolate pot in one hand and cup in the other.

She set them on the table before me. "Just a little something to help you sleep, India."

"That's very kind of you." I eyed her closely, waiting for her to tell me the real reason for her visit.

She poured the chocolate into the cup and handed it to me, smiling. "Drink up."

I glanced at Matt. He merely shrugged. I sipped. It was rather bitter, not like the velvet-smooth chocolate Mrs. Potter usually prepared. "Did you make this yourself?"

"I did. Go on. Drink."

I sipped again to please her, but it was much too bitter for me. Not that I would tell her. She was quite inept in the kitchen, so for her to do this was special. "Thank you. It was very thoughtful of you."

"My pleasure. Goodnight and sweet dreams. Matthew, make sure she finishes every last drop." She patted his cheek fondly then let herself out.

I stood and removed my dressing gown with Matt's assistance. "How odd. She's never brought me chocolate before."

"You're not going to finish it?"

"It's not to my taste."

He picked up the cup, sniffed the contents, and sipped. "I don't mind it." He sipped again then drained the cup.

As he undressed, he said, "Aunt Letitia must have wanted to show her appreciation for the dinner. Her friend seemed to enjoy herself, despite giving Willie a wide berth most of the evening."

"Perhaps that's why she enjoyed herself."

He grinned. "Her niece seemed to like Willie's company well enough."

We climbed into bed and I extinguished the lamp on my bedside table, but Matt left his on. His expression had taken on a faraway look.

"What is it?" I asked.

"What were you and Gabe discussing?"

"His upcoming marriage."

"You looked serious, and that is not a serious subject."

I smoothed my hand over the jacquard bedcover, giving it my full attention so as not to be caught in his intense gaze.

Matt placed his hand over mine. "India?" When I still didn't look at him, he touched my chin and gently turned my face to his. "What's wrong?"

I lifted my gaze. My heart dove at the worry in his eyes. "It was nothing," I said quickly to reassure him. "We were talking about Ireland, that's all."

"Ah. And whether they planned to move there, I assume."

I snuggled into him, resting my head on his chest. The steady rhythm of his heartbeat, as regular as clockwork, always made my own heart swell with happiness. "He says they're staying in London. It was quite a relief to hear it."

He stroked my hair back from my face. "Anything else?"

"Chronos is sicker than he's letting on, but Gabe doesn't think he's dying. Not yet, anyway."

"We'll keep an eye on him. So was there something more you two talked about?"

I tilted my head to look at him. He watched me with an earnest expression. He knew there was more. I didn't want to tell him, however. Matt might one day need Gabe's magic to boost his health again, and if he was reminded of how adamant Gabe was not to use it, he would refuse to ask.

I held no such qualms. Gabe said he wouldn't use his magic to save the lives of *others*. If Matt needed him again, *I* would not hesitate to ask.

I closed my eyes before his intense gaze drilled the truth out of me. "There was nothing more."

He circled me in his arms and kissed the top of my head. I felt rather than heard his deep exhalation, a sure sign that he didn't believe me but wasn't going to press me for an answer. Keeping secrets from Matt was almost impossible, and something I hated doing, but when it came to the matter of his life, I would lie a thousand times and never regret it.

CHAPTER 2

*A*ccording to Mrs. Bristow the housekeeper, Willie returned home at dawn. When Willie finally got out of bed in the early afternoon, I cornered her in the sitting room and asked where she'd gone after our guests left and the rest of the household retired.

She raised the newspaper to avoid looking at me. "Visiting a friend."

"Who?"

"None of your business."

"Brockwell?"

"I said it ain't none of your business, India."

I appealed to Aunt Letitia, sitting on the sofa with her embroidery. Despite wearing spectacles, she squinted as she poked the needle through the fabric. She didn't notice me and didn't appear to be listening to our conversation anyway.

I rearranged the flowers in the vase on the table next to Willie and repositioned the framed photographs on the console table under the window, all the while humming a tune.

When I turned around, Willie was peering at me over the top of the newspaper, smiling. "You really want to know, don't you?"

"Not in particular. I was simply making conversation."

"Ha!"

"I can see you had a good time, and that's all that matters."

Her smile turned secretive. "I had a real good time."

"Speaking of Brockwell…"

"We weren't."

I was pleased to see that mentioning his name didn't diminish her smile. Indeed, it seemed to widen. "Speaking of Brockwell, are you two friends again?"

The last time I'd spoken to her about the detective inspector, she'd informed me that he'd asked her to marry him and she'd refused. Her rejection had resulted in increased tension between them which made both of them miserable. She missed him. I knew that with absolute certainty. But whether she missed him enough to capitulate and marry him was another matter entirely. And I didn't have a clue as to whether he missed her enough to return their relationship to the way things had once been.

Willie looked like the cat that caught a mouse. "Jasper and me are more than friends again."

I gasped. "That's marvelous! Why didn't you tell me? He could have come to dinner last night."

"No, he could not," Aunt Letitia piped up.

Willie and I both turned to her. "Why not?" I asked.

"Because that would have made thirteen, and no dinner party can have such an unfortunate number of guests. Remember that, India. It'll be important when you move to the country and host dinners more often."

I dismissed her with a wave. "It'll be years before Matt inherits Rycroft Hall."

"My brother is getting on in years and his ruddy complexion suggests he's hardly the healthiest individual. You ought to ask that lovely young doctor how long he thinks Richard has left in this world."

"That's a little morbid, don't you think?"

She emitted a small sound of derision through her nose. "It's only morbid if one cares."

Willie lifted the newspaper higher to hide her face as she leaned closer to me and whispered, "Have you noticed how she talks a lot about death lately?"

"Does she?" I whispered back.

"Not her own, but other people's. I reckon she's got a connection to the afterlife on account of her age and the spirits are communicating with her."

I rolled my eyes. "You are quite mad, Willie."

"Me? I ain't the one talking to spirits." She snapped the pages of the newspaper to straighten it and resumed reading. "Can't a person get some peace around here?"

Bristow appeared at the door and announced the arrival of Lord Farnsworth. His lordship sauntered in looking pleased with himself. He bowed to Aunt Letitia and me, and he even shook Willie's hand.

She eyed him warily. "What's going on?"

"I am in an excellent mood this morning. Last night's dinner was superb and the company entertaining. I enjoyed myself immensely and came to thank my hostess." He gave me another bow. "Thank you, India. You are a marvel."

It was my turn to eye him with caution. He was being very effusive, even for him.

Aunt Letitia set aside her embroidery and removed her spectacles. "I am so pleased you enjoyed yourself, Davide. Does your enthusiasm have anything to do with Lady Helen? You two seemed to be getting along splendidly last night."

"She's very jolly. I like her. Indeed, I like her enough to invite her to walk with me this afternoon. I was on my way to Hyde Park now, but thought I'd call here first." He glanced at the clock on the mantel and pushed himself to his feet. "Better not keep her waiting."

Aunt Letitia clapped her hands lightly. "I am so pleased she agreed to see you. It's an excellent sign that her affections are engaged."

He put up a finger. "Don't get ahead of yourself, Letty. It's just a walk." He checked his reflection in the mirror. "Anyway, neither of us will be forced down the aisle before we are ready."

"That's why you like her, eh?" Willie asked, chuckling.

He winked at her. "Say, you look very cheerful today. Enjoyed yourself last night, too?"

Willie's smile widened.

"She saw Brockwell after we all went to bed," I told him.

Willie frowned. "I never said that."

Lord Farnsworth picked up his hat and headed for the door. "Good day, all. Don't bother the staff, India, I'll see myself out." He passed Matt in the doorway and lifted his hat in greeting. "Can't stop, must dash."

Matt watched him go then entered the sitting room. "What was he doing here?"

"I'm not entirely sure," I said.

Aunt Letitia picked up her embroidery again, a smug smile on her face. "He's going to marry Lady Helen."

Willie snorted. "No, he ain't. Neither of 'em wants marriage. Not yet, anyway."

Aunt Letitia clicked her tongue and put on her spectacles. "Don't take what they say at face value. Once they realize how well matched they are, it will be full steam ahead. Both know they risk losing the other if they don't come to an understanding swiftly." She poked the needle through the fabric. "I give it to the end of spring for an announcement, possibly less if they see each other every day."

Willie raised the newspaper to cover her face. She leaned closer to me and jerked her head, urging me to lean in too.

She dropped her voice. "Should I tell her?"

"Tell her what?" I whispered.

"That I was with Helen last night."

I managed to press my lips together before my gasp escaped.

"I climbed up to her window and she let me in. We arranged it beforehand, at dinner."

"So Lady Sloane doesn't know," I said, pointing out the obvious.

"Helen says her family wouldn't approve." She jutted her chin in Aunt Letitia's direction. "Letty doesn't mind as much, so I reckon I should tell her so she doesn't get her hopes up for a quick marriage."

"She doesn't mind what *you* do, Willie, but that's because you're not a young English lady. I think she'll be horrified to find out that Lady Helen prefers women to men."

"And isn't as innocent as she makes out." Willie's lips curved slyly. "I ain't her first."

I cleared my throat and looked down at my skirts, the floor—anywhere but at Willie. "Don't tell Aunt Letitia. She might blame you for corrupting Lady Helen, no matter what you say. But I do think you should tell Davide. He seems to think he has a chance." I frowned. "Why *is* Lady Helen seeing him today if she's not interested?"

"Who said she's not interested?"

"Ah. So she likes both men and women too."

"She just wants to have some fun while she's young. She doesn't want a husband who'll tell her to act conventional. I reckon she'll make that clear to Davide soon enough."

Matt's face appeared above the newspaper, peering down at us. He arched his brows in question.

Willie folded up the newspaper and slapped it into his chest. "I'm going to find Duke."

"He's assisting the iceman with his delivery downstairs," Matt said.

Willie left, and Matt took the seat she vacated. He withdrew a letter from his pocket and handed it to me. "This just arrived. It's from Coyle."

The note was addressed to both Matt and me and informed us that the home secretary and Mr. Le Grand, the spy master, were calling on Lord Coyle at four o'clock. If we wished to be part of the conversation, we could attend as well.

When they'd given the official role of advisor to Lord Coyle, I'd been disappointed they trusted him over me, particularly when I considered him the least trustworthy man in England. He was, however, very powerful, and that power must have attracted them.

"Shall we go?" I asked.

Matt scrubbed a hand over his mouth and jaw. "I don't want anything to do with Coyle."

"But…?"

"But can we afford not to go? What if something important is discussed? Something that affects you?"

I agreed. "The question is, *why* does Coyle want us there? He has the ear of Mr. Matthews and Mr. Le Grand. He is helping form government policies about magicians and the use of magic. He has the power he always craved. He doesn't need me."

Matt gave me a grim smile. "Perhaps he has discovered he does need you. After all, how can one form a policy about magic and not ask England's most powerful magician for advice?"

Perhaps he was right. The only way we'd find out was if we went to the meeting. I glanced at the clock and rose. "He didn't give us much time to think about it."

"I suspect that was intentional."

* * *

FROM THE LOOK on Hope's face as we passed the open door to the Coyles' drawing room, she was not expecting our visit. Matt's cousin jumped to her feet and rushed to intercept us on the landing. Her chest rose and fell with her deep breaths, but not from that small amount of exertion. She was anxious.

"What are you both doing here?" she asked.

"Coyle summoned us," Matt said. "Your butler is taking us to his study."

The butler cleared his throat, a polite directive to hurry us along.

Matt would not be hurried, however. "Do you know why he wanted to see us?"

"No, but Mr. Matthews and Mr. Le Grand are also here."

Hope glanced between us, frowning. "I see that is no surprise to either of you. I am always the last to know, even when events occur in my own house."

"Hope, are you all right?" Matt suddenly asked.

Her jaw firmed and she tilted her chin. "Of course." To admit otherwise would be to acknowledge she'd become weaker through her marriage, not stronger. And Hope loathed weakness.

She had always been proud, but her pride had been dented when her marriage to Lord Coyle began to crumble, almost from the day of their wedding. She might have risen in the world through him, but she no longer exuded confidence. She was as elegant and beautiful as ever, however the hint of vulnerability in her demeanor made her more alluring.

It also brought out Matt's protective instinct. "My offer still stands," he said. "You know where we are if you need us."

"I don't need you. I don't need anyone." It would seem marriage had not matured her. She was as petulant as ever.

I grasped Matt's arm. "You may not *need* anyone, Hope, but having friends can be a comfort in difficult times."

"Don't pretend you are my friend, India."

"India's offer was a genuine one," Matt snapped.

He so rarely spoke harshly to her that she was taken aback.

Matt folded his hand over mine and we ascended the stairs together behind the butler. I resisted the urge to look over my shoulder at Hope.

Both Mr. Matthews and Mr. Le Grand rose from their chairs upon our arrival. Lord Coyle did not. He sat behind the desk and grunted a greeting around the pipe in his mouth. He lifted a finger from the arm of his chair, indicating we should sit.

"Good morning, Mrs. Glass, Mr. Glass," Mr. Matthews said as he resumed his seat. "I trust you are both well?"

"Very well, thank you," I said.

Mr. Le Grand greeted us too, with a little less enthusiasm

than the home secretary, but with more politeness than Lord Coyle. I was pleasantly surprised, although, in truth, I wasn't sure how these men would treat us. Our last meeting had ended in me being disappointed they chose Lord Coyle as their advisor, but the door to collaboration had been left open. They needed me more than I needed them.

Mr. Le Grand did not resume his seat but moved to stand by the bookshelves. By separating himself from us, he was signaling that he was there to observe. With his hooded eyes and casual pose, he could be easily mistaken for a bored civil servant, but I knew better. It was an act. The man was shrewd.

"Now will you tell us why you've summoned us all here instead of meeting in my office, Coyle?" Mr. Matthews asked. He was the epitome of a polished politician but I wouldn't underestimate him. He was intelligent, but he didn't hide it like Mr. Le Grand. He wanted us to know it.

Lord Coyle leaned back, making the chair groan in protest. "I prefer it here."

"Of course, but in future, it makes more sense for you to come to the Home Office."

"Not for me. As to the reason for the meeting, the unrest between magicians and the artless is growing."

Mr. Matthews waited for more, but none came. "And?"

"And you've done nothing about it."

"We've called for calm and the police are doing everything in their power. They've made arrests—"

"They haven't arrested the key troublemakers."

A muscle pulsed in Mr. Matthews' cheek as his jaw firmed. "They're being protected by others, but we'll uncover their identities soon."

"Not soon enough." Lord Coyle removed his pipe and pointed it at the home secretary. "A more important point is to ask what you are doing for the long-term protection of magicians in the city and around the country."

Mr. Matthews' gaze flicked to Mr. Le Grand then back to Lord Coyle. "That's where your advice comes in, my lord."

He sounded somewhat confused, as if they'd been over this before. I got the feeling Lord Coyle was raising the point again for my benefit. "We'll consider it in the formation of our policies."

"Bah! What a waste of time that will be." Lord Coyle plugged the pipe back into his mouth. He sucked and puffed only to have to withdraw it again as a cough racked him. He turned quite red in the face and a thick vein bulged in his neck above his collar. Thankfully the coughs subsided, and he was able to resume speaking. "We need immediate action. I didn't agree to be an advisor to see my advice ignored."

"It's not being ignored." Mr. Matthews might be a consummate politician, but he couldn't hide his irritation altogether. "These things take time. There is a process—"

"Damn the process!" Lord Coyle's words reverberated around the office before a taut silence settled.

Mr. Matthews looked uncertain how to proceed. He might be the head of the Home Office, but he was addressing an earl with as much, if not more, power than he wielded. He was also out of his depth. His knowledge of magic was probably the least of everyone's in the room.

I expected Mr. Le Grand to break the silence, but he seemed more interested in waiting to see how events played out.

It was Matt who spoke first. "So your alliance isn't working out. I'm not surprised, but what does this have to do with India?" He might sound underwhelmed, but there was a tightness in his voice that only those familiar with him would detect.

Lord Coyle leaned forward and set his pipe on the desk. "This is what I propose. The riots need to be broken up before complete anarchy erupts."

Mr. Matthews scoffed. "It won't get that far."

"Won't it?"

Mr. Matthews sucked in a sharp breath. "The police will have them under control soon. Give it time."

"Time." Lord Coyle's gaze shifted to me and he chuckled.

It ended in a rattling cough that momentarily overtook his entire body. When it subsided, he wiped his mouth and moustache with his handkerchief. "Time will not heal, it will only make the divisions wider. The riots need to be stopped now and new laws passed as soon as possible before the city is torn apart."

"Ah. Now I see what you're getting at." Mr. Matthews turned to Matt and me. "Lord Coyle has proposed some new laws regarding the use of magic. Namely, he wants the craft guilds to have no control over a magician's business. A magician should be allowed to use his magic as he sees fit."

It didn't sound unreasonable. So why the tension between these men?

"He also proposes that the government undertake a campaign to ensure the public is made aware that magic doesn't last."

"That will decrease the demand for their wares somewhat," I agreed. "And that in turn will see the de-escalation in tensions between the artless and magicians."

"The value of your magical collection will decrease," Matt said to Lord Coyle. "If everyone can purchase magical objects, they'll no longer remain rare collectibles."

Lord Coyle lifted his shoulders in a shrug. "There is a greater good at stake here. The good of the nation. And what is the point of an old man collecting objects when he has no heirs to leave them to?"

"You have a wife."

Another shrug dismissed Hope with as much consideration as he dismissed a servant from the room.

Matt turned to Mr. Matthews. "There's more, isn't there?"

Mr. Matthews hesitated. Perhaps he hadn't expected to be pressed further. "Coyle also wants a law passed that will ensure Mrs. Glass enhances the magic of a select few magicians."

"What?" Matt exploded.

I placed a hand on Matt's arm to discourage him from storming out. "By enhance, you mean lengthen their magic."

C.J. ARCHER

"And create new spells by combining different magics," Lord Coyle added. "Just as you did with the movement spell that made the carpet fly. The possibilities are endless and—"

"India has already made her stance on that clear," Matt ground out.

"I am not interested," I said, rising.

"No?" Lord Coyle's calmness chilled me to the bone. I got the feeling he was enjoying himself. "Then why keep a list of magicians?"

"We're not," Matt said.

Lord Coyle didn't look at him. He kept his hard gaze on me, as though drilling through my skull to expose my secrets. "Of course you are. Why wouldn't you? It makes sense to collate names for yourselves and for future generations. Magic is, after all, about lineage." He picked up his pipe again. "I know you want to create spells, Mrs. Glass."

"I don't," I snapped. "I like to play with timepieces and use my magic to fix broken ones, but creating new spells is not a calling, my lord. Don't believe everything Fabian Charbonneau told you. He's an excellent liar."

Fabian had lied to our faces for weeks, pretending to be my friend when he'd tried to kill the man I loved and destroy my life in the process. No friend would do that.

But he was partially right when he said performing magic was a compulsion. It was an urge I could sate by performing simple magic, however. I didn't *need* to create new spells.

"It's all right," Mr. Matthews said with a steely edge. "I have told Coyle I'm not interested in his idea. I don't know why he thought bringing you here would change anything. Did you think you could convince her to change her mind, Coyle?"

Lord Coyle didn't rise to the bait. Indeed, he seemed unperturbed by Mr. Matthews' scathing tone. "What do you think, Le Grand?" he asked.

Mr. Le Grand moved out of the shadows and approached. His eyes were no longer hooded; they focused on me. "I admit Coyle's idea is intriguing, on the surface. The potential

THE GOLDSMITH'S CONSPIRACY

for greatness and invention is enormous. Flying carpets are just one idea, but there are many others that could benefit the nation. Bank notes that don't tear. Roads that rarely need resurfacing. Ships that can't sink. There is even the rumor that your magic can be combined with a doctor's magic to keep the wounded alive."

I swallowed but managed to keep my features schooled. Beside me, Matt went very still. "There's no such thing as medical magic," I said. If these men knew what Gabe Seaford and I were capable of, if they knew that Matt was kept alive by the magic in his watch, they might never let me walk out of this room. Making carpets fly was one thing, but healing soldiers wounded in battle was valuable beyond all measure.

Lord Coyle's eyes narrowed ever so slightly.

Mr. Le Grand's smile implied he knew that I lied. "There is one very large flaw in Coyle's idea."

"And that is?"

"You. You are but one woman. You can't be everywhere or do everything. You would become exhausted. Not only that, it's clear you would not be a willing participant in the scheme."

The counter argument was that I could be forced to be a participant. If the government wanted me to do as Lord Coyle suggested, they only had to threaten my family and friends. If they didn't know that, Coyle certainly did.

Lord Coyle removed the pipe from between his lips. "You are a valuable asset, Mrs. Glass. You should be treated as such, just like the brightest scientific minds who work for the good of the nation."

"They do so willingly," I pointed out.

He returned the pipe to his mouth and his lips stretched into a macabre smile around it.

Matt rose. "We've heard enough."

"I am on your side," Lord Coyle said. "I am on the side of magicians."

"You are on your own side," I spat back. "The side of

power. I want nothing to do with you or your schemes." I took Matt's hand and we headed toward the door.

"Wait," Mr. Matthews called out. "One moment, please. Can we return to the most pressing matter? What do you propose we do to end the riots, Mrs. Glass?"

How quickly things changed. They must consider Lord Coyle's advice poor indeed to turn to me now, and in his presence too. It would be easy to gloat, but I kept my features schooled and did not look at his lordship.

"A middle ground that's fair to both parties must be sought. The best way to do that is consult them. I suggest you bring the two sides together for discussion."

Lord Coyle snorted. "They'll never reach an agreement."

"Magicians aren't going away, nor can they retreat into the shadows again. The only way to stop the riots and persecution is to find a middle ground. It won't be easy, and there will be people on both sides who'll remain dissatisfied, but I believe common sense will prevail for the majority."

Mr. Matthews agreed. "Do you have ideas on what the middle ground should look like?"

I opened my mouth to answer, but Matt spoke first. "If you wish to hear my wife's ideas, please call on her at your convenience." It was said for Coyle's benefit. Matt didn't want me revealing anything in front of his lordship for fear he would somehow use it against me.

Lord Coyle grabbed his walking stick and pushed himself to his feet with a wince of pain. That small effort caused his breathing to become shallow. He suddenly looked like an elderly, unwell man. But he quickly recovered and any sympathy I'd felt for him vanished with his sneer.

I strode to the door, wanting to get as far away from him as possible.

"You'll regret shutting me out." It wasn't clear whether he was speaking to Matt and me, or Mr. Matthews and Mr. Le Grand.

Nevertheless, I shivered. Lord Coyle's threats always came to pass.

Matt opened the door, revealing Hope standing there. Her wide eyes stared unblinking up at him.

"Is that my wife, listening in at doors again?" Lord Coyle smashed the end of his walking stick into the floor.

Hope jumped. Her face paled.

"Pathetic," her husband spat. "Pathetic and useless."

"Don't speak to my cousin that way," Matt growled. "She deserves some respect."

"Don't bother to pretend that you care, Glass. You know as well as I that my wife is a manipulative, selfish creature. As soon as she got what she wanted, her true colors were revealed." He limped across the room, leaning heavily on the stick. His face shone with sweat by the time he reached us. "Look at her now, standing there trembling as if I frighten her, as if she is the victim. You were not fooled by her before, Glass, so don't be fooled by her act now. You're smarter than that."

Hope's lips quivered. "Husband, please, stop this. I've done nothing—"

Lord Coyle smacked his walking stick into the leg of a table by the door. Hope and I both jumped. She recoiled and stepped back. There was no sign of her pride now, no hint of the strong woman she'd been when she'd tried to manipulate Matt into marriage. She was still beautiful, but her beauty was that of a butterfly trapped in a jar. Even I wanted to release her from this misery.

"Come home with us," Matt urged her quietly.

She wiped her palms down her skirts and shook her head. "This is my home, and my husband is right. I've made my bed and now I must lie in it. He is the husband I deserve. We all know it."

Matt took a step toward her, but she put up her hands, warding him off. "Don't, please." Tears filled her eyes and she tried to blink them away.

Lord Coyle's sneer returned. "You should be on the stage, my dear."

Hope turned and hurried away, disappearing down a corridor.

I took Matt's hand again. He was rigid, his grip firm as we headed down the stairs. He did not speak as the butler let us out and it was left to me to instruct Woodall to drive us home. Matt waited until we'd driven out of sight of Coyle's townhouse before he slammed his fist into the door. Thankfully it was padded.

I touched his knee. "You can't save her. Not unless she wants to be saved."

He took my hand and pressed it to his lips. He kissed my knuckles through my glove and bowed his head. He heaved a deep breath and let it out slowly. It seemed to help him regain some composure. "I know. That's why I hate this. There's nothing I can do."

CHAPTER 3

 illie loathed the opera, so when she asked to come along with us, I was skeptical about her motives. Her excuse that she was expanding her cultural horizons didn't ring true. Willie's idea of culture was watching a boxing match in the basement of a Mayfair pub instead of an East End one.

The real reason became a little clearer when Lord Farnsworth sauntered into our private box a few minutes before the curtain was due to open. He bowed to Aunt Letitia and me, and shook Matt's hand. He stopped short upon seeing Willie, dressed in her finest gentleman's outfit.

He fingered her tailcoat lapel. "That won't impress her, you know."

Aunt Letitia lowered the program she'd been reading to her lap. "Impress who?"

"Velvet collars and stitched cuffs are out of fashion."

Willie tugged on her jacket cuffs and stretched her neck out of her stiff shirt collar. She wasn't used to wearing formal opera clothes and complained for most of the journey to Covent Garden until Aunt Letitia threatened to have Woodall turn the carriage around and drive home so Willie could change into something more feminine. Willie stopped whining but continued to wriggle in the seat the rest of the way.

"She doesn't care about fashion anyway," Willie grumbled.

Aunt Letitia rapped her on the knuckles with her closed fan. "I demand to know who you're talking about."

"Lady Helen," Matt told her. "They're both trying to win her hand."

Aunt Letitia's lips formed an O.

"It ain't her hand I want," Willie mumbled.

Aunt Letitia smacked her fan harder on Willie's knuckles.

Willie crossed her arms, tucking her hands under her armpits, out of Aunt Letitia's reach. "Me and Davide both like Helen. He's jealous because she chose me."

"She did not choose you." Lord Farnsworth hitched up his trouser legs and sat. "She hasn't chosen anyone yet."

"So what do you call what happened between her and me last night?"

"A diversion. Diversions aren't serious, Willie. They're an aperitif before the main course." He removed a pair of dainty silver opera glasses from his pocket. "Where is she, anyway?"

I nodded in the direction of Lady Sloane's private box where her niece sat with composure and poise, even though she must be aware of the opera glasses focused on her. Dressed in a pale pink and white dress with lace trim at the elbow, and with her hair falling in soft curls around her face, she looked feminine and innocent. There was no hint of her adventurous spirit.

As a wealthy noblewoman and newcomer to London, she was a curiosity and would remain so until more girls filtered into the city for the social season. Her attendance here, and at other events, signaled her availability. If she failed to convince her family to give her time to make a love match, she would find herself engaged very quickly.

I leaned closer to Lord Farnsworth. "If you intend to throw your hat into the ring, I wouldn't delay."

He lowered the opera glasses and dismissed my concern

with a flourishing wave. "I have time. She isn't ready. She wants to have some fun first."

Aunt Letitia clicked her tongue but offered no verbal response.

"Maybe she doesn't want to ever marry," Willie said with a glare directed at both Lord Farnsworth and me. "Some women don't."

"Not all women are free to do as they please," I said. "Particularly noblewomen."

The lights dimmed and the audience hushed. I settled in for an evening of music. Half way through the second act, a soft snore signaled that Willie was asleep. When the lights came back on at intermission, Lord Farnsworth kicked her ankle.

She snuffled and wiped her mouth with the back of her hand. "Is it over?"

"Half way," Matt said, looking just as bored as his cousin. "I'm going to stretch my legs."

Moments after he left the box, we had visitors. Mr. and Mrs. Delancey from the collectors' club entered, all smiles. Dressed in dramatic crimson and black satin and lace, she looked like an injured bat swooping upon us. Aunt Letitia wrinkled her nose when Mrs. Delancey sat in Matt's vacated chair, uninvited.

"What a lovely coincidence," Mrs. Delancey declared. "You don't come to the opera often, India."

"She hates it," Willie said.

"I don't hate it," I countered. "I just prefer the lighter operas of Gilbert and Sullivan. I'm enjoying *Aida* very much, however."

"One doesn't come to the opera for the music, my dear." Mrs. Delancey looked out upon the sea of audience members, both below us and in the boxes. "One comes to watch. Did you see Lady Louisa Hollingbroke? She looks quite forlorn with only her elderly aunt for company. It serves her right, ending her engagement with that scurrilous journalist friend of yours."

Louisa hadn't been the one to end the relationship; Oscar had. But they'd agreed to put it about that she'd finished with him to save her the humiliation. "He isn't scurrilous, merely naïve for thinking his book would benefit magicians."

I watched Louisa, seated in the large private box beside her elderly aunt. The two didn't speak. Indeed, the aunt looked as though she was asleep. No one came to visit, either, which surprised me. Louisa was wealthy and titled, making her quite the catch. Gentlemen ought to want to court her and ladies should desire her friendship. But I'd not known her to associate with anyone outside the collector's club. Perhaps she was considered too old for matrimony, having been on the London social scene for a number of years. Or perhaps she was just considered too odd.

"Damn," Lord Farnsworth suddenly muttered as he peered through his opera glasses.

I followed his gaze to Lady Helen who was now speaking to a short gentleman. I couldn't quite see from this distance, but it appeared as though her aunt was somewhat embarrassed by the presence of the newcomer as she fluttered her fan vigorously.

And that's when I realized it wasn't a gentleman at all. It was Willie. The chair she'd occupied behind Aunt Letitia was vacant. I hadn't noticed her leave.

Lord Farnsworth leapt to his feet and pushed past Mr. Delancey. He was gone before I could advise him not to make a scene.

Mrs. Delancey gasped. "She's looking this way."

"Lady Helen?"

"Louisa."

Louisa gave me a small nod and I nodded back. Then she suddenly turned as a gentleman entered their box. He bowed to her and her aunt. When he straightened, my heart leapt into my throat.

Mrs. Delancey gasped again. "That vile creature. That rotten, horrid, despicable man. How *dare* he show his face!"

It was the first time I'd seen Fabian since he'd tried to kill

Matt outside our house. According to Detective Inspector Brockwell, whose men were watching him, Fabian had been lying low, rarely leaving his house.

Mr. Delancey moved to stand beside his wife and squinted in the direction of Louisa and Fabian. "He must have hoped to avoid notice by arriving during the interval. I would call that a monumental failure."

Mrs. Delancey picked up Lord Farnsworth's opera glasses and peered through them. "Louisa has a nerve inviting him. Indeed, she has a nerve remaining friends with him at all."

That might be so, but it was inevitable that she would choose Fabian's side. With her engagement to Oscar over, she was looking for another magician to wed. She had always had her sights set on Fabian, thanks to his power, but he'd rejected her advances time and again. Now that she was the only friend he had left in London, he might not reject her next time. Perhaps they already had an agreement, hence his presence in her family's opera box.

Fabian's gaze suddenly turned to us. I quickly looked down and studied the program in my lap.

Matt returned just as the lights dimmed. The Delanceys said their farewells, but Mrs. Delancey paused before exiting. "Are those opera glasses magical, India?"

I brushed my hand over the fine silver piece she'd returned to Lord Farnsworth's chair. It was warm with faint magic. But I wasn't going to tell her that. If I did, she would hound me until I learned who'd made it. "Why?"

"They're rather lovely. Do you know any magicians who make opera glasses?"

"No."

"A silversmith magician, then?"

"No, sorry."

She sighed. "Pity. What about a—"

"Good evening, Mrs. Delancey," Matt said stiffly as he held open the door for her. "Enjoy the rest of the opera."

With one wary eye on Matt, Mr. Delancey grabbed his wife's hand and pulled her out of our box.

"Vulgar woman," Aunt Letitia muttered as she relaxed in her seat. "I'm glad you didn't invite her to join us for the second half, India. Do you think Davide and Willie will return?"

Matt sat and took my hand. By the dim light, I could just make out his reassuring smile. "I'm not sure," he said.

"Where do you think they rushed off to like that? It was most odd."

I sighed, grateful her eyesight wasn't good enough to see Willie and Lord Farnsworth with Lady Helen.

Willie and Lord Farnsworth met us only briefly after the show ended. They were going out together in search of nocturnal entertainment. It appeared they'd put their rivalry aside, for now. I was glad to see they hadn't let Lady Helen come between them.

I waited until we were home before telling Matt that Fabian had been with Louisa. He was unsurprised.

"They need each other now more than ever." He lifted my hair off my shoulder and met my gaze in the reflection of the dressing table mirror. He stood behind me in just his trousers, his hands on my shoulders, and kissed the top of my head. "Did I tell you how beautiful you looked tonight?"

"Twice." I tipped my head back and he kissed my mouth. "You looked rather dashing yourself." I picked up my hairbrush and stroked it through my hair. "You're not worried about Fabian and Louisa joining forces?"

He shook his head. "They can't do anything to us. The police have Fabian in their sights. If he puts a foot wrong, he'll be arrested again. And Louisa is harmless."

"She's clever."

"But not dangerous."

I wasn't so sure. I didn't think we should underestimate her.

Matt touched my hand, stopping me brushing. He leaned down so his face was level with mine and regarded me in the reflection with sternness. "Louisa is just a selfish person with one aim—to marry a magician and beget magical children.

Her friendship with Charbonneau might result in them marrying, but if so, it doesn't matter. Not to us. It doesn't make either of them more powerful than they already are. It changes nothing."

He spoke with such confidence that I found myself agreeing. I released a breath, comforted, and sank into his arms.

Our embrace was interrupted by a knock on the door. It was Aunt Letitia, delivering a pot of hot chocolate again. She handed it to Matt with a smile, and he thanked her.

"It's good of you to bring me a cup before bed, Aunt."

"It's not for you!" She snatched the pot and cup from him and set it on the dressing table. "It's for India." She patted my shoulder and left.

Matt shook his head, chuckling, as I poured the chocolate into the cup. I sipped and pulled a face at the bitterness. I passed the cup to Matt. "I won't tell her you prefer it."

"I don't know why she's making you hot chocolate and not me. I am her favorite nephew."

"You're her only nephew. Now drink up and come to bed."

He drank the chocolate in a single gulp.

* * *

WE AWOKE when it was still dark to someone banging on the front door. Interruptions during the night never brought good news.

Matt sprang out of bed before I even had a chance to roll over. "Wait here." He threw on a shirt and trousers and ran out of the bedroom. His footsteps were so light, he hardly made any noise as he ran down the stairs.

Two other sets of footsteps sounded like elephants descending.

I pulled on a house coat over my nightgown and followed. I knew the house well enough not to require a light, but even so, I kept my hand on the stair railing to make sure I didn't fall. A light flickered in the entrance hall below, but as I drew closer, I realized it came from the lantern held by the young constable standing just inside the door. He was barely old enough to be called a man and the oversized coat made him seem even more youthful.

I arrived just in time to hear Cyclops say, "I'll get dressed." He ran past me, back up the stairs. "Morning, India."

"What is it?" I asked Matt and Duke, standing with the constable. "What's going on?"

Matt closed the door, shutting out the cold air. "Cyclops is needed. There's been a disturbance in his jurisdiction and all able-bodied men are required to report for duty."

"All *big*-bodied men," the constable said, removing his hat and bobbing his head in greeting. "Ain't many bigger than Constable Nate Bailey." He stared up the staircase with wide-eyed admiration.

"What kind of disturbance?" I asked.

"A crowd's gathering on Shoreditch High Street to block the morning traffic."

"Is it an artless protest march?"

"It is the artless," Matt said, "but it doesn't appear to be a march. They're setting up barricades."

Barricades usually meant they were going to dig in for some time, perhaps even become violent if their requests weren't met. The barricades would offer protection from the police trying to move them along.

The door suddenly opened and Willie stumbled in, still wearing her formal gentleman's attire, but with the tie stuffed into her coat pocket and her shirt collar half detached. She'd lost her hat. She squinted at the constable then hiccoughed.

He grabbed her arm and twisted it behind her back. "I've got him, sir! He won't get away with breaking and entering."

Either Willie was too drunk or was curious as to how events would play out because she didn't resist. "You're lucky I ran out of bullets."

The constable twisted her arm harder.

"Ow! Let me go or I swear I'll hunt you down and shoot you when I reload."

"You'd better let her go before she wakes my aunt," Matt said. "She's harmless enough."

Duke snorted. "You reckon?"

The constable released her. "She?"

Willie rounded on him, hands on hips. "Aye, I'm a woman, and you're an idiot if you can't tell."

The constable held the lantern closer to her face and studied her from head to toe. With a shake of his head, he apologized.

I wasn't sure if asking my next question was a good idea, but my curiosity won over caution. "Willie, why have you run out of bullets?"

"It was a wager. Helen reckoned I couldn't shoot a tin can from ten feet. So we went to a lane, lined up some tins we found, and I shot 'em." She tugged on her jacket lapel. "I hit two. If I'd had less to drink, I'd have got all six."

"Lady Helen was with you?"

She nodded. "She put on men's clothes and we all went for a drive. Her, me and Davide. We had a real good time. We stopped at a pub and watched a fight. Then we went to a gambling den. I think I lost some money there." She shrugged. "I lost it somewhere."

"How much?" Duke asked.

"I don't know."

"You loaned Helen men's clothes?" I asked. "Whose?"

"Didn't need to loan her any. She had her own, hidden under the bed."

I squeezed the bridge of my nose and groaned. "If she's caught out of the house in the middle of the night with you two, her reputation will be ruined. Her *life* would be ruined."

"Don't be dramatic, India. I reckon it would be the start of her life, not the end. It ain't right for a free spirit like her to be cooped up inside all the time with just her old aunt for company. She needs to get out and enjoy everything London has to offer."

I sighed.

She threw her arm around my shoulders. "Duke and Matt understand, don't you?"

"Don't drag me into this," Matt said.

"Duke?"

He screwed up his nose and crossed his arms. "Leave me out of it too."

Cyclops rushed down the stairs, doing up the buttons of his uniform, his helmet under his arm. "Let's go."

"Be careful," I said.

He nodded, and exited with the constable in his wake. The faint glow of dawn lightened the eastern sky.

Matt locked the door and took my hand. "I doubt I'll fall back to sleep now, but I'm going to try."

We walked together up the stairs ahead of Duke and Willie.

"Next time, take me with you," Duke whispered.

"To the opera?" Willie asked, not even trying to keep her voice low.

"To wherever you go after the opera."

"I thought you were getting too old and sensible for going out."

"I've always been sensible, but I'll never be too old for some fun. Besides, someone's got to make sure you don't make an ass of yourself."

She chuckled. "If you reckon you can stop me, you're a bigger fool than I thought. But I love you anyway, Duke."

I glanced over my shoulder to see her hugging him, and Duke laughing and shaking his head.

* * *

NONE of us could settle to any task throughout the morning. Even Aunt Letitia noticed our agitation and suspected something was amiss. She demanded to know what, and Matt told her. Then she demanded he go to Shoreditch High Street to gather the latest information on Cyclops's welfare.

THE GOLDSMITH'S CONSPIRACY

"If something happens to him, we'll hear soon," I told her gently. "It's best to stay away and let the police do what is necessary to disperse the crowd."

My words were as much for her benefit as Matt, Duke and Willie's. While Aunt Letitia seemed to calm a little, the others continued to pace about the sitting room, drum their fingers, or stare out of the window. Indeed, it was Aunt Letitia who scolded them for straining her nerves.

"Worrying won't do anyone any good," she said in a prim school mistress voice. "I won't allow you to infect us with your gloom. Either cheer up or leave."

Willie continued to drum her fingers on her thigh, but Duke and Matt made an effort and agreed to play a game of cards to keep them occupied.

Aunt Letitia picked up the book she'd been reading and handed it to me. "Will you read to me, India? Then after luncheon you should go for a walk. Moderate exercise is important."

I opened the book to the page she'd marked, but only managed a paragraph when Bristow entered and announced the arrival of Mr. Matthews and Mr. Le Grand. I rose to follow him to the drawing room, but Aunt Letitia caught my hand.

"I don't think you should speak to them. Let Matthew do it alone."

"I need to hear what they have to say. Don't worry. I won't agree to anything unless it's of benefit to me."

Her grip tightened. "But you shouldn't be troubling yourself with their schemes, India. It's not good for your nerves to be worrying about such weighty matters."

I patted the back of her hand then extricated myself from her grasp. I heard her click her tongue as I exited the sitting room.

Duke and Willie had followed us to the drawing room and Matt introduced them as our associates to the home secretary and the spy master. Mr. Matthews, however, asked them to leave.

"Matters of national security cannot be discussed with

civilians of another country," he said in his politician's concil-
iatory tone. "I'm sure you understand."

"I'm a civilian from another country and you have no
qualms speaking to me," Matt countered. "Besides, we'll tell
them everything after you leave so having them present will
save time." He indicated both men should sit.

Mr. Matthews hesitated, but Mr. Le Grand gave a slight
nod and the home secretary sat. The spy master sat too, rather
than melt into the shadows as he usually did.

"You know about the trouble in Shoreditch," Mr.
Matthews began. "Your friend is there with the police force, I
believe."

Willie took a step toward him. "Is he all right?"

"As far as I know but the situation is ongoing."

"Are you expecting me to do something about it?" I asked.
"Is that why you're here? Because I don't see how I can
placate an angry mob of artless craftsmen."

Mr. Matthews shook his head. "That's not the reason for
our visit." He shifted in the chair as if trying to get comfortable and glanced at Mr. Le Grand.

The spy master's approval came in the form of a long
blink. He was clearly driving this meeting, even though Mr.
Matthews outranked him.

"We don't think it's a coincidence that this protest has
come so soon after dismissing Lord Coyle's advice yesterday," Mr. Matthews said.

My breath hitched. "Are you saying Lord Coyle orchestrated it as a form of retribution?"

"It's a possibility but we can't prove it."

"There have been frequent protests," Matt said. "Why do
you think this one was caused by him?"

"It's different," Mr. Le Grand said. "It's a blockade rather
than a march or targeted riot. With the others, we've had
intelligence in the hours beforehand. Not this time. It caught
us by surprise, which implies a different hand is stirring the
pot."

"We suspect that hand is Coyle's," the home secretary

continued. "He was angry after yesterday's meeting. Perhaps angry enough to make trouble in retaliation."

Matt huffed a humorless laugh. "You only have your-selves to blame for that. You asked him to be an advisor then rejected his advice when it wasn't to your liking. If you'd done your job, you would have known he was dangerous." He didn't look at the spy master, but we all knew the barb was directed at him.

Mr. Le Grand remained unmoving, however, not even blinking as he regarded Matt coolly from beneath half-lowered lids.

Mr. Matthews cleared his throat. "There was no founda-tion for the rumors against Coyle. Besides, the benefits of employing him outweighed the negatives."

I threw my hands in the air. "He killed Sir Charles Whit-taker, your own employee!"

Mr. Matthews raised a hand in protest. "There's no proof of that. And if he is as dangerous as the rumors suggest, then how better to keep an eye on him than from within our own ranks?"

Matt leaned forward, resting his elbows on his knees and loosely clasping his hands in front of him. It was a pose often employed by Duke, Cyclops or Willie, while Matt tended to be more upright and English in his mannerisms and stance. Perhaps he was forgetting himself in his curios-ity. Or his concern. "So why are you here? What do you want from us?"

Mr. Matthews turned to me. "We would like to officially ask you to advise us, Mrs. Glass. At Coyle's, you invited us to call on you to hear your ideas." He spread out his hands before settling them on the chair arms again. "So here we are."

"My ideas are simple," I told him. "Lord Coyle was right when he suggested magicians must let the world know their magic doesn't last forever. That can be done through news-paper editorials and advertisements. But magical goods will still be highly sought, so I think there should also be a limit to productivity. Perhaps a cap on quantities manufactured or higher prices assigned to magician-made goods."

Mr. Matthews' eyes lit up. "A tax! Yes. Cabinet will like that idea."

Duke rolled his eyes. "Of course they will."

Matt sat back and gave me a small triumphant smile. The tax had been his idea. We both knew the government would like it. It remained to be seen whether it would satisfy the artless and magicians too.

Mr. Matthews rose and buttoned up his jacket. "I'll speak to my colleagues today."

Matt also rose. "You should set up a meeting between the artless and magicians as soon as possible."

"Not until I have approval from cabinet."

"And how long will that take?"

"I should have an answer by next week."

Matt shook his head. "That's too long. The sooner the two sides can sit down together, the sooner the riots will end."

"I need approval first. There is a process, Mr. Glass. You know that."

Matt's jaw firmed.

Willie wasn't willing to let the matter go, however. "You've got to do something about the riots *today*!"

Mr. Matthews turned away from her. "The police are handling it."

She grabbed his arm, forcing him to face her. "How many will be injured or killed attempting to break it up?"

"We cannot take any proposals to these people without first discussing them amongst ourselves. It would be irresponsible."

"Forget talks. It's time for action."

He shook her off and strode for the door.

"I have an idea," she said.

Mr. Matthews waited by the door. "Le Grand?"

But Mr. Le Grand ignored him. "Go on," he said to Willie. "What's your idea?"

Mr. Matthews' lips flattened in indignation.

Willie turned her back to him as he had done to her. "You think Coyle's behind today's blockade, right? But you have no proof. I reckon we try to get that proof by infiltrating the artless group behind it and find out where they're getting their information from."

"Absurd," Mr. Matthews muttered. "Are you suggesting *you* be the infiltrator? You're not qualified."

Willie bristled. "We used to work for the sheriff back home, and sometimes that meant pretending to be on the side of the outlaws. We were damned good at it too."

The spy master's face was as bland and unreadable as ever, but he didn't immediately reject her suggestion, which I took as a good sign. "I've heard of your endeavors in America. But there is a problem. Glass is known by Coyle, Abercrombie, and the other instigators behind the riots. You all are."

"I infiltrated their ranks before and no one recognized me. I can change my hat, my clothes, even my gender."

Mr. Le Grand hesitated.

Willie poked him in the chest. "You can make it official and agree here and now, or walk out of this house and pretend I said nothing. Either way, I'm doing it and you ain't stopping me."

Mr. Le Grand raised an eyebrow at Matt. Matt smirked. It was all the answer the spy master needed. "You give me no choice, Miss Johnson. See what you can find out from within their ranks. But if you're caught, you are on your own. I won't be sending any men in to help you."

She snorted. "I don't need a man's help."

I watched them leave with a sense of relief washing over me. Finally we were moving forward and my ideas were being given serious consideration. Talks between magicians and the artless would soon alleviate some problems and see an end to the riots.

But not soon enough. Not for Cyclops, and now Willie.

And it remained to be seen how Lord Coyle would react if Willie could prove he was behind today's blockade.

CHAPTER 4

*A*fter Willie left dressed in the clothing of a laborer, our day did not improve. Aunt Letitia insisted we go for a walk for fresh air and gentle exercise, but we returned home after a mere twenty-five minutes. Two acquaintances she'd not spoken to in some time approached us in Hyde Park and wanted to commission me to fix their clocks. Aunt Letitia had roundly admonished them for their rudeness and they'd gone off in a huff. We decided it was wise to leave before a third asked.

It was fortunate that we returned to the house when we did. Detective Inspector Brockwell had arrived while we were out. We found him sipping tea with Duke in the drawing room. Both men leapt to their feet upon our entry and looked grateful to be rescued. I imagined the conversation had been awkward. Neither man was a great conversationalist, and they'd never before been left alone together. The only thing they had in common was Willie.

She was topmost on Brockwell's mind. "Duke tells me you let her go on a dangerous scheme to infiltrate the dissenters' camp."

"We didn't *let* her," Matt said. "She has a mind of her own and there's no changing it when she's made a decision."

"You ought to know that better than anyone," I pointed out.

Brockwell scrubbed his sideburns, his frown replaced by a sheepish twist of his lips.

I indicated he should resume his seat. "I am pleased to see that you and Willie have made up."

"I suppose we have."

"You suppose?"

"One day she's not speaking to me, and the next she's resting her feet on my dining table and is talking to me as if nothing is amiss. I just go along with it."

Duke nodded knowingly. "It's better that way."

"Less tiresome," Aunt Letitia agreed.

"Less complicated," Matt added.

Bristow arrived with extra cups, plates and a fresh pot of tea. I poured while Matt handed out slices of cake. Brockwell set his down without touching it. He still looked troubled.

I refilled his teacup and handed it to him. "Willie will be all right. She's very capable when it comes to missions such as this."

"I know that, but…"

"But you're worried nevertheless."

He lifted a shoulder in a shrug. "I wish there was something I could do."

"We all wish there was something we could do," Matt said.

Aunt Letitia tapped her teaspoon on the side of the cup after stirring her tea. "Have you tried walking, Inspector? Or laudanum?"

We all stared at her, but she sipped her tea as if she hadn't just suggested the very conservative detective inspector take the highly addictive remedy.

Bristow entered and announced two new arrivals. "Lord and Lady Rycroft. Shall I show them in?" He hadn't finished speaking when Matt's aunt and uncle pushed their way past him.

The collective groan from the rest of us wasn't audible, but it was palpable nevertheless. Matt and I rose to greet our guests, while Duke and Brockwell made their excuses and beat a hasty exit from the drawing room.

I signaled to Bristow to bring in another two cups then indicated to our guests that they should sit.

"We won't be staying," Lady Rycroft said, taking a seat by the fire. If her snippy tone didn't alert me to the fact that something was wrong, her scowl certainly did. Even though the skin on her forehead was pulled back tightly by her turquoise turban, she managed to bestow glares upon Matt, Aunt Letitia and me.

Matt's uncle looked less ill-tempered than his wife as he lowered himself somewhat gingerly into a chair, but once he was settled, his heavy brow plunged into a furrow. I braced myself for a berating, although I couldn't think what we'd done wrong now.

"Are you unwell, Uncle?" Matt asked.

"He's upset," Lady Rycroft answered with a pitch so high it made the hairs on the back of my neck stand up. "Upset and hurt at the traitorous way we've been treated by our own family."

I tried to remain as still as possible. Perhaps if I didn't move, they'd forget I was there. This was a topic best left to Matt. He could choose to employ his charms to diffuse the tension, or not. It was his family and entirely up to him as to how to proceed.

"Do go on," he intoned. "I am all ears."

"Don't pretend you don't know what this is about."

Matt looked askance at me. I shrugged.

"Don't *you* pretend she stood a chance," Aunt Letitia snapped. "We all know she did not."

Lady Rycroft gasped and followed it up with a series of heavy breaths, as if she'd received a blow to the gut.

I cast another glance at Matt, arching my brow in question. He mouthed "Charity and Davide" back at me. Now I understood. His uncle and aunt were upset that we hadn't pushed Lord Farnsworth in Charity's direction. They must have been quite set on him taking her off their hands.

Lord Rycroft's face turned thunderous. "You had a duty to your family, Letitia, and yet I hear you introduced that Farnsworth character to Lady Sloane's niece in this very house! No doubt your intention was for them to meet."

"That is generally the intention of a dinner party." Aunt Letitia sat stoically, a steel pole withstanding the storm raging around her.

"How could you betray your own flesh and blood!"

"Keep your voice down," Matt growled. "And do not speak to her that way."

"I'll speak to her any way I bloody well like. She's my sister!"

Poor Aunt Letitia. She'd been subjected to her brother and sister-in-law's cruel words and cavalier disregard for her welfare for years. They'd neglected her when she lived with them, and ignored her once she moved in with us unless they wanted something from her, like now.

Matt wasn't allowing it, however. "Get out of my house." His voice lashed as brutally as a whip, despite remaining level.

Aunt Letitia's high, almost melodic voice was its exact opposite and yet no less effective. "Brother, are you blind or simply playing at being stupid?"

Lord Rycroft's face flushed scarlet. He bared his teeth. "I beg your pardon!"

"Davide is eccentric but not mad. Unlike Charity."

Lady Rycroft squeaked in horror.

"*You've* got a nerve calling others mad, Sister," Lord Rycroft spluttered.

Aunt Letitia clicked her tongue as if admonishing a child for saying something naughty. "A little madness here and there is not a hindrance to a happy marriage or life, of course. Not in itself. But when it comes with a vindictive, cruel and selfish nature…well, I couldn't foist that on Davide. He's such a good, kind-hearted soul."

Lady Rycroft shot to her feet. "*You* are the cruel, vindictive one. Farnsworth was Charity's last chance."

"She's young," I told her. "She'll find another. Look at Patience. She was older when she found love."

"Patience is an agreeable sort. Charity is…challenging." Lady Rycroft sniffed and turned suddenly to her husband. "We're leaving. Come, Rycroft."

But her husband didn't get up. He sat slumped in the chair, his face the waxy gray of a candle stub. He rubbed his upper arm.

Matt strode over to him and crouched beside the chair. "Are you all right, Uncle?"

"Of course I bloody well am." Lord Rycroft pushed to his feet only to lose his balance.

Matt grasped his elbow to steady him. Lord Rycroft drew in a few deep breaths before shaking him off.

I opened the door and called for Peter the footman. "Assist Lord Rycroft to his carriage."

"I don't need anyone's help," his lordship growled. He tugged on his jacket lapels and marched out of the room. He seemed to have recovered from his turn.

"I hope he'll be all right," I said once they were out of earshot.

Aunt Letitia sniffed. "I don't. Honestly, how could they think Charity would be a good match for Davide? He can do much better. Lady Helen will suit him well."

"Because she likes adventure?"

She tapped her temple. "Because she's in full command of her faculties."

* * *

Detective Inspector Brockwell returned to the house at dinnertime, as did my grandfather. I watched Chronos carefully for any signs of illness, but he seemed well enough for an elderly man. He fell asleep in an armchair after dinner and snored softly, much to Aunt Letitia's annoyance. After fifteen minutes, she went to bed.

I tinkered with a clock while Duke, Matt and Brockwell played poker. The detective lost all of his matchsticks very quickly and abandoned the game. He picked up the newspaper and started reading, but remained on the same page for over an hour. I closed the clock's housing and went to sit beside him on the sofa.

"You're worried," I said gently.

He lowered the newspaper with a sigh. "Don't tell her. She'll assume my concern means I think her weak."

"I won't say a word. Would you like a brandy to help settle your nerves?"

"Someone say brandy?" Willie sauntered in with a broad smile plastered on her face. "Evening, Jasper. You come to see me?"

He leapt up and embraced her. She hugged him back then ordered him to stop fussing.

Duke handed her a glass of brandy then poured another for Brockwell. "Have you seen Cyclops?"

Willie downed the brandy in a single gulp then held the glass out for more. "He's fine. There's been some injuries on both sides, but no fatalities. The police haven't broken through the blockade, and I don't reckon they will. Not any time soon. If the military are called, it'll be a different story."

"Let's hope it doesn't come to that," Matt said. "What did you learn?"

She hitched up her trousers and sat in an armchair, cradling her glass in both hands. "Rumor is the main participants are being paid to cause trouble. Some others reckon that's unfair and they should all get paid. I overheard two men discussing it. They didn't know I was listening in."

"Who do they think was providing the money?" Matt asked.

"A rich lord, so they said."

"Coyle," Duke muttered. "It has to be."

Brockwell agreed. "If we can get evidence, I can have him arrested for inciting unrest."

Willie shook her head. "There ain't no evidence, just rumor. The men reckoned whoever it is, his interests aligned with theirs, and he wants the magicians banned from the guilds too."

Coyle didn't care about the guilds or the artless agenda. He only cared about causing trouble for me, and now the government. They'd stripped him of the power he'd gained when he became their advisor, and Coyle didn't like losing power, not even a modest amount.

"What about Abercrombie?" Matt asked. "Did his name arise?"

She nodded. "He seems to be the conduit between Coyle and the troublemakers."

"That's enough to arrest him, ain't it?" Duke asked Brockwell.

The inspector shook his head. "Not unless we can find a witness who's prepared to say they received instruction and payment from Abercrombie. Then we'll have to get Abercrombie to admit he received his instructions and funds from Coyle. It *is* enough to question him, however."

"You can't do anything without going through Matthews and Le Grand," Matt said. "This is a Home Office matter, not merely a police one."

I caught Willie staring at me, but she quickly looked down at her glass then hurriedly sipped. Matt noticed too.

"What is it?" he asked her.

She pressed her lips together as if she would refuse to answer, but at Matt's urging, she gave in. "There was some talk about India. Oscar Barratt, too."

"Go on."

"They think India and Barratt are to blame for encouraging the magicians to come out of the woodwork."

Matt's hand curled into a fist. I suspected he was imagining punching Oscar in the nose as punishment for writing his book. I sat beside him and closed my hand over the top of his. He uncurled his fist, but anger still vibrated through him.

"All will be well once it becomes known that magic fades over time," I said.

Brockwell strode toward the door.

"Where are you going?" Willie asked.

"To call on Mr. Matthews and tell him what you learned."

She set the glass on the table with a thud. "Not without me you ain't. It's my information."

He moved aside to allow her to exit ahead of him. She grabbed his arm, grinning like a debutante stepping out with her paramour, and they continued side by side. "Don't wait up for me," she said over her shoulder. "I'll stay at Jasper's tonight."

The discussion had roused Chronos, although he'd not contributed to the conversation. He announced he was leaving, and Matt called for the carriage to be brought around to take him home.

After we saw him off, we returned to the drawing room with Duke. I was keenly aware of Cyclops's absence. Catherine must be worried. She would have heard about the barricade in Shoreditch by now and would know he was there.

A mere forty minutes later, Willie walked in again. She strode to the drinks trolley, poured herself another brandy and downed it in a single gulp. Matt, Duke and I exchanged glances.

Duke mouthed, "Say something," to Matt. Matt shook his head. Cowards.

It would seem it was up to me to put my head into the lion's mouth. "You decided to come home instead of going to Brockwell's?"

She swung around and pointed at me with the finger of the hand that held the glass. "Did you know, India?"

"Know what?"

"That Jasper was with someone else last night."

"And?"

49

"And he shouldn't be!"

Well, well. Willie was jealous. Not to mention unreasonable. "*You* were with Lady Helen."

She pouted. "That's different. He knows I see other people."

"And he can't? That's hardly fair, Willie."

She finished her brandy and slammed the glass down on the drinks trolley. "I'm going to sneak into Helen's room. If you see Brockwell in the morning, you can tell him I ain't pining for him."

"It seems to me that you are."

She pretended not to hear me and strode out of the room.

All of the tension left with her and I breathed a sigh of relief. Matt and Duke relaxed in their chairs. Sometimes Willie could surprise me. I hadn't expected her to feel romantic jealousy. It stood to reason, I supposed. She was the most emotionally charged person I'd ever met so it made sense that she was capable of experiencing fierce jealousy too.

I hoped it wouldn't ruin her relationship with Brockwell altogether, just when it seemed to be back on track.

* * *

MATT and I called on Mr. Matthews the following morning just as the home secretary received word that the blockade of Shoreditch High Street was being dismantled and the dissenters moved on. It meant Cyclops would soon be heading home, or perhaps to Catherine's shop.

"Thank your cousin for me, Glass," Mr. Matthews said with a smug smile. "Her actions gave us enough information to question Abercrombie, and I believe that's why we can claim victory in this battle."

"What did he say?"

"Nothing to implicate Coyle, unfortunately, but I think we frightened him enough that he decided it was time to end the blockade. I doubt he'll cause us concern again."

"You're a fool if you believe that," Matt said. "Abercrombie won't give up easily."

"He's weak. Men like him crumble under a little authoritative pressure. As soon as he realized we knew he'd been agitating the artless, he backed down."

"He has Lord Coyle on his side," I pointed out. "That will bolster his confidence. But I am pleased that he ordered an end to the blockade. That's a good start."

Matt lifted his gaze to the portrait of the queen, dressed in full regal costume complete with crown, scepter and a disapproving frown. She seemed to be disagreeing with her employee over his opinion of Abercrombie.

"What does Le Grand think?" Matt asked.

The home secretary sat forward and clasped his hands on the desk. "He thinks sending Miss Johnson in disguise into the enemy camp was a master stroke. The object of the exercise was to end the blockade and we achieved that." His smug smile returned, and I suspected Mr. Le Grand had disagreed with the home secretary about Abercrombie fading into the background, but his concerns had been dismissed, just like ours were being dismissed now.

"Are Le Grand's men watching Abercrombie to see if he contacts Coyle?" Matt asked.

"Of course. It's in hand, Glass. This is the beginning of the end of all your troubles."

It was a grand statement, and one that I couldn't believe. Not yet. Not until I knew for certain that Coyle and Abercrombie were rendered powerless.

"I'm glad you stopped by this morning, Mrs. Glass. It saves me from sending you the letter I've been drafting." He stubbed his finger on the paper in front of him. "I want you to speak to the prime minister and cabinet next week about your proposed magic tax."

I blinked hard. "You want *me* to talk to the prime minister?"

"And cabinet. Who better to discuss the tax than the woman who thought it up?"

"Oh," I muttered. "Then yes. I accept."

"It wasn't an invitation, but very well." He plucked his pen out of the stand. "I'll have the details sent to you tomorrow."

I rose only to sit again. "The tax is just one idea. There are more. Can I discuss those at the meeting too?"

"I don't see why not, but don't be surprised if the tax is all *they* want to talk about."

I left feeling light as air, my mind whirling with so many thoughts. Thankfully Matt steered me outside and into our carriage or I might have been standing in the corridor for some time.

It was Matt's kiss on my temple that brought me back to the present. "I'm very proud of you, India. You're going to make those politicians take notice of magicians."

"If I don't stumble over my words and trip over my feet."

He laughed softly. "You'll be fine."

"You Americans always say that. We English are more realistic. I hope I don't ruin everything." I groaned as the enormity of what I'd accepted hit me. I felt sick. "It's not just magicians who're depending on me to succeed, but women too. If I come across as a silly female, I might set the fight for equality back decades."

He put his arm around my shoulders and drew me to him. "Just say the word tax three times and you'll have them eating out of your hand."

I laughed and hugged him tightly. Matt always knew how to dispel my anxiety.

* * *

THE ARRIVAL of Brockwell after luncheon was a welcome surprise. I ushered him into the drawing room where I'd been reading with Aunt Letitia. I checked the landing and corridor to make sure Willie hadn't seen him and closed the door.

She was somewhere in the house, having just woken up after a night out with Lady Helen. According to Mrs. Bristow,

Willie had been drunk when she'd come home just after dawn. Thankfully she'd put herself to bed quietly and not woken the rest of us.

"Tell me what it is you're going to say to her before you see her," I told him. "That way I can determine if anything needs changing."

His brow furrowed. "Do you mean Willie?"

"Some men lack the qualities required for, er, intimate conversation of the nature you need to have with her. Not to mention that Willie is particularly difficult."

Aunt Letitia muttered an agreement.

"So I think it's best if you get an opinion of your speech before you speak to her," I finished.

"You misunderstand, India. I'm not here to speak to Willie."

"But you must! If you don't, she'll think you don't care, and I know you do. Don't give up now. Not when she's finally revealing the true depth of her feelings for you."

His jaw dropped only to quickly close again. He scrubbed one sideburn then switched to the other.

"I think her jealousy can work in your favor," I went on. "You just need to know how to play your cards. Don't show them too soon, but don't hold them too long, either."

My analogy seemed to confound him. He looked dazed. "She's jealous?"

I laughed then realized he was serious. "Couldn't you tell? Honestly, I'm a little surprised. She's not very adept at keeping her feelings to herself."

He nodded slowly. "It does explain why she left without saying goodbye and slammed the door on her way out."

I rolled my eyes. He might be a detective, but he was quite oblivious when it came to matters of the heart.

He cleared his throat. "I'm not here to see Willie. I'm here on a rather important police matter, as it happens. There was a break-in at a jewelry store overnight."

"Was the jeweler a magician? Is that why you're here?"

"No. I mean, I don't know if he was a magician." He

glanced past me to Aunt Letitia, but she appeared not to be listening. He scratched his sideburns again and looked reluctant to continue.

"Inspector," I snapped. "Do go on before I expire from curiosity."

He lowered his voice so she couldn't hear. "Nothing was stolen, but the jeweler was murdered."

"How awful. Have you caught the murderer?"

He nibbled on his lower lip.

"Inspector!"

He flinched. "Dr. Gabriel Seaford was arrested this morning."

I gasped and pressed a hand to my throat. My pulse pounded in time to my erratic heartbeat. "No. There must be a mistake. He can't have done it. Gabe is not a murderer."

"He was known to have argued with the victim about an engagement ring, and he was seen leaving the scene of the crime. We also found bloodied knife and clothing in his home."

I reached behind me and grasped the back of a chair to steady myself. If I let go, I might collapse to the floor. "You know what this means," I whispered.

"It means if he's found guilty, he'll hang. And if he hangs, Matt's life could also be in danger, if the magic in his watch runs out. Yes, India. I know. That's why I came here immediately. Because based on the evidence, Seaford is guilty."

CHAPTER 5

*M*att took the news of Gabe's arrest better than me. His first and only concern was for Gabe's welfare. He wasn't worried for himself at all.

"Where is he now?" he asked Brockwell.

"A holding cell at Scotland Yard. He'll be moved tomorrow morning. You'll want to visit him, I expect."

"Can we?"

Brockwell hesitated. "I can claim that I suspect the victim was a magician and you've been hired as consultants. That will get you past the sergeant on duty." He always followed procedure, so for him to bend the rules for us, he knew how important it was that we speak to Gabe.

I clasped his hand. "Thank you, Inspector."

Willie and Duke emerged from the service area while we were putting on hats and cloaks in the entrance hall. With Gabe's arrest foremost in my mind, I'd momentarily forgotten about Willie and Brockwell's relationship troubles. It wasn't until Willie refused to look at him that I remembered.

Brockwell didn't let her brush-off deter him. He smiled at her. "Afternoon, Willie."

She crossed her arms. "Jasper."

"Where are you going?" Duke asked.

"Scotland Yard," Matt said. "Seaford has been arrested for murder."

Willie's explosion of expletives reverberated around the entrance hall, bouncing off the tiled floor and walls.

Matt ordered her to keep her voice down. "I don't want to worry Aunt Letitia."

"What are we waiting for? Let's go see Gabe!"

"You're not needed. India and I—"

She shoved him in the chest and marched past him. She was out of the door before anyone could stop her. Duke accepted her coat from Bristow and hurried after her to the waiting carriage.

Willie and Duke reluctantly agreed to remain in the carriage after Brockwell insisted he couldn't get all four of us in to see Gabe. Willie let him know her displeasure at being left out by slumping in the corner and pouting.

"Don't take it personally," I told Brockwell. "She's just very protective of Matt and hates that she can't help."

"Gabe's the one we should be worried about," Matt said as he opened the door to the police headquarters.

I went in ahead of him. "Of course, and we all are, but there is the matter of your watch too. If the medical magic in it fades again, and there is no magician doctor to fix it…" Tears pooled in my eyes and couldn't be blinked away.

He touched my chin. "Don't worry about me, India. You know my thoughts on that. This is about Gabe; only Gabe."

Brockwell signed us in at the front desk then we headed through the warren of corridors and rooms to the stairs leading down to the basement holding cells. The cooler air sent a shiver down my spine, and the lack of windows and fresh air made the corridor seem even narrower, the walls closer. I found it hard to catch my breath. Our echoing foot-steps were a signal to the prisoners on the other side of the locked doors that someone passed. One begged us to let him out, and another shouted his innocence.

The sergeant escorting us stopped at a door and unlocked it using one of the keys attached to the large iron ring he carried. Gabe lifted his head and closed his eyes in relief upon seeing us. He stood and shook Matt's hand then mine.

"I am very glad to see you both. Very glad indeed." He indicated the wooden bench bolted to the wall. It must act as both bed and seat, depending on whether the thin mattress rolled up on the end was laid out or not. "Be my guest, India. It's surprisingly clean."

"We keep a tight ship here," Brockwell said, somewhat defensively.

The sergeant closed the door. The *clank* of the tumbling lock was loud in the small room. A sense of doom swamped me and I gladly sat down before I swooned.

Gabe sat beside me. He looked tired, his eyes bloodshot. His hair was neatly combed, however, and his face cleanly shaved. He still wore his own clothes but one of the shirt cufflinks was missing. He may have lost it in a scuffle when the police arrested him.

"Tell us what happened," Matt said. "Why do they think you did it?"

Gabe shook his head. "It's all so confusing. They say they have witnesses who saw me leave the shop where the murder happened, but I wasn't there. I swear to you, I wasn't!"

"We believe you," I said.

"And the bloodied clothing and knife found at your house?" Brockwell asked.

Gabe shook his head again and again, as if trying to clear it. "I don't know how they got there. All I can think is that the police put them there when they searched to implicate me."

I glanced at Brockwell.

"That wouldn't happen if I was in charge of the investigation," he said.

"I wish you were in charge," Gabe muttered. "Then I might stand a chance." He raked his hand through his hair, messing it up, before smoothing it again.

"We'll get you out," I assured him. "Matt and I will investigate."

He gave me a flat smile. "Thank you."

"Have you ever met the witnesses?" Matt asked. "Could they be people you've angered, who'd be prepared to lie to implicate you?"

"No! Certainly not to the point that they want me to hang for a crime I didn't commit."

"You were seen arguing with the victim," Brockwell said. "Can you explain that?"

"I commissioned the jeweler to make an engagement ring for Nancy. I wanted her to have the best, so I thought I'd look for a magician jeweler. To be honest, I wasn't expecting to find one, but I made sure to touch as many gems, silverware and gold pieces in all the jewelry shops I entered. To my surprise, I felt magical warmth in Mr. Goldman's shop. It was faint, but I felt its warmth as surely as I feel the damp in this cell. It was in the gold chains he had on display."

I stared wide-eyed at him. "He was a gold magician? But how can that be? Gold magic died out centuries ago." A man named McArdle once told us as much last year. He was a gold magician, thought to be the last of his kind. He hadn't known any spells and claimed all the spells used by gold magicians had been lost long ago.

Yet Gabe was telling us he felt magic in gold in a London jewelry shop.

"Go on," Matt said. "How did the argument start?"

"I was excited to find a magician," Gabe said. "I honestly hadn't expected to, so I was caught a little off guard. I blurted out my surprise to the jeweler and admitted that I was also a magician and recognized the magical heat in his chains."

"Did you tell him what sort of magician you were?" I asked.

He shook his head. "It never came to that. As soon as I mentioned magic, he told me the price was double what we'd agreed. He said he couldn't possibly sell magical gold for anything less. Naturally, I was angry. Anyone would be." He appealed to Brockwell.

The detective inspector stood unmoving, his face unreadable.

"Then what?" I asked.

"Then I refused to pay and stormed out. Another customer was entering as I left. A woman."

"She must be the one who told the police about the confrontation," Matt said.

"I think the shopkeeper next door also saw me leave in a fury. He was standing in his doorway as I walked past."

"Did you go home?" Matt asked.

"I went to work. My shift was about to start. I didn't return home until three this morning. And before you ask, I didn't see anyone who can vouch for my arrival. No one is up and about at that time. No one who lives near me anyway."

"So conceivably you could have been at the shop killing Mr. Goldman," Brockwell said.

"Except I wasn't," Gabe bit off. "I went straight to bed and was rudely awoken by the police at eight this morning." He lowered his head and dragged both hands through his hair. "This is a nightmare."

"We'll hire a good lawyer," Matt said. "And we'll begin investigating immediately. We'll find the real killer as quickly as we can, Gabe. Don't worry."

Gabe shook Matt's hand then turned to me. His gaze softened. "India, will you do me a favor and call on Nancy? She'll be beside herself with worry."

"Of course I will. We'll take good care of her. You'll be out in no time, anyway."

His smile was forced but at least he tried to put on a brave face.

Brockwell banged on the door and the sergeant unlocked it. We headed silently back the way we'd come, up to the ground floor. Policemen hurried along the corridors; some were in uniform, others in plain clothes. Brockwell nodded a greeting to many, but when he spotted a man with an impressive gray moustache and balding head, he hailed him.

He introduced us to the detective investigating the murder of Mr. Goldman. "What is the latest information?" Brockwell asked.

The detective eyed Matt and me carefully. "I can't tell you that here."

Brockwell followed his gaze and frowned. "They've consulted for us on magical cases before. You know that. You can trust them."

"This isn't a magical case."

"The murdered man was most likely a gold magician and the suspect is—"

"A friend," Matt cut in. "He didn't do it."

The detective grunted. "Evidence says otherwise." He tried to push past us, but Brockwell stopped him.

"You're not looking for another suspect, are you?" he pressed.

"We have our man. Why waste resources when it's a foregone conclusion?"

"Blast it, he's innocent!"

"If he is, then why are there witnesses willing to testify against him? Why were bloodied clothes and the murder weapon found in his house?" The detective pointed a finger at Brockwell. "And don't spout that nonsense about corrupt officers planting evidence and paying witnesses."

"You're denying that corruption exists in the police force?" Matt asked.

"I'm denying that it exists in *this* case. There's simply no reason for any officer to incriminate Seaford or pay off witnesses. Where would they get the money?"

Where indeed?

The detective's features softened as he blew out a breath. He stroked his moustache and glanced around before stepping closer. "None of us want to see a good man hang for a crime he didn't commit, but the evidence against Seaford is overwhelming. There's nothing I can do for him."

"You can keep looking for the real killer," Matt growled.

The detective simply shrugged and walked off.

I watched him go, my heart a dead weight in my chest. How could he dismiss a man's life with a shrug?

The lives of two men.

I glanced at Matt, standing beside me with his hands on his hips, a seething tower of anger. He suddenly turned and strode off. Brockwell and I raced to keep up.

"Well?" Willie asked when we reached the carriage. Both she and Duke stood on the pavement, despite the chilly breeze coming off the Thames and whipping across the Victoria Embankment.

"It doesn't look good," I said.

Willie's face fell. Duke swore. "We've got to do something!" he cried.

Matt turned to Brockwell. "Can you find out the names of the two witnesses who claim to have seen Gabe leaving in the middle of the night?"

Brockwell tilted his head to the side. "You can't speak to them, Glass."

Matt ignored him. "India, you should visit Miss O'Dwyer."

"You're not coming with me?"

He peered up at the topmost level of the imposing red brick building. "I'm going to talk to the commissioner."

I climbed into the carriage ahead of Duke and Willie, neither of whom were particularly interested in calling on Gabe's fiancée. Both wanted to start investigating, but Matt insisted they go with me. Willie only acquiesced when he assured her he'd meet us before he called on the witnesses.

Willie spent most of the journey to Pimlico muttering about injustice under her breath. I tried to ignore her, but with Duke sitting in morose silence, I had nowhere to turn. That left me to dwell on my own misery and consider Gabe's case. The more I thought, the clearer one thing became.

Someone was behind his arrest. Someone had paid police to plant incriminating evidence at Gabe's house and paid witnesses to claim they'd seen him leave Mr. Goldman's shop after the murder. The only man with the financial means to do that, who would have no qualms about murdering an innocent man to implicate another, was Lord Coyle.

I was no longer surprised by the depth of his evil. I wasn't even shocked that he knew how important Gabe was to us. Coyle's tentacles reached into corners we thought well hidden. His spies and contacts could uncover truths we'd tried to bury. Indeed, knowing that Gabe was being targeted because of his special connection to us only confirmed that Coyle was behind this.

He must have discovered that Matt needed Gabe for his own survival. He knew we'd do anything to save Gabe from the gallows. Would he demand something from us to make the evidence disappear?

Or would he let Gabe hang for something he didn't do just to prove that he had the power?

Duke suddenly clicked his fingers. "We can get Charbonneau to use his magic to fashion a key out of iron. Then we'll break Seaford free."

Willie looked at him as though he'd sprouted another head. "That's the dumbest idea you've ever had. Scotland Yard is crawling with police. How will we get past them all? And you're forgetting that Charbonneau's a low-down pigswill who tried to kill Matt."

"I ain't forgetting. I just reckon he's the best option we got. Maybe the only one."

"Fabian is not an option," I said heavily. "He'll demand too high a price."

Fabian might seize the opportunity to demand Matt divorce me so I could be free to marry him instead. I wouldn't put anything past him. If he was desperate enough to attempt to kill Matt, he was desperate enough to make demands I couldn't possibly fulfill.

"Matt ain't worried for himself," Duke muttered. "Did either of you notice?"

Willie kicked the seat opposite and crossed her arms over her chest.

I turned to look out of the window, but saw nothing through the blur of my tears. "Matt thinks he should have died years ago. He considers every day since the shooting at Broken Creek a windfall, one he did nothing to deserve. He has already resigned himself to the outcome if Gabe isn't around next time the healing magic in his watch fades."

Willie kicked the seat again. "That's stupid."

"Yes, it is. But it's what he thinks."

None of us were in the mood to speak to Miss O'Dwyer. We couldn't cheer her up or give her good news. Even so, I owed it to Gabe to support her as much as I could.

She was not at work on the wards at the Belgrave Hospital for Children, so her colleague directed us to the dormitory out the back where the nurses lived. We found Miss O'Dwyer lying on her bed, her eyes closed, clutching a framed photograph of Gabe to her chest.

I sat on the bed and she opened her eyes with a gasp. "It's just us," I said gently. "I've come from seeing Gabe and—"

"Is he all right? Did he say anything? Do you know how the investigation is going?" She swiped at her damp cheeks with the back of her hand as if her tears frustrated her. It was a relief to see she possessed an inner strength. She was going to need it.

"He looks well and is staying positive. The investigation is ongoing. He asked me to check if you needed anything."

"I need him out of prison and by my side." She closed her eyes and pressed her fingers to her temple. "I can't believe this is happening. It's like a bad dream. I keep thinking I'll wake up and all will be well. But it's not a dream, is it?"

I cast a desperate look to Willie and Duke in the hope they could say something to comfort her. I suspected anything I said would simply make her sadder and feel even more hopeless.

Willie sat on the bed on Miss O'Dwyer's other side. "Is there anything you can tell the police that will help Gabe's case? Anything you might have been holding back?"

Miss O'Dwyer frowned. "Why would I keep something from them that might help him?"

"It might be something that could harm your reputation." Willie shot me a speaking glance. "You know what I mean, India. You explain it."

"No need," Miss O'Dwyer said on a sigh. "You're asking if I left with Gabe when his shift finished last night, and if I stayed with him at his house until morning. I didn't. My shift finished hours earlier and I was in here or the dining room in full view of several other nurses at all times. I'm afraid I can't even lie for him. They'll know."

Willie suddenly hugged her. "At least you were willing to lie."

"I'd do anything for him. Anything." Her lower lip trembled.

Duke handed her his handkerchief. "Keep it," he said as she dabbed at her eyes.

We headed back outside to our carriage. A few minutes later, a hansom cab pulled up and Matt stepped out.

"Where's Jasper?" Willie asked.

"Working." Matt held up a piece of paper. "He managed to get the address of the two witnesses while no one was looking."

"That wouldn't have been easy," Duke said, directing a knowing look at Willie. "He's brave, smart and patient."

She snorted. "Are you in love with him too?"

Duke's lips twitched with his smile. "'Too?'"

Willie snatched the paper off Matt. "Let's go before it gets dark."

"What did the commissioner say?" I asked Matt as he assisted me into the carriage.

"That there's nothing he can do if all the evidence points to Gabe's guilt."

"So it's entirely in our hands."

His only response was to kiss the back of my hand before releasing it and climbing in after me.

"We have to succeed, Matt. We can't fail him. We simply can't."

He gave me a weak smile then turned away to stare out of the window.

* * *

GOLDMAN'S GOLD and Silverware shop was shrouded in darkness, the display shelf in the window empty except for a cloth of black velvet lining it. We were more interested in Lowe's Watches and Clocks next to it, however. I recognized Mr. Lowe's name, but had never met him. Even so, I decided to stay in the carriage while Matt questioned him. Mr. Lowe had been a member of the Watchmaker's Guild's court of assistants and one of Mr. Abercrombie's cronies. I didn't know if Mr. Lowe had lost his position on the committee when Mr. Abercrombie was ousted, but it didn't matter. Because of that association, I knew he didn't like me and wouldn't answer our questions if I showed my face.

Willie waited with me, but Duke went inside with Matt. "It ain't a coincidence that he's a watchmaker," she said, peering out from behind the curtain. "If I had money, I'd wager it all on Abercrombie putting him up to this."

Matt flipped the sign hanging inside the door to CLOSED then we lost sight of them. I sat back out of view and looked through the window on the other side. The bakery across the way was already closed, the lights off. According to Brockwell, that was where the other witness, an apprentice baker, worked. He'd been on his way to work early this morning when he claimed he'd seen Gabe emerging from Mr. Goldman's shop.

I checked my watch then checked it again a minute later and a minute after that. Time ticked slowly, but when Matt and Duke emerged, a mere five minutes had passed since they'd entered.

Matt gave Woodall instructions then joined us in the cabin along with Duke. "Lowe claims a loud noise coming from next door woke him up just before four this morning," Matt said. "He came downstairs and looked through his front window. He saw a man pass by in a hurry, and thanks to the lamplight, he got a clear view of his profile. He described the man to the police when they questioned him and they later asked him to identify the fellow in a line-up. He says he was able to easily pick him out."

"Was he lying?" Willie asked.

"I think so. He looked directly into my eyes and hardly blinked."

"He sounded wooden, too," Duke added. "Like he'd learned his part."

Willie slapped her knee. "So he *was* put up to it! Let's go back to Scotland Yard and tell Jasper."

Matt shook his head. "There's nothing Brockwell can do. It's not his case. Besides, unless we can prove Lowe is lying, it'll be his word against ours."

Willie swore.

"I'm going to say something you won't like," Duke hedged. "Especially you, India."

"Then don't say it," Matt said, at the same time that I urged him to continue.

Duke chose to ignore Matt. "I reckon we give Lowe an incentive to tell the truth. We could offer him a bribe."

"Or threaten him at gunpoint," Willie added with a glint in her eye.

"Willie," I chided.

"Just threaten. It's better than beating him up, ain't it?"

"It will look worse for Gabe if his friends are caught offering bribes to witnesses or threatening them," Matt pointed out. "You're also forgetting the second witness."

"No, I ain't. We can threaten him too. I reckon he's lying, just like Lowe."

We arrived at the tenement in which the apprentice baker lived as dusk settled over the city like a blanket. The street-lamps had not yet been lit and, by the look of the broken glass panels on some of them, they would remain unlit in this part of London. Hopefully we wouldn't be long. Spitalfields wasn't a place one wanted to linger after dark. One of the Ripper murders had occurred a mere two streets away. Yet despite the misery and desperation imprinted in the soot-stained walls and muck-filled gutters, smiling children greeted us. There were no adults in sight.

Matt handed out coppers to each of the children as Duke knocked on the tenement door.

A young man dressed in trousers that strangled the waistline of his stout frame answered. "What d'you want?" he snapped. Upon realizing he addressed a gentleman and lady, he mumbled an apology. "I thought it was them brats knick-knocking again."

Matt introduced us as consultants for Scotland Yard. "Are you Jack Crabb?"

"Aye."

"We have some questions about your statement regarding the murder of Mr. Goldman."

"I've already told the police everything."

"Even so, we need to be thorough. Tell us *precisely* what you saw."

Mr. Crabb sucked on his teeth as he regarded each of us in turn. "I was walking to work early this morning when I saw a man leaving the jewelry shop in a real hurry."

"What time was this?" Matt asked.

"Ten minutes to four."

"To have seen the man's face so clearly in the dark, you must have been very close to him."

"Close enough to almost bump into him. We were passing under the streetlamp near Goldman's shop, so there was some light."

I frowned. He sounded like he was telling the truth, not at all wooden. Yet something about his story didn't ring true. "Had you come straight from home?"

"Yes, ma'am. I walk. It takes twenty-five minutes."

"Then why were you walking on the pavement outside Mr. Goldman's shop?"

He gave me a blank look.

"The bakery is on this side of the street. You don't need to cross to the other side where Mr. Goldman's shop is located if you're going directly to work."

His mouth opened and closed but the only sound to come out was a hiss of breath.

"Answer her," Matt snapped.

"I, uh, I can't remember why I crossed the street." He retreated back inside like a turtle into its shell and slammed the door shut.

Willie pounded her fist on it. "You're lying! Come out here and admit you've been paid to lie!" When the door didn't re-open, she pounded on it again. "An innocent man's going to hang for a murder he didn't do because of you! Come on out and admit you lied."

The door remained firmly shut. Willie went to pound on it again, but Matt caught her wrist.

"You're wasting your breath."

"Maybe but it makes me feel better."

We returned to the carriage and Woodall drove us home. There was nothing more to do. We were deflated, defeated, and frustrated beyond measure. It was almost impossible to put on a brave face for Aunt Letitia, but we all tried. Except for Willie. She went straight to her room and stayed there. We sent dinner up to her and left her in peace.

Cyclops had returned home in the late afternoon after calling in briefly at Catherine's. He'd gone directly to bed, according to Aunt Letitia. After being on duty all of yesterday and last night, he was exhausted. He didn't sleep through the night, however, and came downstairs at ten o'clock. Aunt Letitia had retired so we were able to talk freely and tell him about Gabe's arrest.

He realized the implication for Matt immediately. It was obvious from his pained look.

"Don't," Matt said, handing him a glass of brandy. "Don't worry for my sake. Worry for Gabe's."

"I can't help it," Cyclops muttered.

"None of us can," Duke added quietly.

Willie strode in, her face set hard until it crumpled when she saw Cyclops. She threw her arms around his neck and hugged him fiercely.

He chuckled. "I'm pleased to see you too."

She drew back. "Have you heard about Gabe?"

He nodded. "So what are we going to do?"

"Nothing until I've got a Bourbon in hand."

Matt poured her a drink and handed her the glass. "I'm going to look around Goldman's shop," he announced. "Tonight."

"You're going to break in," I said flatly.

"I'm coming with you," Willie declared.

Duke and Cyclops insisted on going too.

"What do you hope to find there?" I asked.

"Something," Matt said heavily as he sat on the sofa beside me. "Anything. There has to be a reason behind his death. I can't accept that he was killed merely to implicate Gabe. It's just too…" He shook his head in disbelief.

I touched his knee. "We may have to accept that implicating Gabe *is* the entire reason. Coyle would do it, simply to hurt us. He may have got the idea when he heard about Gabe's argument with Goldman."

Matt sat back with a sigh and tapped his finger on the side of his empty glass. He had not asked for it to be refilled. He rarely drank more than one at a time, having had trouble with drinking to excess in the past. "There is also the possibility Goldman's murder is related to him being a goldsmith magician, and Gabe is merely the scapegoat."

Cyclops had been about to sip but now lowered his glass and stared at Matt. "I thought the gold magician lineage ended when McArdle died."

"McArdle might have been mistaken when he claimed he was the last one."

It was a possibility, although I couldn't think why anyone would want to kill a goldsmith magician. I agreed with Matt. A search of Goldman's premises might provide a clue.

"We shouldn't go before midnight," I said. "And we must all wear black."

It was a testament to how well they knew me that no one tried to tell me I couldn't accompany them.

Or so I thought.

"Don't look so smug," Willie said. "You're only coming because you're the only one who can detect magical heat."

* * *

THE LOCK on the back door of the shop was complicated. It took Matt over twenty minutes to open it with his tools. When he eventually did open the door, we were faced with an iron grill and another lock, just as complicated as the first. Matt went to work again, using the light from my lamp to guide him. When it finally swung open on silent hinges, I breathed a sigh of relief.

Willie, Matt and I entered, while Cyclops remained in the rear lane to keep watch. We'd left Duke standing at the shop's front entrance, leaning against a lamp post as if waiting for a friend.

The back rooms appeared to be used for storage, with one entire room occupied by a large safe. A smaller safe was tucked into the corner of the workshop, alongside rows upon rows of locked drawers. The jeweler's tools of pliers, tweezers, magnifiers and others I didn't know the names of were neatly lined up on the bench beside a marked wooden mandrel used for ring sizing. While the bench was pristine, the floor around it was littered with metal filings.

It was the shop itself that interested me the most, however, so I left Willie behind to see what she could find. Matt followed me. We covered our lanterns and blocked the window with the black cloth we'd brought, ensuring there were no gaps at the edges. Then we uncovered the lamp and began our search.

The shop was small with one long counter and several glass cabinets, all locked. The most valuable pieces had been put away by Mr. Goldman after he closed up for the last time. It occurred to me to check if the safe had been tampered with. Perhaps this was a simple case of a robbery gone awry.

Although considering the false witness testimonies implicating Gabe, I doubted it.

Matt found the order book and sat on the floor to read it. I kept looking, not particularly sure what I was searching for. The space behind the counter was mostly filled with locked wooden coffers. The only unlocked ones were used to store different colored ribbons and strips of leather, most likely to attach pendants to.

I rifled through the leather, only to quickly jerk back my hand. "Magic." I touched the silk ribbons. "These have magic in them too." Closer inspection revealed the fine workmanship on all the pieces.

I passed Matt one of the locked boxes. "Can you use your lock picks to open this?"

He pulled the slender tools out of his pocket and got to work.

"Do you think you can open the safe next?" I asked.

"I'm afraid safe cracking is beyond my skills."

"And here I thought you could do anything."

"Almost." His crooked smile made him look devilishly handsome in the low light.

I looked through the pages of the order book while Matt worked on the lock but didn't recognize any customers' names.

Moments later, he flipped open the lid of the box just as Willie emerged from the workshop. She announced she was going upstairs to search Goldman's residence and then she disappeared again.

I scooted closer to Matt to investigate the contents of the box with him. It was filled with gold chains of different thicknesses and lengths. I fingered them and immediately felt the magic warmth. But it was very faint, like a fireplace filled with ash rather than coals.

"It's incredibly weak," I whispered. "The magic must have been put in it a long time ago."

"How long ago?"

"Impossible to say, but I think years. Many decades or even centuries."

"So Goldman isn't a magician?"

"It's unlikely he put the magic into these, but he could be the descendant of a gold magician. Try another box and see if we find something with stronger magic."

Matt unlocked a second coffer, this one containing silver chains. The magic heat swamped me before I'd even touched a single piece.

"These have magic too, but it's much stronger than the gold."

"So he was a silver magician who also happens to deal in gold that contains old magic?"

We continued searching through the boxes, only to reveal more of the same. Gold pieces with faint magic, and silver items with strong magic.

Willie rejoined us and announced she'd found nothing of interest upstairs. "Ready to leave?"

"Not quite." Matt stood and put out a hand to assist me to my feet. He headed back into the workroom but I hesitated.

On a hunch, I ran my hand along the polished wooden surface of the counter, but felt no magic. Nor had I felt it in the wooden boxes. I rounded the counter and touched one of the display cabinets, expecting the same result. It was warm. I asked Willie to bring the lantern closer. The light struck the cabinet's feet, carved into the shape of a lion's paws. The work was so fine, they looked lifelike.

I straightened and looked around the shop. My gaze fell on the stack of business cards and I returned to the counter. I touched the top one. Magic. Strong magic, going by its heat.

Willie and I joined Matt in the workshop. He stood at the filing cabinet, the drawer labeled SUPPLIERS opened as he read a file.

He closed it and slotted it back into the drawer. "He only has one silver supplier."

"That's odd, ain't it?" Willie said.

"I assume so. Even odder is that he has recorded a name but no address."

"What about a gold supplier?" I asked.

"There are dozens upon dozens, scattered throughout the

country. His other suppliers are limited in number, just like the silversmith, but unlike for her, he has recorded their addresses. There are two leather suppliers, two furniture makers, a ribbon maker, and a silk embroiderer. Do you remember Abigail Pilcher, the former nun? The embroidery on those silk ribbons was done by her."

"Did you see a supplier for his business cards?"

Matt nodded. "It was Hendry, listed at his former address so he must have made them for Goldman before his arrest and subsequent disappearance."

Willie muttered an expletive under her breath. "I ain't never going to forget him. Murder by a thousand paper cuts." She held the lantern high as she led the way to the back door. "What's it all mean? Was Goldman a magician or not?"

"My guess is he wasn't," Matt said. "He had suppliers for all of his items. *They* were the magicians, not him. He was some sort of collector, but unlike those from the Collectors' Club, he sold his wares."

I agreed with some of his assessment, but not all. "I think he *was* a gold magician but, like McArdle, he had no spells. He could use his magic to detect gold magic in objects, but not put it in himself. That's why he had gold suppliers from all over the country. It's likely they didn't even know they had gold pieces with magic in them, but he did. He was also able to feel the magic in other objects and so sourced only those for his shop."

"But he didn't raise his prices," Willie pointed out. "Except when Gabe told him he felt the magic. So what was the point?"

I didn't have an answer to that. She was right. There seemed no point to selling magic pieces if he wasn't going to charge a higher price for them until someone told him they knew they contained magic.

"I think I know," Matt said darkly. "And if I'm right, then I also know who killed him."

CHAPTER 6

*A*fter I added Mr. Goldman's name to our list of magicians the following morning, noting DECEASED next to it, I scanned the page to the top. I'd spent most of the night thinking about Matt's theory that Mr. Goldman did something similar. Like us, he collected the names of magicians. But instead of locking his list away in a safe place and telling only a few trusted souls of its existence, he gave his list to Lord Coyle.

And Lord Coyle used it to bolster his collection of magical objects, as well as his collection of information about magicians. Information he used to gain power. Matt suspected Mr. Goldman told Lord Coyle that Gabe was a magician after their encounter, and together they'd worked out he was a doctor magician. Lord Coyle must have then guessed that Matt's survival in Broken Creek and here in London after being involved in a carriage accident and then a shooting was a result of Gabe's magic. To punish us, he had made sure Gabe was the main suspect in the murder of Mr. Goldman.

There was no doubt in any of our minds, Coyle had then killed his accomplice, Mr. Goldman. But the question remained—why?

We weren't going to get answers by confronting Coyle, but we had to do something or Gabe would never be freed.

Another thought occurred to me, one that had me hurrying out of Matt's office and down the stairs. I found him at the breakfast table with Cyclops, Duke and Willie.

"Shouldn't you be at work?" I asked Cyclops.

"I've taken the day off," he said without looking up from the slice of toast he was buttering. "I'm working with you to find Goldman's killer."

"We don't know what to do next," Matt said from the sideboard where he was filling his coffee cup.

"I have an idea." I joined him and poured myself a cup of coffee. I breathed in the bitter aroma, drawing it into my lungs. It helped wake me up after a terrible night's sleep. "There was an address for all of Mr. Goldman's magician suppliers—gold, leather, silk, wood and paper. But not the silversmith. He recorded just a name."

Matt leaned back against the sideboard, cup in hand. "So he didn't know where she lived. She must have come to him. He never called on her." He lifted a shoulder and shook his head. "How is that important?"

"I don't know, but it's a deviation from his pattern of recording names *and* addresses for his suppliers. Why should she be different?"

Duke tapped his temple. "Maybe he didn't need to write down her address because it was up here. He knew it well. Maybe they were close."

"Yes! If they were friends, perhaps she can shed some light on his relationship with Coyle and what went wrong between them. Mr. Goldman may have told her something important before his death, something that implicates Coyle."

Matt nodded slowly as he considered my theory. "We need to speak to her. Perhaps another jeweler will tell us where we can find her."

Willie wrinkled her nose. "You're going to make Duke, Cyclops and me go to all the jewelers in the city and ask 'em, aren't you? That's going to take days!"

"There may be another way," I said. "Lord Farnsworth's

silver-plated opera glasses were infused with magic. We can ask him where he purchased them."

Willie shoved a piece of toast in her mouth, gathered up the remaining rashers of bacon from her plate in one hand, and picked up a sausage in the other. She waved it in the air, signaling for us to follow her.

"India hasn't eaten yet," Matt said.

She didn't stop.

Matt went to protest again, but I shook my head at him. I drained my coffee, grabbed a slice of toast and exited behind Willie. The less time we wasted, the better.

* * *

Lord Farnsworth was still in bed when we arrived at his house, but Willie convinced the butler to wake him up by threatening to go upstairs and drag him out herself. A few minutes later he returned to the drawing room and announced his lordship would be down in a moment.

Lord Farnsworth arrived dressed as immaculately as ever. Even his hair was parted as straight as an arrow down the middle. The only telltale sign of a late night were his blood-shot eyes and an overwhelming smell of lavender and musk that he must have splashed over himself before coming down.

"Good morning, Friends. What a lovely surprise. Do you want breakfast?"

"We already ate," I said. "Davide, where did you purchase your opera glasses?"

He took my odd question in his stride, as if it was an everyday occurrence to have friends visit out of the blue and ask him where he bought things. "From a gentleman's shop on Bond Street. They sell umbrellas, walking sticks, handker-chiefs, that sort of thing. There was a collection of rather exquisite silver accessories on display that day, including the opera glasses. The engraving was so fine, I simply had to have it." He rocked back on his heels, a smug smile on his face. "Do you know, I wouldn't be surprised if it's magician-made, it's that beautiful."

"It is," I said. "I felt the magic in it the other night at the opera. We're looking for the magician who made it. Can you tell us the name of the shop where you bought it?"

"Mallard and Son. Do you think he's the magician?"

"We're not sure."

"How thrilling. May I come?"

"Not this time," Matt said, extending his hand. "Thank you for the information."

Lord Farnsworth gave a disappointed sigh but didn't press the issue. He shook my hand too, then Duke and Cyclops's before we filed out. When he came to Willie, he blocked her exit.

"You missed having a grand time with Lady Helen and me last night. I took her to a gambling den then we went and saw a fight." He frowned. "Or was it the other way around?"

I gasped. "You took Lady Helen out? Just the two of you? Good grief, if anybody found out, she'll be ruined."

"I'd just have to marry her sooner than we would both like. But I would do it."

"If she'd have you," Willie pointed out. "I don't think she cares for you *that* much."

Lord Farnsworth laughed. "You're just jealous that I'm going to win her and you're not."

Willie tried to push past him but he continued to block her way. "So where were you last night?" he asked.

"I had something more important to do."

"What's more important than an adventure with two amusing friends?"

"Murder."

He stared at her, then turned that stare onto each of us. When none of us elaborated, he faced Willie again. "Who did you kill?"

"A fool who got in my way." She shoved him in the arm.

The force wasn't enough to move him, but he hurriedly stepped aside. "That was a joke. Wasn't it?"

"I don't joke about murder, Davide." She patted his cheek. "I'm going to be busy most nights for a while. Tell Helen I'll miss her and I'll see her in a few days."

"If you don't go to prison, you mean." He laughed, but it died when he realized no one laughed with him. "I'll tell her. And do try not to kill anyone else, Willie. Unless they deserve it, of course."

* * *

As SOON AS we mentioned Lord Farnsworth's name to Mr. Mallard, he was keen to assist us in any way he could. When we asked if his silver wares were made by a silversmith by the name of Marianne Folgate, he didn't ask why we needed to know, he simply said that he had been getting his silver from her for over a year. When we asked for her address, he didn't hesitate to give it to us. Lord Farnsworth must be a good customer indeed.

Marianne Folgate lived in a boarding house run by a heavyset woman with a pronounced limp who wheezed when she asked Matt and me what we wanted in a no-nonsense school matron's voice.

"We're looking for Marianne Folgate," Matt said. "We believe she lives here."

"You're too late."

Oh God.

"What happened to her?" Matt asked.

"She moved out."

I blew out a relieved breath. "Where did she move to?"

"I don't know. She didn't leave a forwarding address."

"Then how do you send on her mail?"

"I don't. I throw it out." She crossed her arms and addressed her next question to Matt. "Why do you want to know?"

"We want to buy some silver off her," he said. "Wholesale, for our new business venture. Are you sure you don't know where she went?"

"I wouldn't have said I don't if I did, would I? All I got was a letter and a week's extra board. Not even a by your leave, if you don't mind."

"Would anyone else who lives here know where she went?" I asked. "Perhaps she had a particular friend amongst the other tenants?"

The landlady signaled for us to follow her inside. "Miss Calendar might know. She spoke to her more than anyone."

She led us to a large kitchen at the back of the house where a young woman wearing an apron was doing the washing up in a tub. A stack of dirty dishes formed a tower on the bench next to her. It must be all the breakfast dishes for the tenants. A respectable boarding house like this was not a common sight in London, although I'd heard of a few springing up in recent years. Run by a woman of good repute, they attracted young female tenants from middle class backgrounds who'd come to the city to find work but knew no one. Shop assistants, governesses, and artists were welcomed, as long as they lived by the landlady's strict rules, agreed to help with the chores, and could afford the boarding fee. In my experience, the price was rather steep for a small bedroom and two meals a day, but paying it was better than the alternative. Young women without employment or friends ended up in the workhouse, whorehouse or on the street.

"This is Miss Calendar," the landlady said. "Miss Calendar, Mr. and Mrs. Glass are asking about Miss Folgate."

"Oh?" The young woman smiled at Matt. She gave me one too, but it was more of an afterthought.

Matt smiled back. "We're looking for Marianne Folgate to commission her to do some work for our new shop. Do you know where she went?"

Miss Calendar shook her head. "I'm afraid I don't. One day she was here and the next she was gone. She left me a note saying she had to leave. She didn't give a reason, but I've been worried about her since. She's quite young, you see, although she's wise beyond her years."

"Did she often keep things to herself?" Matt asked.

"She didn't speak much about her family, but she was open about everything else. She wasn't talkative, but she was cheerful, content. She had a love of life, in her own quiet way." She shook her head, reconsidering. "I'd call it more of an appreciation for life rather than love. Anyway, she changed in the weeks leading up to her departure. She kept more to herself and seemed troubled. I asked her what was wrong, but she wouldn't say." Miss Calendar frowned in thought. "She did say something odd which has stayed with me. She told me she wished she'd been more careful. When I asked what she meant, she didn't answer."

"She was a silversmith," Matt said. "Did she work out of her room?"

The landlady bristled. "Of course not. This is a respectable boarding house, not a workshop."

Matt arched his brows at Miss Calendar. "You can't get her into trouble now."

Miss Calendar shook her head. "Mrs. Drewery's right. Marianne didn't do any work here, or anywhere for that matter. She had some old family silver she brought to London with her after her parents died. She sold it off, mostly to a particular jeweler, but sometimes to other shopkeepers."

"Do you know the name of the jeweler?" Matt asked.

She shook her head. "I did see him here once. Short, dark-haired fellow in his forties. They spoke out the front, shook hands, and then he left. It was all very civil. And respectable," she added for Mrs. Drewery's benefit.

"Did anyone else visit her?"

"No."

"What about that man in the carriage?" Mrs. Drewery said. "Large man, white moustache. Very rude he was when I asked what he wanted with Miss Folgate."

Lord Coyle had been here! It was the link we needed to connect him to Mr. Goldman. The goldsmith must have introduced Coyle to his new silver supplier once he realized her silverware contained magic. It didn't explain why Coyle would kill the goldsmith, however.

"He told me to mind my own business. Very rude indeed," she added in a mutter.

"When was this visit?" Matt asked.

"A number of weeks ago. Perhaps two months. I can't recall. The days roll into one when you're my age."

"And how did Miss Folgate seem after the meeting?"

"I can't say I took much notice."

When neither had any more to offer, we returned to the carriage. Matt asked Woodall to drive in any direction he pleased until further notice, then he climbed into the cabin and sat beside me.

I couldn't wait to tell the others and blurted out what we'd learned. "I think Goldman introduced Coyle to Miss Folgate once he realized he'd found a silver magician, just like he'd introduced Coyle to the leather magicians, wood, silk and any others he'd come across over the years."

"The doctor magician being his latest find," Cyclops added.

"So we have him!" Willie cried. "We can tell Jasper that Coyle knew Goldman and that's how he found out about Gabe."

Matt shook his head. "All we've done is establish that Coyle knew Marianne Folgate and *she* knew Goldman. It's not enough to implicate Coyle in Goldman's murder. We need a direct link."

"And a reason for Coyle to kill Goldman," Cyclops added. "We don't even know if Goldman had an opportunity to inform Coyle about Gabe. Gabe let it slip to Goldman that he was a magician before going to work. At four the next morning, Goldman is killed. That's only a matter of hours."

Willie nodded along, a determined set to her jaw, her eyes flashing. "So we need to prove Coyle saw Goldman at some point in those hours."

"How are we going to do that?" Duke whined.

"We ask someone who lives with Coyle," I said. "We'll invite Hope to tea."

* * *

WE SENT our footman to the Coyles's townhouse with an invitation for Hope to join us for afternoon tea. He came back with the handwritten note still in his pocket. He hadn't been allowed to see her in person so had followed Matt's instructions and not delivered it.

"Her companion said she was indisposed," he went on.

"Companion?" we echoed.

"Looks like Coyle's got someone watching her every move now," Duke said.

"He's keeping her prisoner," Willie added. "I want to punch her in the face sometimes, but I don't like this. He can't stop his wife from leaving the house."

Matt dismissed Peter with instructions to send for the carriage. "I'm going to call on her myself," he told us.

"And if Coyle's there?" I asked.

"I'll tell him Hope is coming home with me."

To my great relief, Lord Coyle was not at home when Matt and I called on his wife. But his absence didn't make our task any easier. Hope's so-called companion, Mrs. Fry, was a towering woman with broad shoulders and a square jaw. A deep vertical line between her eyebrows gave the impression she'd never smiled in her life. She certainly wasn't smiling at us as Matt requested to see Hope.

"Lady Coyle is indisposed," she said in a loud voice that echoed around the grand entrance hall.

"I don't believe you," Matt said.

Mrs. Fry's nostrils flared and her eyes narrowed ever so slightly. She didn't look like someone who expected, or liked, being questioned. "You may leave a message with me—"

Matt pushed past her and headed for the staircase. It happened so quickly, Mrs. Fry was caught off-guard.

She raced after him, her black skirts getting tangled around her ankles in her haste. "Wait! You can't go up there."

Matt paused on the lower step as a tall, young footman emerged from the shadows at the rear of the entrance hall.

The butler stood alongside him, his hawkish features set hard.

"I don't see anyone here who can stop me," Matt said with a defiant arch of his brows.

The footman swallowed hard. The butler merely stepped forward. "Is everything all right, Mrs. Fry?"

"Mr. and Mrs. Glass don't believe me when I say Lady Coyle is not available," Mrs. Fry said.

The butler addressed Matt. "I'm afraid her ladyship has locked herself in her room."

Matt's lips stretched into a tight smile. "Either you fetch her or I go up and break the door down and get her out myself. I don't care which of you does it, but I suggest the one with the key."

Mrs. Fry and the butler exchanged glances and Mrs. Fry headed up the stairs. The keys dangling from her chatelaine jangled with each stride.

A few minutes later, Hope joined us in the entrance hall. The dark circles under her eyes amid her otherwise pale face were a testament to how poorly she was sleeping. Dressed in a white and ice-blue silk dress, trimmed with delicate white lace, she looked like a fragile snow queen, still regal but moments away from melting into a puddle of despair.

With her head held high, she greeted Matt and me with strained civility.

"May we speak alone, Hope?" Matt asked.

"No," Mrs. Fry said. "Lord Coyle has instructed me to stay with Lady Coyle at all times. It's for her health, you understand."

"Is she ill?"

"No," Hope said with the measure of the defiance I expected from her.

Mrs. Fry clicked her tongue at her charge. "The doctor says she's suffering from hysteria. Her nerves are frayed and if they break altogether, she'll go mad."

"Perhaps if she wasn't held prisoner, she would be fine," I pointed out.

Mrs. Fry's nostrils flared again, as if annoyed I'd spoken at all. "Apparently madness runs in the family. There is a sister—"

"My sister is eccentric, not mad." It was the kindest thing I'd heard Hope say about Charity.

"I'd like to speak to my cousin alone," Matt growled.

"That won't be possible," Mrs. Fry snapped. "Anything you have to say, you can say here, then I would ask you to leave. Lady Coyle needs her rest."

Matt pressed his lips together.

"Hope," I begged. "Dismiss her. You don't have to be a prisoner in your own home."

"Lady Coyle does not employ me," Mrs. Fry said with a defiant tilt of her lips. "His lordship has given me instructions that his wife is not to be disturbed. So if you wouldn't mind…" She nodded at the butler to open the door.

"We're not leaving here without her," Matt said.

"Then Lord Coyle will have no alternative but to have you arrested for kidnapping."

"Not if she comes with us willingly."

"I'm afraid Lady Coyle is in no fit state to make that decision. Her mind is too fragile, and she's too easily swayed by those who would wish to control her. Only her husband has her best interests at heart, and he has put her into my care."

Matt grabbed Hope's arm. She flinched and he immediately let her go. "Hope, you don't have to stay here."

"Legally, you do," Mrs. Fry told her. "If he kidnaps you, it won't go well for either him or you. Remember what happened when you tried to sneak out of the house?"

Hope wrapped her arms around herself. The muscles in her face tightened as if she was barely managing to school her features. "Go, Matt," she whispered. "There's nothing you can do."

"I'll engage a lawyer and get you out of here."

Hope closed her eyes and swallowed hard.

Mrs. Fry grabbed her by the elbow. "A woman cannot divorce her husband without a valid reason. Besides, it will only prove she's going mad, since only a madwoman would want to divorce such a caring, devoted husband."

"He can't keep her prisoner!"

"Matt, stop, please," Hope begged. "Just go. It's for the best."

"Sir, your presence is upsetting her. I must insist!"

Matt scrubbed a hand over his jaw. He hated being powerless to help someone in distress, particularly a family member he felt obliged to protect. But Hope was right. There was nothing he could do, and staying was just going to make it worse for her.

I took his hand and together we exited the house. He instructed Woodall to drive to his uncle's place.

"Do you think her parents will have better luck talking to her alone?" I asked.

"I don't know what I think. All I know is, she needs to get away from Coyle. He's destroying her."

I sighed. Hope was in an impossible situation. A husband had absolute control over his wife's life; that was why it was so important to marry a good man. If he wanted to control her spending, he could. If he wanted to limit her contact with the outside world, he could ban visitors. If he found doctors to testify that she was insane, he could have her committed to an asylum for the rest of her life. Her relations could try to find their own doctors to refute such claims, but getting one into the house to see her was going to be difficult, if not impossible.

Even so, Matt tried to convince his aunt that Hope needed help. Lady Rycroft simply told him she would speak to her husband when he returned home, but we both knew from her tone that she wasn't worried. Hope had made a good match, as far as she was concerned, thus ending their parental duty.

"Pssst." The hiss came from just outside the drawing room. I had remained standing by the door when Matt ventured in further to speak to his aunt, and so was the only one to hear it. "Pssst, India."

I checked to see that Lady Rycroft wasn't looking my way,

then surreptitiously stepped toward the door. Charity stood in the corridor and signaled me to come closer.

"What is it?" I whispered.

"I overheard what Matt said about Hope being held prisoner. I want to help him get her out."

"I don't see how you can."

"Through her bedroom window." She said it so matter-of-factly that I almost giggled at the absurdity of it. But Charity looked utterly serious. "Tell him to meet me out the front here at midnight."

"I don't understand. Why does he need to meet you?"

She rolled her eyes. "He doesn't know which room is hers. I do."

"You plan to kidnap her?"

"It's escaping, not kidnapping."

The idea wasn't entirely preposterous. I suspected Matt might like it when the only alternative was to attempt to free Hope via a lengthy and public legal process. "Why don't you just tell me which is her bedroom window and I'll let him know?"

"And miss all the fun?"

"India?" Lady Rycroft strode toward me. "India, who are you speaking to? Is that Charity?" She peered around the doorframe, but Charity had vanished.

Matt brooded for much of the journey home, too angry with his aunt, Lord Coyle and the dreadfully unfair laws that meant he couldn't help his own cousin. All I wanted to do was see his mood lift, and there was only one way to do that.

"I think you should break into her room tonight and get her out," I said.

He blinked at me. "I think so too, but I wasn't sure you'd like the idea."

"I hate it, but I know you'll never forgive yourself if you do nothing."

He scrubbed his hand over his jaw. "Coyle will know it was me."

"He can't do anything about it if there are no witnesses. She'll have to go into hiding, of course."

"I'll arrange for her to travel to France. Breaking in won't be easy. Climbing up won't be a problem, but I expect the windows will all be locked, and I don't know which is her bedroom."

"Charity does, and she wants to help."

"That's a first."

"She wants you to collect her at midnight then she'll help you break Hope free. I would suggest you take one of the others with you, but I'm not sure if more hands would be a help or hindrance in this situation."

"Probably a hindrance." He leaned across the gap and grasped my hand. Already he looked as though a weight had been lifted from his shoulders.

I, however, was more worried than ever. If Lord Coyle caught Matt breaking into the house, he would have no qualms having him arrested.

CHAPTER 7

I tinkered with an old watch in the sitting room while I waited for Matt to return. The process calmed my agitated nerves, and it also allowed me to block out Willie's whining over losing at cards. Between them, Duke and Cyclops had won almost every round of poker.

When Matt finally walked in just after one, Willie was the first to leap up and greet him. "Well? How'd it go?"

I peered past him. There was no sign of Hope.

He sat on the sofa with a heavy sigh. "She wouldn't come. She didn't want to be running from him for the rest of her life."

"But if she stays, she'll be his prisoner," I said.

He shrugged. "She insisted she'll be fine. I didn't want to leave her there, but Charity also insisted. She'd given me a letter and small parcel to deliver to her sister, and Hope wrote a letter back to her. After she read it, Charity told me that Hope didn't want to come with us."

"So that's that." Willie dismissed Hope's plight with a wave of her hand. "Did you ask her about Coyle meeting Goldman in the hours before his death?"

He nodded. "She saw a man matching Goldman's description come to the house and meet with Coyle in his office."

"That proves it, then. Goldman told him about Gabe being

a magician." From the resigned tone of Willie's voice, it was obvious she knew there was nothing we could do with the information. We couldn't take it to the police. Not unless Hope had overheard them speaking about Gabe, and not if she couldn't testify. Coyle would have the court believing his wife was insane, rendering her testimony worthless.

Willie poured herself a bourbon at the drinks trolley, downed it in a single gulp, and licked her lips. "Right. I'm going out."

"Where to?" Duke asked.

"To see if Helen wants some fun. Want to come?"

"Depends on the kind of fun you plan on having."

She smacked the back of his head as she passed him. "The adventuring kind. I feel like a night out drinking and gambling with friends. What about you, Cyclops?"

"I've got to work tomorrow," he said as he rose. "Does your sudden hankering to go out with Lady Helen have anything to do with competing with Farnsworth for her attention?"

She barked a laugh. "If it was a competition then I'd win. I'm more fun than him."

The three of them filed out of the sitting room, arguing over whether Willie was indeed fun to be around, or simply impossible to ignore.

Matt sat back with a sigh, drawing me with him. I snuggled against his chest and closed my eyes. The steady rhythm of his heartbeat calmed me. I hadn't realized how tense I'd been as I waited for his return.

I wanted to ask him what happens next; not just with Hope but with Gabe. But I didn't want to spoil the moment, and I suspected he didn't either. After a few minutes of comfortable silence, he picked me up and carried me upstairs like we were newlyweds.

* * *

CYCLOPS WAS CALLED into work very early the following morning when another riot broke out in his jurisdiction. According to the newspapers, which we scoured over breakfast, there'd been several marches in London and other cities around the country as artless craftsmen protested against the magicians. They wanted them banned from guilds, their licenses revoked and their shops shut down. According to several reports, many guilds had already ousted known or suspected magicians.

There was no news on what subsequently happened to those magicians.

Duke threw down *The Times* in disgust. "It's all one-sided. The magicians need to protest too or they're going to lose their livelihoods."

Matt folded the newspaper and picked up his coffee cup. "They're disorganized. The artless have their guilds and the guild masters are rallying the troops. They have the names of their members at their fingertips, and can quickly disseminate information or appoint someone to speak to the journalists. Magicians have never joined forces. They've acted alone for so long, never knowing any other magicians outside their family circle. It'll take weeks, perhaps months, before they get organized enough to have their own protests."

"They know India."

Matt glared at him over his cup. "India has enough on her plate."

"I'll put their case forward to the prime minister when I speak to him," I said. "In the meantime, I'll speak to Oscar. He can report the effect the riots and protests are having on magicians to garner public sympathy."

Matt passed me the newspaper he'd been reading. "He's already doing that."

Oscar Barratt's article made up half of one column on page five of *The Weekly Gazette*. It wasn't long enough or prominent enough to have any effect.

"My meeting with the prime minister and cabinet needs to

be brought forward," I said. "I'll write to Mr. Matthews this morning."

I was about to leave the dining room but stopped when Willie and Brockwell entered. Instead of her usual buckskins or trousers, she was dressed in a police constable's uniform that was too large for her small frame. It would seem they'd had an interesting night. It was wonderful to see them together again. At least something was working out for the better.

But the sheepish look on Willie's face and the scowl on Brockwell's gave me pause. Willie never looked sheepish.

She went straight to the food on the sideboard, but Brockwell hovered in the doorway. I invited him in but he shook his head. Oh dear. Something was very wrong.

"What's the matter?" I asked.

"Not another lover's tiff," Duke said with a roll of his eyes.

"Shut it, idiot," Willie snapped.

Matt appealed to Brockwell with an arch of his brow. If we wanted a sensible answer, the detective inspector was the only one who'd give it.

"I was called to the Yard at six this morning." He nodded at Willie, her back to us as she stood at the sideboard. "She had them send for me."

"Why were you at Scotland Yard?" Matt asked her.

"It was nothing." She sat at the table, her plate piled with bacon and fried eggs. "Let's just forget it happened. Jasper says no charges will be laid, so that's the end of it. Now, leave me in peace. I'm starving."

Duke crossed his arms and regarded her with a smirk. "What *did* you do?"

"According to the arresting constables, she was pulled out of the river with a French flag stuffed down her shirt. She'd stolen it from a vessel moored at St. Katherine's Dock. She was given dry clothes at the Yard."

Matt dragged a hand over his face. "Give me strength."

Duke looked as though he was trying very hard not to

smile. "When I left you and Helen, you said you'd be coming home too, as soon as the poker game finished. How did you go from being dry in a gambling den in Bermondsey to wet in the Thames?"

Willie shoveled bacon into her mouth.

"She told me she had to steal the flag on account of it being for a wager, and she couldn't afford to lose," Brockwell said.

"Then don't take the bet," Matt growled.

Willie bent over her plate of food, not meeting anyone's gaze.

"Did Lady Helen get home all right?" I asked.

Brockwell nodded. "One of the constables escorted her."

I turned to Willie. "If her aunt finds out, Aunt Letitia will never forgive you for corrupting the girl."

Willie swallowed. "Me corrupt her? She's the reason I got arrested!"

"Do tell," Duke said with a smug smile.

"Helen made me take the bet," she mumbled.

"No one can force you to take a bet," Matt said.

"She can. She's knows just what to say to make me do things I don't want to do. Like use up all my bullets the other night on tin cans. That ain't something I usually do. Nor is this. I don't like water."

"What did she say when you got arrested?" I asked.

"Not much. She was too busy laughing."

We all turned to Brockwell.

He nodded. "She was laughing at Willie and flirting with the younger of the two constables, apparently."

Good lord. She was more trouble than Willie. I pitied her poor aunt.

"I managed to have Willie's arrest quashed," Brockwell went on. "She was let off with a caution, but I won't be stepping in again. I have my reputation to consider."

Matt stood and shook his hand. "Thank you, Brockwell. Will you stay for breakfast?"

"No, thank you. I best be going."

"You're going back to the Yard?" I asked.

"I've got the day off."

"So you have time to enjoy breakfast."

"If it's all the same with you, I prefer not to stay." He gave me a flat smile.

I suddenly recalled that Willie mentioned he'd been seeing another woman. Perhaps she was waiting for him at home.

But going by the look of profound disappointment he gave Willie, I suspected his reluctance to stay had more to do with her. He'd finally reached his breaking point with her antics.

Duke waited until we heard the front door close then turned a glare onto Willie. She bent further over her plate of food, pretending not to notice.

"You went too far, this time," he said. "Brockwell's had enough."

"It ain't my fault!"

"It is your fault, and it's time you accept it. No one's responsible for your actions except you. If Helen brings trouble to your door, then you've got to keep your distance from her. If you don't, you won't see Brockwell again."

Willie slumped in her chair, her lower lip protruding with her pout. "He doesn't want me no more anyway. He's got himself another woman."

Duke pushed his chair back and stood. "And that's another thing. Make up your mind. If you want Brockwell all to yourself then you've got to let him know. If you don't show him he's important to you then why should he commit to you?" He snatched up his plate and returned to the sideboard where he helped himself to seconds.

Willie poked her food around her plate with her fork, her pout even more pronounced.

Matt leaned toward me and lowered his voice. "The children are finally growing up. Soon they'll be flying the nest altogether."

I wasn't sure I liked the sound of that. I rather enjoyed having our motley brood live with us.

* * *

I DECIDED to call on Mr. Matthews at his office instead of sending him a note. With Matt attending Gabe's trial, I went alone. Upon seeing me waiting in the outer office, he asked his assistant to notify Mr. Le Grand. The spy master joined us a few minutes later. I wasn't sure why he was needed, as he spoke very little during our meeting.

"I'm glad you came here today, Mrs. Glass," Mr. Matthews said after he closed the door. "I have news that you may find very welcome. Abercrombie has had his license revoked."

I could hardly believe it and had to ask him to repeat it.

He smiled. "The Watchmakers' Guild has revoked Abercrombie's license. He can no longer sell watches and clocks in London."

"But that means he'll have to close his shop."

Neither Mr. Matthews nor Mr. Le Grand responded. They simply watched me, as if waiting for the monumental news to click into place.

"Why did the guild do it?"

"They were made to understand the benefits of ousting him from the guild."

I gasped. "You put pressure on them, didn't you? Is that wise, considering the tensions in the city?"

"It was done in such a way that the government can't be linked to it. The current guild master understood that it was in his best interests to remove the one bad apple from the barrel."

He probably didn't need much convincing. Abercrombie's stock would now be sold off very cheaply and, being the guild master, he was in prime position to have first pick. Considering I was the only timepiece magician in the country, and I wasn't selling magical clocks or watches, the guild members would have no need to participate in the agitating antics of Abercrombie. Their businesses were not threatened by magicians.

"I'm not sure having his membership and license revoked

will put an end to the riots," I said. "It might have the opposite effect."

"Not if he leaves the city," Mr. Matthews said.

"Why would he leave?"

Again, Mr. Matthews and Mr. Le Grand remained silent,
leaving my question hanging in the air like unpicked fruit.

"So, to what do we owe the pleasure of your company this
morning, Mrs. Glass?"

"I wanted to ask you to bring the meeting with the prime
minister and cabinet forward. The riots are getting worse.
Lives are in danger and businesses are being disrupted.
Surely the prime minister can see that the earlier we convene,
the better."

"He has been traveling the country and is on his way back
to London as we speak. I'm sure once he arrives, and sees the
trouble first-hand, he will want to hear your solutions immediately. Don't worry, Mrs. Glass." Mr. Matthews gave me a
benign smile, one designed to placate. "With Abercrombie
gone, it clears the path for calm. Without him fanning the
flames, the other artless will be open to your ideas instead of
making trouble for trouble's sake."

I hoped he was right.

"Is there anything else, Mrs. Glass?"

I had debated with myself on the journey to the Home
Office whether to come clean about Gabe's importance to
Matt. Mr. Le Grand had already implied he knew that
medical magic may exist, but I wasn't sure I wanted to
confirm it for him, or tell him how it had saved Matt's life. It
was not just our secret but Gabe's too.

On the other hand, perhaps the information he wanted to
keep private was the very thing that could save him.

I decided to say as much as necessary and as little as
possible. "There is something else, as it happens. Something
very important to me that I hope you can use your influence
to resolve in our favor. A dear friend of ours has been arrested
for murder, but we know he didn't do it. His trial began
today."

Mr. Matthews sat back with a heavy exhalation. Standing beneath the portrait of the queen, Mr. Le Grand didn't move. "If the coroner found just cause to send your friend to trial, then there's nothing I can do," Mr. Matthews said.

"There was no coronial inquest. The police insist he did it."

"Then why are you so sure he didn't?"

"Because we know our friend. He's a good man. In fact, we believe Lord Coyle is behind his arrest. Not only did he commit the murder, but he set Gabe up."

Mr. Matthews's face was not usually animated, but all at once, his brows shot up, his lips parted and his eyes widened. "Are you sure?"

"Quite sure, but we have no definitive proof. The police believe they have the killer and won't look at anyone else unless we can prove Gabe is innocent beyond doubt. Even if we found proof against Lord Coyle, it's unlikely he'd be arrested. He's too powerful."

Mr. Le Grand moved away from the wall and approached. "Why does Coyle want your friend found guilty?"

I lowered my gaze so that I didn't come under the influence of his intense one. "Because Coyle wants to punish me."

"You have other friends, ones you are closer to than Dr. Seaford." I hadn't given him Gabe's full name. He must already be familiar with the case and Gabe's friendship with us. "Mr. Glass's American cousin gets herself into quite a bit of trouble with the police, I believe. It would be quite easy to set her up for murder. So why Dr. Seaford?"

I schooled my features. "You'd have to ask Lord Coyle that."

His gaze held mine for a long moment. I kept my breathing steady, but it did little to settle my rapid heartbeat. The silence stretched for what seemed like several minutes but was probably just seconds, until he retreated to the wall once again.

I tore my gaze away from Mr. Le Grand to focus on the

home secretary. "Will you help my friend, Mr. Matthews? Will you speak to the police commissioner?"

"I'm afraid I can't interfere with the justice process. It would be political suicide if it got out."

"But he's innocent!"

"Then the jury will acquit him."

"Coyle has paid witnesses and set Gabe up. The jury will have no choice but to find him guilty." When he merely shrugged, I stood and slammed my fist on the desk. "Can you not do this for me now that I am helping you?"

Mr. Matthews moved his hands to his stomach and regarded me coolly. My outburst hadn't even made him flinch. "I have removed Abercrombie for you, Mrs. Glass. Is that not enough?"

"You removed him for *your* sake, not mine. Make no mistake, I am well aware of whose side you are on."

I stormed out of his office and down the stairs, yet Mr. Le Grand still beat me. He must have taken a more direct route, because he was waiting in the carriage without having broken a sweat.

"Don't blame your driver," he said. "He was reluctant to allow me to join you, but I told him it was in your best interests and you'd want to hear what I had to say."

"What do you want?"

"To help your friend the doctor."

I turned to him fully. "You'll help get him released? Thank you, thank you."

He shook his head and my heart sank. "I can't get him released. But I can help you to help him escape."

"Escape? But if you're caught helping us, won't that jeopardize your position at the Home Office?"

One corner of his mouth lifted into the closest thing to a smile I'd seen from him. "I'm sure you can appreciate the necessity to keep what I'm about to tell you to yourself." He glanced past me and out of the window then sank further into the opposite corner.

"You have my word I won't tell Mr. Matthews or the police," I said.

"Your friend will be lodging at Newgate tonight. These days, the prison is only used for criminals attending trial at the Old Bailey or condemned to execution so there are not many guards on duty. A warden by the name of Wellings begins his shift at seven. Tell him Fletcher Bell sent you and you want to speak to Dr. Seaford alone in his cell. You'll also need to pay him a significant sum to look the other way."

"Wait a moment. You're planning his escape *from Newgate*? But that's impossible."

"Not impossible, just not easy. He won't simply be able to walk out in his prison uniform. You'll need a disguise."

"Who is Fletcher Bell?"

"A man who needs to speak to prisoners from time to time to gain information without going through the proper channels. He has never helped a prisoner escape before, however, so Wellings won't be expecting it."

"What if the warden wants a description of Fletcher Bell to verify we know him?"

Mr. Le Grand hesitated before saying, "He looks remarkably like me."

I blinked slowly, feeling quite overwhelmed. My head was thick with a kind of fog that I couldn't see through to the other side. If Matt were here, he'd have a dozen questions for Mr. Le Grand, but I could think of none. They'd probably come to me five minutes after he left.

He opened the door and stepped out. He tugged on his hat brim, partly in deference and partly to cover his face. "Good luck, Mrs. Glass."

I put out my hand to stop him closing the door. "Why are you helping us?"

"It's in my interests to do so."

I sat back as the carriage jerked forward, and I was left staring out the window at the blur of buildings streaming past. I was right in that dozens of questions now crowded my head. But they were not questions to ask Mr. Le Grand. They were questions about my own sanity.

Because I was seriously considering doing as he suggested and breaking Gabe out of Newgate, and surely only a madwoman would think that possible.

* * *

Matt returned late in the day with a gloomy shadow dogging him. I'd just returned home myself from a walk with Aunt Letitia. The fresh air had cleared my head, but one thought dominated all else. We had to take this opportunity to free Gabe. It might be the only one we got.

I waited until Aunt Letitia was out of the room before asking Matt about the verdict, even though I could tell it wasn't good.

"The jury took only a few minutes to find him guilty," he said. "There was no other finding possible. Not with the evidence presented to them. Gabe had no viable defense."

I felt sick. There was no point asking him about the sentence. Murderers were hanged.

Matt raked his hands through his hair and down his face. When they came away, he looked as though he was being led to the gallows himself. "This is all my fault. A target was put on Gabe's back as soon as Coyle learned of his importance to me."

I touched his cheek and forced him to look at me. "If that's what you think then it's *my* fault. Coyle's problem is with me, not you. But I don't accept that anyone is to blame except Coyle." I tried to offer a smile despite the anxiety threatening to overwhelm me. I suspected I failed miserably. "I know of a way to get Gabe out."

He sat up straighter. "You have new evidence to get the conviction overturned?"

I shook my head. "I have a way to get him out of Newgate. The idea came from Le Grand."

I told him what the spy master had told me. By the time I

finished, Matt's expression matched what mine must have looked like during my conversation with Mr. Le Grand.

"That plan is…" He shook his head slowly, as if he couldn't quite believe it. "It's risky."

It wasn't an outright refusal. That meant he was considering it. I was glad I didn't have to go behind his back.

"Do you trust Le Grand?" he asked.

"We don't have a choice."

"No," he said darkly. "We don't." He got to his feet and paced the length of the sitting room. When he reached the wall, he turned back, and raked his hand through his hair again. Matt only showed this much agitation when he was deep in thought.

Willie entered, only to stop and frown at him. "What's going on?"

Duke came in behind her. "Why're you pacing?"

Matt stopped. His eyes shone in the light of the nearest lamp, his breathing quickened. "Close the door."

Willie rubbed her hands together as she sat. "You've got a plan to free Gabe, haven't you? You only get this excited when you're onto something big and right now, there ain't nothing bigger than getting Gabe out of prison."

Matt and I told them what Mr. Le Grand had told me. Then Matt laid out a plan. It did not involve me going anywhere near the prison. In fact, Matt was the only one entering Newgate and he would be wearing a false moustache and beard so that he couldn't be identified.

"Nope," Willie said with a determined shake of her head. "You ain't going in alone. I'm coming."

"And me," Duke said.

But Matt would not be swayed. "Any more than one person will rouse suspicions. If Le Grand uses the disguise of Fletcher Bell to gather information from prisoners, then the warden will expect the person Bell sends in his stead to follow the same procedure."

Willie swore under her breath.

Duke gave a reluctant nod. "That'll get you in, but how

will you get Gabe out? Wellings won't be expecting two to leave. Not when only one entered."

Willie clicked her fingers. "We create a disturbance near the entrance, something that'll distract Wellings long enough for Gabe to get out, but not enough to call other guards."

"A drunken fight ought to do it," Duke said. "You and me can do that, Willie. While Wellings is busy with us, Gabe slips out. Cyclops can be waiting for him around the corner with the carriage. Matt helps Wellings disperse the fighters then leaves."

"What if Wellings looks around as Gabe's running off?" Willie asked. "Or what if someone sees him? Those prison uniforms are real distinctive. I reckon we should get him a disguise. Matt can take it in to him and he can change in his cell."

"I'll pack some of my clothes," Matt said.

But I had a better idea. "Willie, you still have the constable's uniform they gave you when you were arrested, don't you?"

Willie's eyes brightened. "Aye, and I like your idea, India. Passersby won't take notice of a constable leaving Newgate. They'll think he was there on official business."

Matt smiled. "It'll also be useful for walking through the prison itself. If other guards see him, they won't stop us."

Cyclops chose that moment to enter, but halted when we all looked at him. "What's happened now?"

"Go and change," Willie ordered. "We've got a plan to get Gabe out of prison, and I reckon we should enact it as soon as possible while it's dark but not late. No one will expect an escape in the early evening."

Cyclops groaned. "I knew I should have accepted Mrs. Mason's dinner invitation." He didn't try to talk us out of it, however. He might be a policeman now, but he knew Gabe's arrest was wrong.

We filled him in on the plan then I told them about Abercrombie's dismissal from the Watchmaker's Guild and how Mr. Matthews and Mr. Le Grand would see that he left

London altogether. In the excitement of discussing Gabe's escape, I'd almost forgotten about him. For the first time in days, I felt lighter. Finally things were going our way. Finally the tunnel didn't seem quite so long and dark.

Cyclops left to change out of his uniform, passing Bristow in the doorway. The butler handed me a note.

"It's from the home secretary," I said as I read. My heart sank. I knew the situation was too good to be true and that something would go wrong. I'd hoped it wouldn't go wrong quite so soon. "It's Abercrombie. He's gone missing."

Matt peered over my shoulder. "How could he be missing? Didn't Le Grand have spies watching him?"

"This doesn't say. But Mr. Matthews points out that if they can't find him, I should be careful. Abercrombie will be angry at being forced out of the guild." I lowered the note to my lap with shaking hands. "And he'll blame me."

CHAPTER 8

*M*att's plan involved me waiting at home. I refused to be left out, however, as it would have been torture on my nerves. We compromised and I waited in the carriage instead, parked within sight of the prison door but far enough away that our conveyance didn't look conspicuous. Cyclops looked like all the other coachmen waiting for his passenger. The street was well lit and it would have been suspicious if we'd shut off the external carriage lanterns. I closed the curtain and sat in the dark, peeking out from time to time.

The prison entrance was quiet with no one coming or going. The governor had gone home and the warden, Mr. Wellings, was in charge overnight. Stationed in the front office, he would be enjoying a cup of tea or nodding off beside the fire.

Matt headed up the four steps to the front door, his figure padded from the extra clothing he wore. He'd already deposited the constable's helmet in a nearby doorway where Duke and Willie pretended to be sleeping off a drunken stupor.

Matt tugged on the bell and the door was opened. He spoke to a man whose face I couldn't see then, after what seemed like a terribly long time, he disappeared inside.

I couldn't sit still. My mind reeled with all the ways in which our plan could go wrong. There was only one thing I knew would work perfectly—our watches, all synchronized by me before we left, kept correct time.

I checked the time in the finger of light reaching through the gap in the curtains. In my head, I counted down the minutes, then checked it again. Duke and Matt would be doing the same.

On cue, Willie and Duke lurched out of the shadows of the nearest recessed doorway and argued rowdily, advancing on unsteady legs until they were just outside the prison door. The door jerked open and Matt and the warden emerged to move the drunkards on. Duke swung a fist at Willie and lost his balance, grabbing hold of the warden's lapels as he went down. He made sure the warden's line of sight was on him and not on the constable exiting behind.

The constable strode past the recessed doorway and picked up his helmet then continued until he reached our carriage. He climbed in, and shut the door as Cyclops urged the horses forward at full speed.

I couldn't contain my relief and threw my arms around Gabe, knocking off his helmet. He returned my embrace somewhat awkwardly. When I drew back, he was smiling.

"I don't know how to repay you for this," he said.

"You already have." I peered through the rear window but we'd turned the corner. "That went well."

Gabe looked like he hadn't slept since his arrest, but his eyes now held a spark of hope, whereas they'd been dull when we saw him in Scotland Yard's holding cell. He breathed heavily, as if he'd just run a race, and his hand trembled. But his smile slowly slipped off as his predicament dawned on him.

He might be out of Newgate, but he wasn't free.

"Where are you taking me?" he asked. "Not to your house, I hope. That's the first place they'll look."

"There's a hotel near King's Cross Station that doesn't ask

for guests' details at check-in. It's not very clean or comforting, but it's just for tonight."

"And tomorrow?"

"Matt will call on you at the hotel with instructions. He'll arrange for your passage to America as soon as possible. We think that's the best place for you to hide. You'll travel under an assumed name and should probably keep that name for… for the time being."

I'd been about to say forever, but stopped myself. Gabe guessed, however. The hope in his eyes vanished as he realized he could never use his real name again. As soon as his absence was noticed, the train stations and docks would be alerted, and the authorities in ports around the world wired with a description of their fugitive. It's why Matt would buy passage for Gabe on a vessel that preferred to land at private docks to avoid customs duties.

"I can never return to England," he murmured.

I blinked back tears. The tears were not just for Gabe. They were also for me. Because wherever Gabe went, Matt needed to go too.

"Will you speak to Nancy for me?" he asked.

"Of course."

"Tell her goodbye."

"It doesn't have to be goodbye. She may want to join you, after a safe period of time."

He drew in a shuddery breath. "I hope so, India. I very much hope so."

* * *

I TOSSED and turned all night. Gabe should be safe under a false name in the hotel run by a manager of dubious character, but what if a reward was offered? I hoped it would take time for the newspapers to print Gabe's likeness, but even so, whenever I closed my eyes I imagined the police knocking on our door.

And then, in the morning, they did.

It was so early that Aunt Letitia wasn't out of bed yet. Matt and the others had already left to secure passage to America for Gabe. Poor Bristow tried to tell the detective that I was indisposed, but he wouldn't listen. As I came down the stairs, I saw him directing the constables to search the house. One rushed past me, avoiding eye contact.

"What are you doing?" I demanded. "You can't disrupt my household like this."

The detective touched the brim of his hat, but didn't look in the least contrite. "Good morning, Mrs. Glass. I am very sorry for this, but it's necessary. You may be harboring a fugitive."

"I assure you we are not."

"Perhaps unbeknown to you."

"What fugitive?"

"Dr. Seaford escaped from Newgate last night. It's likely he had help."

I did my very best to look surprised, innocent and outraged all at once. I may not be the best actor, but I think I did rather well. I *had* to succeed. Lives were at stake.

"And you think *we* helped him? Why?"

"He's a friend of yours. You visited him when he was being held at Scotland Yard."

"To offer him legal counsel."

Bristow cleared his throat. "Fossett and I will follow the constables to make sure they don't steal anything."

The butler headed toward the service area while the footman took two steps at a time to catch up to the constable. He stopped as he passed Aunt Letitia on her way down, bade her good morning, and continued up.

"India, why is there a policeman outside my bedroom?" she asked, her voice quavering.

I took her hand and assisted her down the final few steps. It was the moment I'd been trying to avoid. We'd kept Gabe's arrest from her for fear it would upset her. But we could hide the truth no longer. "Dr. Seaford has been falsely accused of murder."

She gasped and clutched her throat.

"He escaped from prison last night and this detective thinks we helped him."

She lowered her hand and her entire demeanor changed from fragile to imperial in a heartbeat. If there was one thing Aunt Letitia was good at, it was snobbery. And she was not going to let someone of a policeman's standing get away with treating her family with disrespect.

"My nephew is the future Lord Rycroft. Do you know what that means?"

"No, but I do know it means he can't get away with helping a prisoner escape."

"He is a friend to your commissioner *and* the home secretary. Indeed, Mr. Matthews was recently drinking tea in this very house!"

The detective gave her a tight smile. "Thank you for enlightening me." He turned to me. "Mrs. Glass, would you mind telling me where you were last night between the hour of nine thirty and ten thirty."

"I was here."

"They all were," Aunt Letitia added. "We played cards after dinner. Ask the servants if you don't believe me."

"I will, ma'am."

I kept my features schooled, even though my heart raced. Although I was sure the servants would lie for us, they might not be good at it.

The constables returned to the entrance hall then the detective asked to speak to each servant alone in the library. We waited as he did so. My heart was in my throat, pounding out a mad rhythm.

It seemed to take an age, but finally Mrs. Bristow emerged with the detective in tow. She retreated to the service area with the other servants and the detective gave orders for his constables to leave.

We were not under arrest. I released a long-held breath.

The detective slapped his hat on his head. "Thank you for your assistance. Good day, Mrs. Glass, Miss Glass."

Bristow opened the front door wide, his nostrils flared in indignation.

The detective stepped over the threshold but paused. "One more question. Where is your husband this morning, Mrs. Glass?"

"Conducting business. I don't know where."

Aunt Letitia sniffed. "A gentleman never discusses commerce with his wife, Detective."

He touched the brim of his hat then trotted down the front steps. Bristow did not shut the door immediately, but waited a few moments.

I took Aunt Letitia's arm and steered her toward the staircase. "Will you have breakfast with me? I could do with some company after that."

She didn't respond and I worried she'd lapsed into a state of confusion, as she often did during tense incidents. But her gaze was sharp as she focused on Bristow, now closing the door.

"What is it?" she asked him.

That's when I noticed his frown too. "The detective left in his conveyance," he said. "But the constables have remained behind. They are standing across the street, watching the house."

Aunt Letitia lifted her chin. "Kindly tell them to move along."

"Let them be," I said. "They won't learn anything." Thank goodness they had not arrived earlier to see Matt and the others leave. One of them could have tried to follow. Not that he would have been following for long. Woodall would relish the opportunity to drive at speed and attempt to lose a constable dogging them in a hansom cab.

I was right to expect one constable to remain outside the house and one to follow anybody who left, because that's precisely what happened when I departed late morning. I considered not calling on Nancy O'Dwyer but decided that's precisely what I ought to do to not appear suspicious. If I'd just learned of Gabe's escape, it would be natural for me to speak to his fiancée. No doubt she would have had a call from the police too and would now know of his disappearance.

Indeed she had, but only one constable watched the hospital entrance.

"Oh, Mrs. Glass, I am so grateful to you for calling on me." Dressed in her nursing whites and with her face drained of color, Nancy looked every bit the heroine from a gothic novel in distress over her lost love. "Have you heard?"

"I have." Another nurse walked past, pushing a trolley stacked with bedpans. "Is there somewhere quiet we can talk?"

She bit her lower lip. "Dr. Olsen is doing his rounds of the wards. We can use his office." She led the way down a corridor and we slipped into a small room filled with shelves of medical books and an untidy desk.

Although we were alone, I kept my voice low. "There is a policeman outside watching to see if you leave."

An angry flush flooded her cheeks. I was relieved to see she wasn't going to crumble into a heap on the floor. "I saw him there after that detective left. He asked me where I was last night. Thankfully I was here and quite a few of the other nurses saw me."

"It's standard procedure to ask. As Gabe's fiancée, you are a suspect. As are we, his friends. The detective called on me this morning and asked about our whereabouts too."

"The nerve! I hope you put him in his place."

"Matt's aunt did."

Tears pooled in her eyes and she looked as though she'd break down. I clasped her hand and she collected herself. "Lord, I hope he gets away. I hope he leaves the country and doesn't come back. But it's my greatest fear that he'll try to see me before he flees and if he does, he'll get caught as surely as you're standing here."

I glanced at the door and stepped closer. "You believe he's innocent, don't you?"

"Of course! I know it in my heart. Gabe is a gentle soul. He'd never hurt anyone."

"I'm glad to hear that, because it means I can trust you."

She tilted her head to the side. "What do you mean?"

"He's safe and will be leaving the country shortly. He'll send for you when he has reached his final destination."

She closed her eyes and drew in a deep breath. A look of relief washed over her. "I know thanks will never be enough, but it's all I can offer. Thank you, India. You and your husband are great friends to Gabe."

"He has been a great friend to us, too. It was the least we could do."

She squeezed my hand. "If you get an opportunity to speak to him before he goes, tell him I love him and I'll wait for him. I'll wait for him forever, but I'd be grateful if he writes sooner than that."

I smiled. "I'll call on you when I have news."

The constable watching the hospital was still there when I left, and the one who'd followed me from Park Street followed me back home again. Matt still wasn't there.

Waiting for him was an excruciating exercise in patience. To alleviate our frustrations, Aunt Letitia and I went for a walk in the afternoon. The sun was out which meant the ladies were out too, ambling in groups of two or three, some with maids walking behind. Nannies pushed perambulators or laid out picnics for their small charges. The energetic rowed hired boats on the glistening waters of the lake and the fashionable made sure they were seen on the backs of high-stepping horses. Wherever one looked, the eye was met with an artist's palette of colors. Chestnut trees burst with cream and pink blossoms, and crocuses poked their purple and golden heads above the earth, announcing the arrival of warmer weather.

The air should have been filled with the scent of spring, but the all-pervading smells of smoke spewing from the city's many chimneys overrode everything. One day, when all this was over and Gabe was safe, we would leave London and have a holiday in the country.

That day might come sooner rather than later, and the

holiday would most certainly be a permanent departure not just from London, but from England altogether. Wherever Gabe went, we must follow. I was as sure of that as I was of my love for Matt.

We would start anew. People traveled to America or the colonies all the time, leaving behind their lives. We could do it too. It would be an adventure.

Or so I tried telling myself. But a sense of gloom settled over me, despite the sunshine. This could be the last time I saw spring in my city.

I placed my hand over Aunt Letitia's as she clasped my arm to help steady herself. I didn't want to think how our departure would impact her. It would be devastating.

"This is Willemina's fault," she said, proving she was thinking about it too. "If she was kind to Detective Inspector Brockwell, Gabe would never have been arrested."

"This has nothing to do with their relationship," I said. "Brockwell can't overrule another detective's investigation."

She clicked her tongue. "I'm sure it is at least partly her fault."

Shortly after we arrived home, Matt, Willie and Duke walked in. It was an enormous relief to see them all smiling, albeit cautiously. Aunt Letitia was so relieved, she plied them all with tea the moment they sat. I plied them with questions.

"It was a success then?"

Matt accepted the cup from Aunt Letitia. "We've secured him passage, but the packet ship doesn't leave for three days. He'll have to lay low until then."

A lot could happen in three days. If Gabe's likeness was printed in the newspapers, the hotel staff might alert the authorities. "You need to take a bribe to the hotel along with Gabe's food this evening," I told Matt.

He nodded.

"And leave the house in disguise," Aunt Letitia added.

"We saw the constable outside, and Bristow said you had a visit from the police," he said.

Aunt Letitia waved her hand in dismissal. "We dealt with

that ill-mannered boor. Honestly, Willemina, you need to be friends with Brockwell again. He must be made to take over the investigation."

"We are friends," she muttered, somewhat unconvincingly.

"Where's Cyclops?" I asked.

"He went to work," Matt said. "We thought it wisest considering we'd be suspects in Gabe's escape. The more we keep to our regular routine, the less suspicious we appear."

Bristow brought in some newspapers and a quick scan of the front pages confirmed what we'd dreaded. They all mentioned Gabe's escape from Newgate and included a likeness of him. They also included a likeness of Matt, but it matched the disguise he'd worn. No one would associate "unkempt dark hair and beard, thick moustache and a stoop" with the clean shaved, handsome and broad shouldered man sitting opposite me.

Except one person did.

Brockwell arrived just after dusk to tell us what we already knew—that we were suspected of helping Gabe escape. "It's fortunate you wore a disguise last night, Glass, or your description would be enough to have you arrested."

It was as if the air was sucked out of the room and no one dared move for fear of shattering a thin veneer we'd tried to keep up in Brockwell's presence. But the detective inspector was too clever, and he knew us too well. We couldn't keep the truth from him.

Which meant we had to trust him.

He sat on the sofa and eyed off the teapot until I rose and poured him a cup. "I'm afraid it's a little cold."

Willie intercepted the cup and saucer before it reached his outstretched hand. "You ain't getting this until you promise you're on our side."

"That's quite a promise to make just for a cup of tea."

"You want more?"

"Depends on what you're offering."

THE GOLDSMITH'S CONSPIRACY

THE GOLDSMITH'S CONSPIRACY

She thrust her hand on her hip. "You make the promise and we'll see."

He considered the proposal then stretched out his hand. "I promise I won't divulge your role in Seaford's escape."

"And if you learn where he is, you won't tell a soul, especially that brick-headed detective."

"I promise. May I have my tea now?"

"In a moment." She set the cup down on the table.

Brockwell sighed and tore his gaze from the refreshments. "What other terms do you need me to agree to?"

Willie threw herself onto his lap and kissed him thoroughly. Brockwell's eyes widened and his cheeks flushed, but his arms circled her waist.

Aunt Letitia clicked her tongue. "When I asked you to be friends with him again, I didn't mean for you to display that friendship in so vulgar a fashion."

Brockwell gave Willie a little push and she stood, picked up his teacup and passed it to him with a smile. He cleared his throat and straightened his tie as he attempted to hold his smile back. He failed miserably, and Willie strutted to her chair with a smug look on her face.

After a fortifying gulp of his tea, Brockwell cleared his throat again. "I need to point out that you are Scotland Yard's main suspect, Glass. I'll do my best to hinder the investigation, but I can't make any promises."

"It's better for you if you stay well out of it," Matt said. "I also don't think it's likely they'll find any hard evidence to link me to the escape, and they won't find Gabe."

"Unlikely, but not impossible."

Aunt Letitia made a small sound of distress and her teacup rattled in the saucer.

I took it from her. "It's time you dress for dinner, Aunt." I indicated to Duke to send her maid Polly up to her room.

Matt assisted Aunt Letitia to her feet and she allowed me to steer her up the stairs and along the corridor. She stared straight ahead, her gaze empty. She'd descended into her past again, where life with her late brother had been carefree and happy.

At her door, she put her hand on my arm. "India, are you and Matthew leaving me?"

Her sudden focus caught me off-guard. It took me a moment to gather my wits, but when I opened my mouth to tell her a comforting lie, I found I couldn't utter a single word. The last thing I wanted to do was lie to her, but telling her that we needed to go with Gabe would devastate her.

"I can't live with Richard and Beatrice again," she whispered through trembling lips. "But I don't want to leave England either." Her grip tightened. "Are you leaving England, India?"

I swallowed hard. "We'll be with you for as long as you need us."

Polly arrived and gently led Aunt Letitia into her bedroom. I closed the door and headed to my own bedroom. I couldn't return to the drawing room with the others. Not with tears streaming down my cheeks.

* * *

MATT KNEW something was wrong the moment he saw me at dinnertime. But he didn't have an opportunity to ask until we were alone in bed. I lay with my back to him, encased in his arms. The touch of his warm body and the steady beat of his heart was the comfort I'd been craving.

But it wasn't enough to completely chase away the shadow that hung over us.

As usual, Matt didn't need to ask me what was wrong. He already knew. "Next time, you can reassure her and tell her we're not going anywhere."

"I can't lie to her."

"It's not a lie."

I turned in his arms to face him. Despite the darkness, I could just make out his gaze, watching me with an intensity that was so familiar yet worrying too. "Matt, we're following Gabe, no matter where he ends up. We have to."

"We're not leaving England. This is my aunt's home, your home—"

"I don't care where I live as long as it's with you. *You* are my home. And Aunt Letitia will get used to America."

His arms tightened around me. "She has lived here all her life and would hate living somewhere else. We can't ask her to leave. Besides, England has become my home too. I also have responsibilities here, not just to my aunt but to the title and estate."

I sat up. "Matt, you can't be separated from Gabe!"

"India—"

"No! I won't accept your excuses. This isn't about responsibilities or livelihoods. This is about your life. If the magic in your watch fades again, I can't fix it alone."

He sat up too. The bedcovers puddled at his waist, but I wouldn't be distracted by the sight of his bare chest. "Last time, I had months to find a doctor magician. This time, the watch is stronger, thanks to your magic, so there's no reason to think it'll fade quickly or any time soon."

"And what if it's not the same next time? What if you suddenly become ill? Or if you're in an accident again? You won't have months in those instances, you'll have mere hours, if that."

He cupped my jaw. "Then so be it."

I shoved his hand away.

"India, I've told you how I feel, as has Gabe. He doesn't like using his magic to extend someone's life."

"He has promised me that he will in your case since the decision to keep you alive was made by his father."

"That doesn't mean he likes doing it. Besides, I'm already on borrowed time."

"Stop it."

"I shouldn't be here."

"Stop it, Matt! Of course you should be here. You should be living until old age."

He shook his head. "You make it sound like I want to die. I don't, I assure you. I have so much to live for." He cupped my cheek again and stroked it with his thumb, catching my tears as they slid down. "But people who want to live die all the time. It's not fair that I should be the one to live because of Gabe's magic. We can no longer expect him to keep me alive and not others. He sees death every day in the hospital. Don't you think he'd like to keep every single one of his patients alive? But he knows it's not right. I know it too. As do you."

I jerked away and lay down again, pulling the covers up to my chin. My tears soon dampened the pillow, but dashing them away wouldn't stop them. They would keep coming until I had none left.

Matt put his arm around me and I tried shoving him off again, but he wouldn't budge. I gave up. I wanted to feel his touch anyway. I wanted him near me, for as long as possible. Because one day, he wouldn't be there. I hoped that day was a long way away. I hoped my magic was strong enough to extend Gabe's magic, because I knew I could never change Matt's mind.

When Gabe left English soil, it would be the last time we'd see him.

CHAPTER 9

*W*e needed to get news and supplies to Gabe the following morning. I was reluctant for Matt to go to the hotel, but he insisted it must be him. He planned on a disguise and would leave through the back entrance of the house, but it wasn't enough to soothe my anxiety. The police had sent a third constable to watch the coach house and mews.

"I'll send for the carriage," I said over breakfast. "One of the constables will have to follow it. I'll go shopping at Harrods to make the journey appear authentic. Just after I leave the house, Willie will leave via the rear entrance, drawing that constable away from his position. Then Matt, you slip out in your disguise."

"What about me?" Duke asked.

Willie slapped him on the shoulder as she passed on her way to refill her coffee cup at the sideboard. "You can help Letty with her embroidery."

Duke pouted. "Why don't I get the fun jobs anymore?"

"Because Letty likes you better than me."

With Cyclops maintaining his usual routine of going to work in the mornings, Willie and Duke had been left to their own devices, more or less. Taking out the third member of their trio had changed the dynamic of the household. I

117

suspected Duke and Willie were beginning to grate on each other's nerves. They needed Cyclops to add balance and a distraction.

Aunt Letitia was quiet this morning as she settled into the sitting room with Duke. Even after Matt spoke to her about his plan to stay in England, she still seemed distant. I suspected she was worried about him being away from Gabe too. She might sometimes be selfish, but she wouldn't want Matt staying in England for her sake if it meant putting his life in danger.

When Woodall brought the carriage around, Matt assisted me into the cabin himself to show his face to the two constables standing on the opposite side of the street. I scanned the street but couldn't see any more policemen. That didn't mean there weren't any.

"Be careful," I said to Matt.

He kissed the back of my hand. "Always."

* * *

AUNT LETITIA DIDN'T like Harrods. She claimed it lacked the personal touch and preferred the specialty shops on Bond Street. But I liked the anonymity of the large store, and its lack of pretension. I also liked that I could buy almost anything under one roof.

I purchased some handkerchiefs for Matt, bottles of perfume for myself and Aunt Letitia, and a pair of gloves each for Willie, Cyclops and Duke. With the goods in my basket, a suitable amount of time had passed and I felt I could return home without raising the suspicions of the constables. I couldn't help walking through the department that sold watches and clocks, however, just to hear their rhythmic ticking.

"India? India, is that you?"

I turned to see Louisa approaching. My insides recoiled at the sight of her. I'd never liked her much, but I liked her even less after seeing her at the opera with Fabian. I forced myself to smile and greet her then made my excuses.

She followed me, however, and stopped me as I reached the exit. A doorman dressed in the green and gold livery of Harrods opened the door for us. I felt foolish making him stand there while we talked so I indicated to Louisa to join me on the pavement outside.

"Did you enjoy the opera the other night?" she asked.

So it would seem we were going to exchange pleasantries as if nothing had happened. "Yes, and you?"

"Fabian and I enjoyed it very much."

I looked away, searching for Woodall among the carriages parked along the street. I spotted him and waved, but he didn't see me. He was distracted by something behind him. I squinted to see, but could only make out the traffic slowing to a halt at the end of the street. Soon it was one long river of carriages and horses, with drivers growing more agitated by the moment.

Then I heard it too—shouted voices in the distance. With the carriages now blocking my view, I couldn't see what was happening. But I didn't have to. The shouts were many and they grew louder with every step the mob took in our direction.

As they approached, I could just make out their grievance. "Down with magicians!" they chanted, over and over.

"Back inside!" the doorman ordered. "Everyone, come back. It's not safe out here."

With the road blocked by traffic, the mob spilled down the pavements like a floodwater. The sound of glass breaking sent some of the horses into a panic, and it took great efforts from the coachmen to keep them from injuring themselves and those on board.

Shoppers on their way to Harrods or who'd just left raced back inside. It wasn't the wisest move. I suspected the department store was the target of the angry mob. But a second mob was approaching from the other end of the street, cutting off escape routes. There was nowhere else to go except back into the building. The constable who'd followed me in a hansom from the house was nowhere in sight.

Louisa grabbed my hand and together we hurried through the door. A few other frightened shoppers entered after us then the doorman closed and bolted the door.

"Move away from the windows!" he shouted. Other staff members repeated the order until it reverberated around the vast space like a drum beat.

"Come on, India." Louisa tugged my hand, but I didn't move.

"This is unnecessary," I said. "These riots don't need to happen. If only they knew…"

"Knew what?"

"Legislation will be created to protect the artless businesses."

"Protect the artless?" She scoffed. "Why should the legislators get involved? The market will sort itself out. Naturally there will be some losers, but those craftsmen who cannot compete with magicians will find other work. It's not the fault of magicians. They shouldn't have to compromise. Would you ask a beautiful woman to make herself uglier? An intelligent man to stop solving complicated equations?"

I was about to remind her that we were not talking about beauty or brains, but about livelihoods and causing financial difficulty to those whose incomes depended on the craft they were trained for, but the sound of glass shattering sent everyone ducking.

Those near the window screamed. People shouted orders, both from within the store and out. The mob's chant of "down with magicians" continued as the door splintered, sending the doorman stumbling backward. Over it all, the high pitch of a policeman's whistle pierced the air.

But it was too far away to save us.

The mob needed to be dispersed now, before they destroyed the store. Those at the front of the crowd pushed on the damaged door until it gave way. They spilled through like a horde of wild animals.

The floor walker bravely stepped in front of them. "Please, stop! Go home!"

"You sell magician-made hats and scarves!" one of the rioters shouted.

"No! No, I assure you, we don't!"

A woman spat on him and a man pushed him aside. The floor walker stumbled and fell, hitting his head against a display cabinet.

Louisa pulled hard on my hand. "India, you have to get back. If they recognize you…"

"No one knows me." But I had no confidence in my own words. I'd met members from the different craft guilds during the course of our investigations. Some would recognize me.

And of course Mr. Abercrombie knew me very well. I couldn't see him, however, but that didn't mean he wasn't staying out of sight in the middle of the crowd.

Now that they'd all spilled into the shop, I realized the mob wasn't as large as I first thought. I guessed there to be fewer than a hundred. It was smaller than the previous riots I'd seen first-hand.

But that was cold comfort when every one of them rushed into the confined space of the store, shouting angrily and waving clubs and fists. When one pushed over a display of perfume bottles, it was a signal to the others to cause as much damage as possible.

One man smashed a hammer through a glass display cabinet. Another swept his arm across a counter-top, scattering the pots of face creams that had been carefully stacked into a pyramid. A third raided the cash desk. The poor shop assistants cowered as far away as they could, some crying, others screaming.

I had to do something. If they only knew their concerns would be heard very soon, they'd calm down. I was sure of it.

I wrenched my hand free of Louisa's grip and thrust it into the air. "Listen! Listen to me! This is unnecessary!"

No one heard me over the din.

"Stop and listen to what I have to say!"

"Get out of the way or you'll get hurt, lady," one of the mob growled.

"The prime minister and cabinet will soon sign off on new laws to limit the sale of magician-made goods. If you would be patient—"

Someone rushed past me, slamming into my shoulder. I stumbled, but regained my footing before I fell. If I was going to make myself heard, I had to get their attention.

I eyed the nearest counter. If someone could assist me onto it I could use it as a pulpit, of sorts.

And then I heard it. The warning chime of my watch inside my reticule, nestled among my purchases in the basket over my arm. I didn't need to hear it to know I was in danger from the mob. If they found out who I was, they would turn on me.

A round of cheers followed by screams erupted as another display cabinet was smashed to pieces. I had to do something and do it now.

I searched for a stool to stand on and was about to ask one of the terrified shop assistants to help me, but my arm was suddenly gripped hard. I dropped my basket.

"Louisa, I—"

The slap across my face stunned me into silence. Tears blurred my vision, but when it cleared I saw Mr. Abercrombie's rat-like face sneering back at me.

"Well, well. Isn't this a fortuitous meeting? I believe I owe you for your interference."

My purchases and reticule had scattered when I dropped the basket. I spotted the reticule near the display of hats on a hat stand that had miraculously remained upright. Trampling feet got much too close to it.

"Let me go!" I tried to wrench free, but Abercrombie held on too tightly.

"Finally, I have you." His lips parted, baring his teeth. He'd always presented a gentlemanly façade, even at his worst. But it had been stripped away along with his guild membership, revealing this cold-hearted and cruel creature.

"Terrible things happen to innocent bystanders in frenzied mobs. They get hurt. Trampled on. Kicked and beaten to death."

I tried to search for Louisa but she was lost amid the chaos somewhere.

Over the din, I could just make out the frenetic chiming of my watch. It was desperate to get out of the reticule, to save me from this man. But my magic couldn't save me when the reticule was closed.

"I'm going to enjoy this." Abercrombie's tongue flicked out and licked his lips. "What a shame you got in the way of a mob in the grip of mania."

The mob swelled around us, ignoring us. They were too intent on doing damage, on having their angry voices heard. They drowned out my pleas and didn't care when I was shoved to the floor near their feet.

Abercrombie thought he was winning, but I'd landed near my reticule. Just a few more inches and my outstretched fingers would reach it.

A shoe struck my hip. Pain flared, despite the layers of clothing that offered some protection. I instinctively curled into a ball to protect myself, but that meant I was further away from the reticule.

I fought through the pain and pushed to my hands and knees, only to receive another kick to my side. It knocked me onto my back. Abercrombie rose above me, his shoe descending over my face.

Operating on pure instinct, I rolled out of the way. His foot slammed into the tiles beside my head.

I scrambled on hands and knees, edging closer to the reticule. I reached for it, only to have my arm stomped on by Abercrombie. I cried out as pain spiked along my arm to my shoulder.

Even through the shouts and sounds of smashing glass, I could hear his cruel chuckle. He was enjoying this.

But I wasn't beaten yet. I still had my wits and one good hand. That hand was in reach of the reticule. The tips of my fingers touched its drawstring and I was able to tug it across the floor toward me.

Just as Abercrombie's foot rose above my head.

My watch vibrated and chimed madly, jumping inside the silk embroidered reticule like a frog. My trembling fingers fumbled with the opening and I managed to widen it, but not enough to set my watch free.

Or so I thought.

The watch did the rest, somehow wriggling its way through the small opening. It launched itself at the man who was about to stomp on my head. The chain wrapped itself around his ankle and jerked his foot backward.

He lost his balance and fell heavily beside me, his eyes wide as he realized what had happened. "Witchcraft," he hissed.

I snatched my watch back and got to my feet. Every place he'd kicked me hurt like the devil, but there was no time to inspect my wounds. I had to get away. There would be no reasoning with this mob, not with Abercrombie fanning the flames of their anger and discrediting me.

Someone grabbed my hand and I tried to jerk free before I realized it was Louisa.

"The staff are directing as many shoppers as possible to the loading bay out the back," she said, pulling me alongside her. "We can leave that way too."

"It's her!" Abercrombie had risen and now pointed a finger at me. "It's Mrs. Glass, the leader of the magicians!"

Only those closest heard him. They quieted and turned to me. "Is that really her?" one asked.

Mr. Abercrombie's sneer turned slick. "It is. It's India Glass. Magician. Witch. Your predicament is *her* fault. If it weren't for her, you'd still have your livelihoods!"

"They haven't lost anything!" I cried, even as Louisa pulled me away.

"Not yet," snarled one of the rioters. He charged toward us. "Don't let her leave!"

I turned and ran, pushing my way through the crowd. My

watch chimed in my closed fist, its magic throbbing. I didn't want to unleash it. It would only draw more attention to me, and lead them to brand me as a witch as Abercrombie had done. The watch couldn't save me from them all.

"Through here." Louisa dragged me after her, through the drapery department where few of the mob had reached. We wove around counters and rack after rack piled with bolts of fabric, only to get to the end and realize we were facing the way we'd come.

Louisa swore.

"This way," said a sales assistant clutching a measuring tape. "Take the exit behind the brocade display. I'll tell them you went a different way. Go!"

Louisa and I ran for the cornflower blue curtain display which hid a door marked STAFF ONLY. I pushed it open, hissing in pain when I knocked my bruised arm.

The door started to close behind Louisa, but not before I saw Abercrombie. While the shop assistant directed our pursuers away from the exit, he'd spotted us.

"This way!" he shouted.

My stomach roiled and I thought I'd throw up. They would easily catch us now.

The door slammed shut just as several police whistles blasted the air. They were as tuneful as a symphony to my ears. Some of the whistles had come from inside the shop, but more came from the constables running through the loading bay in which we now found ourselves. Joined by some of the staff, they streamed past us and cut off the rioters emerging through the entrance to the shop. The constables pinned them to the ground and disarmed those carrying weapons.

Abercrombie wasn't one of them.

Louisa and I slowed our pace. Breathing hard, we exited the loading bay. Once back on Brompton Road, I spotted Woodall standing up on the driver's seat, looking toward the front entrance of Harrods.

We approached from behind and I called out to him. A

look of relief flooded his face when he saw me. "Get in, Mrs. Glass. I'll get you out of here."

"May we offer you a lift?" I asked Louisa.

"If you wouldn't mind." She gave Woodall her address then climbed into the cabin behind me.

We both breathed enormous sighs as we sank into the seats. I winced a little as my sore hip touched the side.

"Are you injured?" Louisa asked.

"A few bruises only."

"It was that horrid rabble-rouser, wasn't it? I saw him attack you, but was too far away to do anything. I couldn't get to you. I'm sorry."

I blinked at her in surprise. This sympathetic woman was not the Louisa I was familiar with. "It's not your fault."

"I loathe being useless. Did he know who you were?"

"His name is Abercrombie. He's the former master of the Watchmaker's Guild, and he despises me. We think he's colluding with Coyle to fan the flames of the artless."

"Coyle working with the artless? Good lord. Whatever for?"

"He wants to force magicians back into hiding. He wants to be their voice to the government so he can manipulate policy."

"To his favor. Yes, I see now. I wish I'd confronted that Abercrombie fellow in Harrods. A swift kick to the nether regions wouldn't stop him helping Coyle, but it would certainly make me feel better." She frowned. "Why are you smiling?"

"You remind me of Matt's cousin." How I wished Willie had come shopping with me today.

"The odd little American? Fabian calls her a wildcat."

I recoiled at the mention of his name, but didn't berate her for speaking it. I was suddenly too tired to do even that. Our escapade had utterly exhausted me.

But Louisa wanted to talk about him. "He's a good man, India. I know what he did to your husband was deplorable, but he was desperate to…to forge an alliance with you. He lost his sense of perspective for a while, but I believe he has it back now. He regrets his behavior."

I watched her from beneath half-closed lids. "He's not the only one with a warped perspective. Yours is skewed too. You believe magic is the most important thing in the world."

She turned to the window. "Not the most important thing. There is love too."

For the first time, I believed she truly was in love with Fabian and not merely wanting to be with him for his magic. Knowing that warmed me to her a little more, although I still didn't particularly like her. Her help today meant I now respected her, however. She had not run off frightened. She had stayed with me, even though I was dangerous to be near.

"You're courageous," I told her.

She gave a self-deprecating smile. "I was terrified in there."

"Then why didn't you leave me when you had the opportunity?"

She looked at me askance. "India, you are the most powerful magician in the country! You must be protected! Particularly now."

I frowned. "Now?"

She nodded at my hand, resting on my stomach. "When you could be carrying the next generation's most powerful magician in your womb."

I lowered my hand to the seat. "I'm not with child."

She looked genuinely disappointed. "My mistake. I do apologize."

We traveled in silence until we reached her house, both of us lost in thought. Her footman opened the carriage door for her and assisted her down the step to the pavement.

"Thank you, Louisa," I said before he closed the door. "I do appreciate what you did today."

She nodded and lifted a hand in a wave as we drove off.

* * *

News of the riot at Harrods arrived at number sixteen Park Street at the same time as me. It was fortunate that it hadn't reached Matt's ears first or he would have been sick with worry and gone to the department store himself to find me.

After I admitted to being caught up in it, everyone insisted I sit down. Aunt Letitia plied me with tea while Duke cut me a thick slice of butter cake. Even Willie fussed, asking if I needed a cushion at my back.

And I hadn't even told them about Abercrombie yet. I knew I couldn't avoid the topic altogether, however, particularly when Matt noticed the awkward way I was sitting, favoring my bruised side.

"Do you recall how Mr. Matthews wrote to us about how they couldn't find Mr. Abercrombie, and everyone assumed he'd left the city? Well, he hasn't. He was there, urging the rioters on. He saw me and we had words. Louisa was shopping there too, as it happens, and helped me escape. I've just taken her home." The short version was for Aunt Letitia's sake.

She was the only one who didn't believe there was more to the story, however. After I finished my tea, I made my excuses. Matt followed me into the bedroom and shut the door.

"Take off your clothes," he ordered.

"Matthew Glass, it's the middle of the day!"

My attempt at light-heartedness fell flat. His lips didn't even twitch. He crossed his arms and repeated his order.

I showed him the bruise on my arm first, then the others. He swore loudly then swore again, under his breath, as he gave them a thorough inspection. As he crouched before me, I told him what Abercrombie had done and said to rile up the crowd.

"My watch saved me from him, and Louisa helped me escape. She was marvelous, actually."

He gently helped me put on a house coat over my underclothes. "You need to see a doctor."

I was about to protest that I was fine, but changed my mind.

His hands skimmed my arms, above the bruise. "Get some rest while I fetch him." He kissed my temple. When he drew away, his jaw was set hard, his eyes ominously dark.

I knew that look. He wanted the culprit to suffer as he'd made me suffer. The problem was, Abercrombie would be in hiding again. "Where are you going?"

"To speak to the home secretary. This should never have happened. If the meeting with the prime minister had already taken place… If Le Grand had done his job properly and followed Abercrombie…" He dragged his hand through his hair and down his face then thumped the bedpost.

I clasped his face in my hands and softened the sharp lines of his cheeks with my thumbs. "I won't ask you not to go, but I will ask you not to do or say anything you'll later regret."

He expelled a breath. "I'll try."

"And please be here when the doctor comes."

"That I can promise." He kissed me gently then left the room.

Once he was gone, I opened my diary and flipped back through the pages.

* * *

After a warm bath that soothed my aches, Matt returned with the doctor. He checked my bruises and declared that no bones had been broken, then prescribed rest.

As he closed up his bag, I cleared my throat. "There's one more thing I want to ask you, Doctor."

"Ask me anything, Mrs. Glass."

"Could I be with child?"

Matt's head jerked up. He'd been sitting on a chair beside the bed and now sat forward. "You think you might be?"

I described how I felt very tired all of a sudden, and sometimes a little nauseous. My courses were also late, which I'd failed to notice with all the drama in our lives of late.

Without a definitive test to say if I was or wasn't, the doctor preferred to assume that I was with child as a precaution. "But you won't know for sure until you start to show. That could be some weeks away."

Matt saw the doctor out then returned to the bedroom. He gently scooped me into his arms and kissed me thoroughly. When he drew away, he couldn't hide his smile. It wasn't his usual smile. It was rather unsure, like a youth about to ask his first love if he could walk with her. For a man who'd been filled with anger and frustration moments before, it was quite a change.

"Do you think you are?" he asked.

"As the doctor says, we'll just have to wait and see."

"Can't you tell?"

I laughed. "Not really."

"Some women know and some don't," he said with all the authority of a midwife with twenty years' experience. "Just in case you are, you must rest now. I'll bring dinner up to you."

"I'll be well rested by then."

He kissed me again, quickly, then stood. "Just humor me for today."

"Very well." As he turned to go, I said, "I think it's best if we don't tell the others until we know for sure. After today's scare, they'll be unbearably cloying."

"Agreed. One unbearably cloying member of the household is enough." He knelt on the bed and kissed me again. "I'm referring to myself, by the way."

I chuckled. "I know. Now go so I can rest then bring me something delicious for dinner. Tell Mrs. Potter I'd like something with a little spice."

CHAPTER 10

*W*ith all the excitement of the previous day, I'd not had a chance to ask Matt how Gabe had seemed when he called on him at the hotel. I asked after breakfast as we waited for Woodall to bring our carriage around.

"He's anxious," Matt said. "He just wants to leave as soon as possible."

"Did you tell him I called on Nancy?"

"He was very grateful to you for reassuring her."

I sighed. "To think, this all evolved from something that ought to be a wonderful time in their lives. Gabe should be slipping that ring on Nancy's finger and setting a date for their wedding, but instead he's in hiding, his life in peril."

Matt circled his arm around my shoulders and kissed my temple. "His life in America won't be so bad. He'll grow to enjoy it there, as will Nancy. Boston and New York are full of Irish immigrants so she'll have a lot of support."

While I was relieved for them, it gave me no comfort to think of them so far away from Matt.

Woodall pulled up outside and Bristow, who'd been waiting on the porch, opened the door for us. We traveled to Whitehall and met Mr. Matthews and Mr. Le Grand in the home secretary's office. They were not alone.

A man I'd met only once stood upon our entrance. Dressed in a well-cut woolen suit of the same steel-gray color as his hair, he looked a little nervous as he extended his hand to me then Matt.

"We weren't expecting to see you, Mr. Stocker," Matt said. "But we're glad you are here."

The master of the Worshipful Company of Woolmen visibly relaxed. He must have been expecting a tense greeting. A few weeks ago, we'd given false names in order to speak to him about Mr. Pyke, the wool magician he'd expelled from the guild just before he went missing. They'd been close friends until Mr. Pyke informed Mr. Stocker that he was a magician. Upon the urging of Abercrombie, the woolen guild master had revoked Mr. Pyke's membership, although we'd got the impression he was uncomfortable at the role he'd played in ruining his friend's business.

A business that Mr. Pyke had since closed. Without guild membership, Mr. Pyke had no license to sell his woolen rugs, and he'd been forced to stop trading.

Mr. Stocker's presence today was an intriguing development and I waited eagerly for the explanation.

It came from Mr. Matthews. "Mrs. Glass, are you aware that your husband called on us yesterday?"

"I am. He mentioned that I was caught up in the Harrods riot?"

He did. "I trust you are recovering from your injuries?"

"Yes, thank you."

"Good, good. Did your husband also tell you that he made it *very* clear that something must be done immediately?" Mr. Matthews adjusted his tie and avoided Matt's glare.

I suspected that meeting had been far less civil than this one. Matt had wanted to blame someone for my injuries, and in the absence of Abercrombie, Mr. Matthews was next in line.

"Mr. Glass urged us to find Abercrombie and bring him to justice," Mr. Matthews went on.

Matt addressed Mr. Le Grand, standing to one side. "And have you done that?"

"We're yet to find him," the spy master said evenly.

A muscle in Matt's jaw pulsed, but he kept his opinion to himself.

"Your husband stressed that we must act now to calm the dissenters," Mr. Matthews said. "I happen to agree that things are taking too long so I took matters into my own hands and called on as many guild masters as I could yesterday after-noon. I invited them to come here this morning to listen to your proposals, Mrs. Glass. Mr. Stocker was the only one to take me up on the offer."

My heart sank. One man wasn't enough. It wasn't nearly enough to affect change quickly.

But it was all we had. "Thank you for coming, Mr. Stocker. I don't think you'll leave disappointed after you hear what I have to say."

He gave me a flat smile. "Since I last saw you, I've had time to think about the situation and an opportunity to talk to guild members. Mr. Pyke is a popular fellow and well respected. No one wants to see him suffer. While some have urged me to continue with his ban, most have insisted he be allowed to rejoin the guild."

"And what did you decide?"

"I'm still considering the options, and whether the guild constitution must be changed. Did you know that Pyke and Mr. Fuller want to form a business arrangement?"

"The other rug maker? I did not."

"They plan to sell Pyke's rugs. The Fullers are very good sales people, but Pyke had the better quality product. He failed to sell many rugs, however, since he didn't enjoy customer interaction. They think combining their skills will work better for them both."

It lifted my heart to hear it. For the artless and magicians to become partners was the best outcome for all. But the arrangement wouldn't suit every artless or every magician.

Mr. Stocker nodded at the home secretary. "I agree with Mr. Matthews. Something must be done or the city will descend into chaos before the week is out. That's not good business for anyone, artless or magician. He told me you have some compromises that might see an end to the troubles."

Mr. Matthews indicated I should go ahead and I outlined my ideas to Mr. Stocker. I told him about the cap on the number of magician-made goods that could be sold, and a tax. Like the home secretary, he preferred the latter idea. I also offered to speak to journalists and have them report that magic didn't last.

"Your suggestions won't be popular with the magicians," Mr. Stocker warned.

"No tax is popular at first," Mr. Matthews assured him. "But it will be accepted, in time, particularly when the magicians realize they have no alternative. If they wish to trade at all, then they must accept it."

"And the guilds themselves?" Mr. Stocker asked. "What role do you propose we play in this?"

"The same role you always have," I said. "You issue licenses to your members, and offer them benefits. In fact, I suggest you turn this into an opportunity to look at how you can best meet the future needs of your members. Some question the benefits they receive from their membership."

Mr. Stocker nodded slowly. "Our relevance has eroded over the centuries, it's true. We used to have more sway in policy-making."

"You used to financially support those members who needed help during illness or catastrophe," Matt added.

Mr. Stocker cleared his throat. "We have a lot of members now and the cost of living has risen… It's just not viable to financially support members who face difficulty, unfortunately. But I agree we must do something to prove we are still relevant, and revoking the licenses of magicians won't do that. It will ultimately decrease our relevance further."

Matt nodded but stayed silent, thankfully. Now wasn't the time to discuss the abolition of licenses altogether which would in turn render the guilds completely pointless. Perhaps when things had settled, but not while so many artless members were angry. We needed them on-side.

"What say you, Stocker?" Mr. Matthews asked in his friendly politician's voice. "Do you agree to take Mrs. Glass's proposals to your guild committee?"

"I will, and gladly. I'll call a special meeting for tonight. They'll want to know when these proposals can be implemented."

"The prime minister is due to arrive in London shortly. Mrs. Glass will tell him everything she has just told you, then we'll ask all the guild masters to attend a special meeting to nut out the details. Will that be sufficient for you to take to your members, Mr. Stocker?"

"It is. And I will send word to other guild masters too. Perhaps the city will be calmer within days." He pushed himself to his feet. "We are on the right track. I'm sure of it. Thank you for your time, Mrs. Glass, Mr. Glass." He shook each of our hands, but when he took Mr. Le Grand's, the spy master wouldn't release him.

"Just one thing before you go," Mr. Le Grand said in that calm way he had, as if he were going to ask about the weather or something equally bland. I wasn't fooled, however, and neither was Mr. Stocker, going by the way he tensed. "Did Abercrombie pay you or your guild members to agitate the crowd during any of the riots?"

Mr. Stocker glanced at Mr. Matthews, but the home secretary remained seated, his hands clasped loosely over his stomach, his expression polite, non-committal. Mr. Stocker gave a small nod and Mr. Le Grand released him.

"Will you be willing to testify in court?" Matt asked.

Mr. Stocker put up his hands in surrender. "No, no, I can't. I don't dare."

Mr. Le Grand arched a brow. "Are you afraid of him?"

The guild master chewed on the inside of his lower lip.

"Mr. Abercrombie wouldn't dare harm you," I said. "He's a weak man. He only attacks those he thinks are weaker than himself." Abercrombie would not have attacked me if I wasn't alone.

"It's not Abercrombie who worries me. It's the man behind him."

"Who?" Le Grand barked. He stepped closer until he was mere inches from Mr. Stocker. It was the most interest he'd ever shown in any conversation I'd been a party to.

Mr. Stocker backed away. "I—I don't know. I'm sorry, but all I know is that someone with money must have funded him. He gave away a lot to the main agitators, and once he mentioned that his lordship won't like it if he failed. He was afraid of the man. And if he's afraid of him, it's probably wise if we all are. I cannot afford to make a powerful enemy, Mr. Le Grand. I have a family, and a business that relies on the patronage of the nobility. Based on what Abercrombie said, I expect this lord can ruin me, and worse." He backed away to the door. "I'd rather stay out of it. Testifying against Abercrombie is more than I am willing to do. I am sorry. Good day to you all."

He left quickly. Mr. Le Grand closed the door and turned, keeping his back to it. Blocking our exit. "We can safely assume Coyle is the man behind Abercrombie and that he's hiding Abercrombie after yesterday's Harrods attack."

"Agreed." Matt steepled his fingers under his chin as he thought. "There are only two reasons why Coyle would hide him. Either Abercrombie is still of use to him or he's worried Abercrombie would crumble under interrogation and implicate him."

"If it's the latter then Abercrombie could be dead," I pointed out. "If he has fulfilled his duty and is now a liability, Coyle will get rid of him." The thought chilled me to the bone.

Matt thumped his fist on the chair arm. "You need to find Abercrombie before that happens."

"I am well aware of that," Mr. Le Grand bit off.

Mr. Matthews moved his clasped hands from his stomach to the desk as he leaned forward. "This speculation is all well and good, but Coyle is a peer. The case against him has to be airtight. If there are any holes, it will be thrown out. Many in the government would prefer that than seeing the reputation of an earl sullied."

"Only those in the House of Lords, frightened it will mean they too will be held accountable for their actions," Matt said.

Mr. Matthews looked away and Mr. Le Grand moved aside. We left.

* * *

I WAS BACK at the Home Office that afternoon to meet with the prime minister and cabinet. The meeting was as productive as I hoped it would be and it felt immensely satisfying to get my point of view across. Having seen the unrest in the city for himself, the prime minister was prepared to consider all options and move quickly. Mr. Matthews stressed the importance of the latter.

I returned home in time for afternoon tea with an unexpected visitor. I hadn't seen Louisa since our escape from the Harrods riot, so I was glad she called on me. It gave me another chance to thank her properly for her assistance.

"It was quite an ordeal yesterday," she said. "I do hope you have recovered, India."

My bruises hurt to touch and my thighs ached from sprinting, but with the success of the day, I'd almost forgotten about my pains. "I'm feeling quite well. And you?"

"Invigorated. It was frightening at the time, of course, but now I feel only immense satisfaction at being able to outwit our pursuers and escape relatively unscathed." Her blue eyes were as big and bright as the summer sky and she could barely contain her enthusiasm. Physical exertion coupled with danger agreed with her. "Imagine living life like that every day."

I laughed, despite myself. "No thank you. Cake?"

We sat alone in the drawing room. Matt had taken Aunt Letitia for a drive, while Willie and Duke were spying on Coyle's house in the hope of seeing Abercrombie coming or going. We all doubted they'd spot him. Indeed, Abercrombie probably wasn't there at all, even though we were quite sure Coyle had orchestrated his disappearance. He would be holed up somewhere else entirely, rather like Gabe staying at a hotel with no links to us.

Louisa nibbled the edge of her sponge cake, her brow furrowed in thought. I suspected this wasn't entirely a social call, but I waited for her to be ready to say what she came to say. It took her quite some time to get to the point, however, and it was only after a long silence that she eventually decided it had to be said.

She put down her teacup and saucer and regarded me with the seriousness that I often associated with her. "I have something important to tell you, India. Something which I am rather reluctant to mention, but…" She shook herself, as if trying to shake off the reluctance. "But you must be made aware, given that we suspect Coyle is encouraging the riots."

"The city will calm down soon."

She didn't seem to hear me and continued on as if I hadn't spoken. "I saw Coyle leaving Fabian's house."

"When was this?"

"Just now. I came straight here to tell you."

"And you think this means they're colluding somehow?"

She blinked. "What else can it mean?"

What indeed. Fabian hated Lord Coyle. Coyle had tried to destroy his relationship with his brother and had been behind the theft of the rug and moving spell from Fabian. It was unlikely they would collude, but it was not impossible. If their interests aligned, they might decide it was best to work together.

The thought chilled me.

"How did Coyle seem?" I asked.

"As smug as always. Fabian looked pleased too as he saw him off. What do you think they have planned?"

"Nothing good." I eyed her closely as she retrieved her cup and sipped. Why was she telling me this when she wished to marry Fabian? They'd been seen at the opera together so they were friends again, so why would she tell me something which could make me think even less of him? It didn't quite make sense.

She met my gaze over the rim of her cup. "I know what you're thinking, India. You're not very good at hiding your thoughts."

I tried to school my features, but that only made her smile.

"You want to know why I'm telling you," she went on. "I admit that I almost didn't. But I detest Lord Coyle and I don't want him anywhere near Fabian. Ever since you cut off all contact with him—"

"He tried to kill my husband!"

"I understand your reasoning," she said gently. "But the fact is, he's now rather lonely. Indeed, he's starved of magical company."

"So he invited an artless lord over for tea?"

"I doubt he invited Coyle, but simply admitted him when he came calling. Coyle does know a lot of magicians and perhaps Fabian saw it as an opportunity to connect with some of them. Naturally Coyle would want something in return, and that is what I'm hoping to protect Fabian from—Coyle's influence and hunger for magical power. Without your friendship, Fabian is vulnerable."

"That is not my fault," I said tightly. "I don't see what you want me to do with this information."

She sighed. "I don't know either. I just thought you ought to be aware of the connection. If a friendship develops between them, it could be dangerous, and I'm worried Fabian will get sucked into Coyle's sphere." She rose to go. "Thank you for the tea and company."

I smiled and tugged on the bell pull to summon Bristow. My thoughts were still on Louisa's piece of news, however. "Did either of them see you?"

"I'm not sure," she said. "Do you think I should worry if they did?"

I gave her a reassuring smile. "I doubt it. Fabian won't expect you to come here and tell us what you saw. He knows you adore him, and it would never enter his head that you'd betray him."

She lay a hand on my arm. "You won't tell him, will you? The situation between us is nice, comfortable. I wouldn't want to damage what we have."

"Of course I won't."

She smiled a secretive little smile. "I've shown him another side to me lately, and I believe he is on the cusp of falling in love with me."

I almost told her that I was pleased to hear it, before stopping myself. I ought not encourage her toward an attempted murderer. It was insanity to wish those two together. But she would not appreciate my advice, nor would she take it on board, so I didn't tell her to avoid Fabian. She knew what he was, and if she still wanted to be with him, then so be it.

Matt entered the drawing room and gave Louisa a short bow before stepping aside so she could pass him. Bristow met her and escorted her to the front door.

Matt helped himself to a slice of cake while I poured tea. "What did she want?" he asked.

"She saw Lord Coyle visiting Fabian. She's worried Coyle is influencing Fabian."

He frowned as he studied his cake before taking a large bite.

"I didn't say this to her," I went on, "but I wonder if Coyle is hiding Abercrombie at Fabian's place. Fabian would only help Coyle if Coyle offered him something in return. Matt, I'm worried what that offer might entail. I'm sure it involves us, in some dreadful way. Or, rather, you."

He set the cake plate down and moved to sit beside me on the sofa. He drew me against him and placed a hand on my belly. There was nothing to feel yet, but he seemed to need the connection. "No harm will come to me, India."

"You can't know that."

"Charbonneau ran out of steam once he realized you wouldn't have him even if I were dead."

I lifted my head off his shoulder to look him in the eye. "Matt—"

He kissed me to stop me talking.

But I would not be stopped. I gently pushed him away. "This is yet another reason we should follow Gabe to America. To get as far away from Fabian as possible."

"India," he purred. "We've already discussed this. You can't change my mind."

I flattened my hand over his. "Not even now?"

Aunt Letitia entered the room and we sprang apart beneath her disapproving glare. "The drawing room is not the place for frolics and afternoon tea is not the time." She stood in front of the glowing coals in the fireplace as I poured her a cup.

We chatted about their drive until she nodded off in the chair. Matt signaled for me to leave the drawing room with him.

"I'll tell Polly to sit with her while she naps," he whispered.

"Matt," I chided. "I'm not in the mood."

"We're going out."

"Where?"

"To speak to someone who might know what Fabian and Coyle are up to."

* * *

PROFESSOR NASH WAS NOT ALONE when we called on him at his University College office. Oscar Barratt sat at the desk with a faraway look on his face that quickly vanished upon seeing us. He extended an ink-stained hand to Matt then gave up his chair for me. As there was only one other chair, the three men remained standing.

"We were just writing down some ideas for our research," Nash said with a wave of his hand that encompassed the piles of notebooks, papers and texts on the desk. "We're expanding my chapter from his book and co-writing a volume on the history of magic."

Oscar rocked back on his heels, looking pleased with himself. I'd never seen him quite so happy. Ending his relationship with Louisa agreed with him. "I was deep in thought just now, considering how the ancients used magic."

"And I've been going through my books, looking for any references I can find." The professor sighed as he surveyed the bookshelves crammed with tomes of all sizes. "I own a few about magic, yet I know others exist. It's just a matter of finding them. I suspect many are in private libraries."

"What will you do when you do find them?" I asked.

"Buy them, of course. Although I'll need funding."

One of the books on the shelves tipped into the gap left next to it from a missing volume that was most likely on the desk. "You're going to run out of space," I pointed out. "Do you think the university will agree to more funding?"

The professor pushed his glasses up his nose and grinned. "I suspect now is an excellent time to approach the board and ask for money. Magic is quickly becoming an important area of study." He patted Oscar on the shoulder. "All thanks to the excellent book written by our good friend here."

Oscar blushed. "You're too kind, Nash."

"The problem is, I'm not sure I want the college to own the library. Whoever owns it, controls it. What if they decide to limit access and only allow certain people to look at the books?" He sighed and fell silent.

Matt cleared his throat. "We have a question for you, Professor."

Nash straightened. "How can I be of service?"

"Have you seen Charbonneau lately?"

"Oh. No, I haven't. I can't bring myself to call on him. He hasn't made contact with me either, so I suspect he knows our acquaintance has ended. Why do you ask?"

"Louisa told me Lord Coyle visited Fabian," I said. "Matt thought you might provide us with an insight into Fabian's state of mind. In the past, he would never team up with

Coyle, but now we're worried he is desperate enough to do so."

Nash placed a hand to his throat. "You think he still wants to kill you, Glass?"

"No," Matt said, at the same time I said, "Perhaps."

Oscar and Nash exchanged glances.

"There could be any number of reasons why they're working together," Matt pointed out. "Charbonneau's motive is not clear, but we believe Coyle might be using him to hide Abercrombie."

"The former master of the Watchmakers' Guild?" Oscar asked. "Good lord."

Matt explained how Coyle was paying artless craftsmen to make trouble, using Abercrombie as his conduit to keep himself one step removed. He also told them about the assault on me at Harrods and how Mr. Abercrombie had since disappeared.

Professor Nash crouched beside my chair and took my hand in both of his. "My dear Mrs. Glass, what a dreadful experience for you. The man deserves a thrashing." He looked up at Matt. "When you find him, Glass, be sure to give him an extra punch from me."

I blinked in surprise. He was the last person I'd expected such a bloodthirsty response from.

"It's absolutely despicable," Oscar said. "I hope you find the cur, Glass, but I'm not sure you'll find him at Charbonneau's house."

"You have an insight into Charbonneau's state of mind?" Matt asked.

"Not his. Louisa's." At our questioning looks, he added, "Have you considered she may be lying in order to hurt him?"

"She told me she wants to protect him from Coyle," I said.

"You can't believe a word she says." As her former fiancé, and the man she made sure was dismissed from a job he loved, Oscar had a right to be bitter. He also knew her better than anyone in the room.

Matt was certainly taking him seriously. He didn't look surprised by the suggestion. He'd probably already considered the possibility that Louisa lied. "You think he rejected her again and this is her way of getting back at him? If he finds out, it would end any chance she has with him, once and for all."

Oscar merely shrugged. "She would do it if she was angry enough. It's precisely the sort of spiteful thing she'd do, in fact. She hates *not* having her own way and if he rejected her yet again, it could have been the last straw."

I wasn't so sure. "I agree with Matt—it would end any chance she possibly has with him. I do think she loves him and would hate the thought of never getting that chance back."

Oscar's top lip lifted with his sneer. "If it is love then it's the twisted kind, like one of those jungle vines that winds its way around the host tree in order to reach the sunlight only to eventually strangle it once it no longer has a use for it."

Nash shuffled away from Oscar, his lips forming a silent "Oh."

Matt held his hand out to me and I rose. "Thank you for your opinion," he said, a hint of amusement in his voice.

Oscar followed us to the door. "What will you do about it? Confront her? Tell her you know what she's up to?"

"We can't be sure if she's lying or not so, for now, we're going to do very little."

Oscar didn't look satisfied with Matt's answer, but he made no further comment. Even he must see that we needed to determine if Louisa was lying or not. If there was a chance Coyle and Fabian were colluding, we must follow that line of investigation.

Instead of giving Woodall instructions to drive home, Matt told him to take us to Fabian's house, but not to park directly out the front.

"I don't think confronting him is a good idea," I said.

"We're not confronting him. We're going to ask the

constable stationed there if he has seen a man matching Coyle's description."

It was an excellent idea and would save us considerable time. "I'd forgotten the police were watching him. I wonder how much longer they'll do it before they decide it's a waste of resources." The thought troubled me. What if the only thing keeping Fabian from attempting to kill Matt again was the fact the police were keeping an eye on his movements?

As it turned out, my concerns were justified. The plain-clothed policeman was easy to spot as he lounged against a lamp post, pretending to read a newspaper. He informed us that once his shift ended that day, no others would be assigned to replace him.

When asked if he'd seen anyone matching Coyle's description call on Fabian that afternoon, he shook his head. So Louisa *was* lying. She'd lied to my face and wasted our time. I wanted to drive to her house and give her a piece of my mind.

Matt was more composed, however. "It's not wise."

"This has nothing to do with wisdom and everything to do with letting her know that we know she lied. The nerve of her!"

He pressed his hand to my lower back. "It's not good for the baby for you to be riled like this."

I turned to him, hand on hip. "A little anger isn't going to harm the baby. If there is one. We don't know for certain."

He stepped closer, squashing my skirts against my legs. His eyes warmed and his lips curved with his seductive smile. "I'm certain."

I sighed. "Matt—"

"India! India, may I speak with you, please?" Fabian trotted down the front steps of his townhouse and hurried toward us.

Matt stepped in front of me but I didn't need his protection from Fabian. If anything, *he* needed protecting.

I moved out of his shadow. "What do you want?" I was

not inclined to greet Fabian with civility or exchange pleasantries.

From the earnest look on his face, pleasantries were not on his mind either. He approached with his hands in the air, and the resemblance to a fugitive captured by the authorities wasn't lost on me.

"Thank you for waiting," he said on a rush of breath. He addressed me, but his gaze flicked constantly to Matt. Perhaps he was worried Matt would lash out. "There is something I must tell you. It concerns Lady Louisa Hollingbroke."

"Go on," I said.

"You should expect a visit from her, but I beg you not to believe a word she says." When I didn't respond, he continued. "She will tell you that I have had a visit from Lord Coyle, but this is not true. I haven't. I swear to you, he and I are not friends. He has not called on me and I have not called on him. You can ask the constable there." He pointed to the policeman, standing several feet away. "He has been watching me for days, but Louisa doesn't know that."

"We've already confirmed with him," I said. "Louisa came to me this afternoon."

He expelled a long breath. "So you believe me when I say I am not working with Coyle?"

"We believe he hasn't called on you here." I wasn't going to let him off the hook completely, but I would admit to that much. "Why does she want to hurt you? I thought you two had become friends again, and I know she hoped for more. Why ruin that?"

He lowered his head and shook it. "She asked me to marry her again today, and I refused. She was very upset. More than the last times. I think she finally admitted to herself that there is no hope. She threatened me, and said I must marry her or she will make my life very difficult. When I told her my life is already difficult…" He glanced at Matt. "She said she will tell you that Coyle has called on me and that we are working together to hurt you, India. She gave me one more chance to agree to her proposal. When I told her no, she left, promising to go to you. I did not stop her." He nodded at the constable. "I knew the policeman would confirm Coyle has not been here. But I was still worried you would believe her."

"Why do you care if we believe her or not?" I asked.

"Because I am ashamed of my actions and I hope one day you can forgive me." He addressed himself to me, not Matt. That made me dislike him more. "Louisa said if I changed my mind and accepted her, she would tell you she'd made a mistake and it wasn't Coyle she'd seen here. She is trying to blackmail me."

"She is indeed," I murmured.

Fabian waited, but I had no more to say and Matt didn't seem to want to comment at all. So Fabian gave me a shallow bow then, as an afterthought, nodded at Matt. He turned on his heel and walked back to his house.

I took Matt's arm and together we returned to the carriage. Neither of us spoke. There was no more to say. Louisa had lied, and she had been caught out in that lie. I'd never believe a word she said again.

It was rather satisfying to know that she'd ruined her chance with Fabian entirely. Whether she was in love with him or not, I didn't care. She didn't deserve to get what she wanted. She was poison, and I was going to stay well away from her.

We returned home as dusk settled on the city. Willie and Duke arrived in time for dinner after watching Coyle's house all day. While Aunt Letitia changed, we met with them in the library and they confirmed that Coyle had not left the house. It was impossible for him to have called on Fabian.

"Did anyone else come or go?" Matt asked. "Was there any sign of Abercrombie?"

Both shook their heads. "That doesn't mean he ain't hiding inside somewhere," Duke said. "Coyle's servants are loyal and won't dare speak against their employer."

Matt scrubbed a hand over his jaw. "He could be hiding

anywhere in the city. We proved how easily it can be done with Gabe. The police are none the wiser."

"The police ain't the best investigators." At Willie's sharp look, Duke quickly added, "Except Brockwell, of course."

I glanced at the clock on the mantel. It was time I dressed for dinner too.

"There's something else," Willie said as I rose. I sat again, my heart sinking. Her tone was ominous. "We overheard Coyle shouting at Hope."

Matt tensed.

"Couples argue," I pointed out. "It doesn't mean anything."

But the look on Willie and Duke's faces was grim. "He shouted real cruel things at her," Willie went on. "Called her names. Told her she was greedy, that she married him for his money. It was nasty."

"I could hear her shouting back," Duke added. "Until she didn't. She suddenly went quiet."

I glanced at Matt. "That's not like her."

Matt's hands curled into fists and his jaw was rigid.

The only reason Hope would have quieted was because she was incapacitated or frightened. Coyle may have struck her or threatened to.

Matt shot to his feet and stormed off toward door. Duke, Willie and I sprang up too and raced after him. We had one aim—to stop Matt from confronting Coyle.

But from the determined look on his face, it was a near-impossible task.

CHAPTER 11

"*M*att!" I called as he strode out of the library. "You can't go. It's foolish to confront Coyle now. He will only deny it."

"I can demand to see her."

"Every time you have asked her if she is all right, she says she is. This will be no exception."

"He may have harmed her."

"You've offered her sanctuary more than once. She has refused you and will refuse again. The only thing you'll achieve is to reveal you've had his house watched. Is that what you want?"

He reached the bottom step of the staircase but went no further. He lowered his head and his shoulders stooped. He knew I was right, but he hated doing nothing.

Willie passed him and stood two steps higher up. She was still shorter than him. "You can't go there now. You've got to be smart about this, Matt."

Duke joined her. "When Willie is telling you to be smarter, you know you're acting foolishly."

Matt heaved a sigh. "Fine. I won't go. But I want one of you to scale the wall and look in on her."

"I'll do it," Willie said. "Duke, you stand below to catch me if I fall."

He snorted. "You ain't a feather."

"It was a joke because I ain't going to fall. I've done this before and I'm younger and more athletic than you."

"Easier to catch, too."

They agreed to go after dinner when Hope should have retired for the evening. Hopefully Mrs. Fry's duties as a paid companion and jailor didn't extend to sleeping in the same bedroom as her mistress.

Matt joined me as I changed into a dress more suited for dinnertime, something I only did to satisfy Aunt Letitia. She liked the tradition, but I thought it a waste of time. At least when it was just us, we weren't as formal as when we had guests.

As it turned out, I needn't have bothered. I met Aunt Letitia emerging from the service area just as we were about to enter the dining room. She still wore her day dress. "I thought you were changing."

"I had to speak to Mrs. Bristow," she said.

"About what?"

"Oh, look, here's Cyclops." She greeted him as he came up the stairs, his constable's helmet tucked under his arm. "You do look tired. I think you should have an early night."

"I won't argue with you about that." He kissed her on her upturned cheek. "But not until I've eaten. I'm famished."

Over dinner, we told Cyclops about our meeting with Mr. Le Grand and Mr. Matthews, and how they were looking for Abercrombie. I went on to tell him about the success of my meeting with the prime minister, and the strange visit from Louisa and subsequent discussion with Fabian.

He didn't seem interested in Louisa's predicament, and his next question proved it. "So we're relying on the spy master who lost Abercrombie in the first place to find him again?" He shook his head as he sliced into the chicken pie but spoke no more as he ate.

"I don't like it either," Matt said. "We need Abercrombie. If we want Coyle blamed for paying the rioters, Abercrombie's our best chance. But even then, he might not testify against him."

Indeed, it was unlikely. Coyle would have come to an agreement with Abercrombie, or perhaps threatened him to ensure his silence.

"Getting Abercrombie to talk is the only chance we have," I said matter-of-factly. "So everyone must stop being so negative. I'm sure Mr. Le Grand will find him. He has more resources at his disposal than us. Now, eat up and enjoy Mrs. Potter's pies. That's enough talk of troubling matters." I glanced at Aunt Letitia to get my point across, but she seemed quite all right with us discussing a topic she would usually consider too "vulgar" for the dinner table.

Even so, I steered the conversation away to the lighter topic of Cyclops's wedding.

Later, after Aunt Letitia retired and we sat in the sitting room, the rest of us were quiet, lost in our own thoughts. Even Willie, surprisingly. She usually hated silence. Indeed, she seemed quite glum as she slumped in the armchair, staring into her glass of Bourbon.

When she finished it, I rose and offered to get her another. "Is everything all right?" I asked.

"My glass is empty."

"There's something else, isn't there? Does it have to do with your love life?"

She merely shrugged.

I perched on the chair arm. "Does it involve Brockwell?"

She sighed. "I went to see him before I joined Duke across the street from Coyle's house. We talked."

"About what."

"About that other woman he likes."

"I thought he didn't like her as much as he likes you."

She stared down at her empty glass, cradled between both her hands. "I told him not to give her up."

"Why would you do that?"

She sniffed. I couldn't see her face as her head was lowered, but I was quite sure she was tearful. It was most unlike her. She may be emotional, but she usually covered it by getting angry.

"You hate the thought of him with another," I prompted.

"I do not."

"You do. It's quite obvious. So why did you tell him not to give her up?"

"Because he won't leave England, and I can't stay now. Not with you and Matt leaving when Gabe's settled in the States."

I lifted my gaze to Matt's. He was watching us. They all were. And they'd heard.

Matt seemed reluctant to repeat his conviction about us not leaving. Indeed, he seemed to need fortifying. He drained his glass then set it down with a *thunk* on the table.

I could have told them we were not leaving, but I didn't want to make it easy for him. He'd made the foolish decision not to stay in England, and now he must face the music.

"We're not following Gabe," he finally said.

Willie's head jerked up. She blinked away her tears and stared at him. "What d'you mean?"

"You have to!" Cyclops said. "You need to go where Seaford goes."

Matt shook his head. "England is my home now. We're not leaving."

Duke scoffed. "But you need the doctor."

"Not anymore. I feel strong. The magic in the watch will last longer this time, I'm sure of it. I have years—"

"You stupid, pig-headed idiot!" Willie shot to her feet and stomped across the floor to stand in front of Matt. She stabbed her finger at him, inches from his nose. "You're going to America too, and that's final."

Matt caught her wrist and shook his head.

She jerked free. "Speak to him, India!"

"I've tried," I said heavily. "He won't listen."

Duke stormed out of the room. Cyclops rose too, but didn't leave. He paced the floor, eventually coming to stop beside Willie. "You *think* your watch will last longer, but what if it doesn't? What if you need Seaford and he's on the other side of the world?"

"Then I will find him, if I have time."

"And if you don't?"

Matt leveled his gaze with Cyclops's. It was filled with sympathy for his friend. "Don't grieve for me yet. I'm still alive."

Cyclops swore, something he rarely did. "This ain't a joke."

Matt crossed his arms. "My decision is final. My home is here. And don't blame India," he said with a stern glare for Willie. "She wants me to go too. But my ancestral estate is here. I belong here. England is where I want to live my life and raise my family."

Cyclops shook his head and strode out of the room.

Willie threw herself into the armchair. She looked as though she was about to burst into tears. "You could have told me this before I told Brockwell he should be with that woman."

"I'm sorry," Matt said. "I didn't realize you planned to follow us to America if we went."

She threw her hands in the air. "Course I was going to follow you! You really are an idiot sometimes, Matt."

He opened his mouth to speak, but I caught his attention with a shake of my head. He closed it again.

Willie glared at her empty glass as if it were the source of all her problems. She rose to refill it at the drinks trolley, but I intercepted her. "No more. Not if you're climbing up to Hope's room later."

She returned to the chair in a strop, arms crossed over her chest, and stewed in her own bad humor.

I returned to the seat beside Matt on the sofa. "Is everything set for Gabe's departure tomorrow afternoon?"

He nodded. "He knows where he has to be and I've given him a disguise to wear, money and false papers. None of us need to go anywhere near him."

It would be a lonely departure with no one to farewell

him. Poor Gabe didn't deserve that, but nothing could be done about it. We were still being watched, as was Nancy O'Dwyer, and we had to stay well away from Gabe, the hotel where he was staying, and the departure dock.

Bristow entered with Brockwell and bowed out again. The detective inspector shuffled forward, clutching the rim of his hat in both hands. He cleared his throat and did not meet Willie's gaze.

She sat up straighter and unconsciously touched the hair at the nape of her neck. I smiled to myself. She would be horrified to know she had some coy feminine mannerisms.

"Good evening, all." Brockwell cleared his throat again. "I trust I haven't interrupted you."

Matt rose and indicated the detective inspector should take his place in the armchair by the fire. "You're always welcome. Brandy?"

"That will do very nicely, Glass. Thank you. And you, India? Are you well?"

"Very well, thank you." I smiled and waited, but Brockwell didn't say anything further. He accepted the brandy from Matt.

One of Matt's eyebrows lifted in an unspoken question while his gaze darted in Willie's direction. Brockwell frowned in confusion.

"Ask her how she is," Matt whispered.

Brockwell's cheeks pinked. "Yes! Willie! How are you?"

"Fine." Her voice pitched high and she blushed too. She studied the four corners of the room in turn, avoiding everyone's gaze.

These two needed a little help. Perhaps a lot of help. Since Matt didn't seem too interested in doing it, it was up to me. "Actually, Willie has something to say to you."

She glared at me, her eyes narrowed to slits.

Brockwell took a large gulp from his glass.

"In private," I added. When Willie didn't get up, I made a small shooing motion.

She blew out a breath and pushed to her feet. "Come on, Jasper."

"Of course, of course." He took another gulp, finishing the brandy, and stood. "Pleasant evening, this, don't you think?"

"Can't say I've noticed."

He put up his finger. "I almost forgot the reason I came. Glass, I have the addresses of some of Coyle's London properties, both in his name as well as properties listed under company names associated with him. I've checked some myself, but there was no sign of Abercrombie."

"And the rest?" Matt asked.

"I thought it would go faster if we split the remaining ones between us. There are quite a few."

"Have your discussion with Willie then we'll head out."

I waited for them to exit the room before turning to Matt. "I'm coming with you."

He hesitated and I knew precisely what he was thinking. He wanted to tell me I couldn't go, but knew that would only make me more determined.

I decided to make it easier for him. "Very well, I'll stay home. It's been a long day and I'm feeling a little tired anyway."

He kissed my cheek. "I'd like it noted that I didn't ask you. You changed your mind."

I arched a brow and he grinned then kissed me again.

"Oh my!" came the musical tones of Lord Farnsworth. "This is rather awkward."

Matt and I moved apart. I was about to welcome Farnsworth when I saw his companion. "Lady Helen! How delightful."

Lady Helen strode in wearing trousers, shirt and jacket. The masculine clothing suited her tall frame and wide shoulders. Unlike Willie, there was an elegance about her that men's clothes couldn't hide, but it was a serviceable disguise and would make it easier for her to escape through her bedroom window.

"I assume your aunt doesn't know you're here," I said,

trying and failing to keep the disapproval out of my voice. While I didn't care what she did or how she dressed, I didn't want to be dragged into her social ruin. If she was discovered wearing men's clothes and out with a gentleman in the evening unchaperoned, ruination was precisely the outcome. But I'd rather nobody found out she'd called in here first.

"She does not." She pressed a hand to her heart. "I do apologize for coming, Mrs. Glass, but Davide insisted we collect Willie before we ventured out."

"Is she here?" Lord Farnsworth asked, looking around.

"She's speaking to Detective Inspector Brockwell, as it happens."

Lady Helen gasped. "That shooting incident wasn't her fault!"

Lord Farnsworth chuckled but offered no explanation.

"He's not arresting her, they're friends," I said. "Good friends."

"*Very* good friends," Lord Farnsworth added with a wink.

Lady Helen's mouth turned down with her pout. "I see."

Willie and Brockwell entered, looking happier than when they'd walked out. It was an excellent sign. Hopefully he now understood why she'd pushed him toward the other woman.

"Helen! Davide!" Willie stopped in her tracks. "What're you two doing here?"

"We're taking you out for an evening of entertainment," Lord Farnsworth declared. "Unless you'd rather stay in."

"I, uh…" Willie glanced at Brockwell.

He nudged her with his elbow. "Go. I don't mind."

"I know you don't, but I promised Matt I'd do something for him. I'll meet up with you after and help search the properties." She turned back to Lady Helen and Lord Farnsworth. "I can't join you tonight. You two go out and try not to get into trouble without me."

Lord Farnsworth hooked his arm through Lady Helen's. "I'm sure we'll find a suitably tame activity to pass the time." He winked at nobody in particular and chuckled.

Lady Helen did not join in with his laughter. She extricated herself from Lord Farnsworth and took both of Willie's hands. "Are you sure you won't join us?"

"I am." Willie stood on her toes and kissed Lady Helen's cheek. "Real sure."

Lady Helen sighed. "Shall we go out again another evening?"

"Sure. Someone's got to keep you two in check."

Lady Helen was about to join Lord Farnsworth, waiting for her by the door, but I signaled for her to join me in a quiet tete-a-tete instead. I pulled her aside, out of earshot of the others.

She shot me a warning look. "I'm about to receive a lecture, aren't I? I must warn you, I don't enjoy being lectured."

And I didn't like being cast in the role of lecturer. It made me feel old. But someone had to talk sense to the girl and stop encouraging her to step onto the tightrope.

"You're flirting with disaster, and since neither Davide nor Willie have a penny's worth of common sense between them, it's up to me to warn you. If you're caught—"

"I won't be. My disguise is excellent, is it not?" She posed with hands on hips, thrusting out her bosom. It only made her look more feminine. "Dear Mrs. Glass, do stop worrying. I appreciate your concern, but I feel so trapped in that stuffy old house with my stuffy old aunt. I need some amusement before I settle down with whichever stuffy old man she picks for me."

"Perhaps you don't have to marry someone either stuffy or old." I indicated Lord Farnsworth, resplendent in a crimson tie with matching cloak over his arm as he chatted to Willie and Brockwell.

She pulled a face. "Good lord, I'm not going to marry Davide. He's fun and sweet, but much too ridiculous. I need a husband I can respect, not one who will spend more time in front of the mirror than me." With that, she kissed my cheek and turned on her heel to join him.

With a flourish of his cloak as he tossed it around his

shoulders, they left as if by magic. I watched the empty doorway where they'd just been, blinking and trying to regain my sense of equilibrium.

Matt caught my elbow. "Are you all right?"

"Yes, thank you. It's just that I can't decide what to make of those two sometimes. Are they clever or stupid? Sensible or outrageous? It rather makes my head hurt just thinking about them."

"Then don't. Ask Brockwell for the addresses while I go in search of Cyclops and Duke. I want to speak to each of them alone anyway."

It was a good idea. Both Cyclops and Duke were worried about Matt, so learning he wasn't following Gabe to America had come as a shock. He would know the best thing to say to dissolve their anger, but not to stop them worrying. Not even Matt's charming manner could do that.

* * *

As the evening wore on, I grew more and more tired. When the clocks chimed midnight, I decided not to wait up any longer. My pillow felt rather lumpy and I had trouble sleeping. The more I tried, the lumpier it felt. It was as if there was something inside it, or under it.

I turned on the light beside the bed and lifted my pillow. I almost fell off the bed altogether in my haste to get away from the mouse. When it didn't move, I ventured closer. The poor creature was dead, somewhat squashed from the weight of my head. By the look of it, it had died some time ago.

Which meant someone had put it there, after its demise.

Willie was going to get a piece of my mind in the morning. In fact, why wait until then? I used a handkerchief to pick up the mouse by the tip of its tail and carried it to her room. Instead of putting it under the pillow, I placed it on top. She couldn't fail to notice it.

I fell asleep and awoke mid-morning alongside Matt. He stirred and rolled over, snuggling into me.

I rested my head on his chest. "Any luck?"

"Abercrombie wasn't hiding at any of the properties," he mumbled.

"What about Hope? Did Willie see her?"

"Apparently she's fine." He lifted his head and glanced at the clock on the mantel then dropped back onto the pillow with a sigh. "Only twelve more hours."

We would both be watching the time tick slowly by today as we waited for Gabe to depart this evening. Every hour that passed was one closer to his freedom and safety. But until I knew he'd docked in America, anxiety would never be far away. So much could go wrong, not just in London, but on the boat too. If the police suspected he'd left the country, they would wire their American counterparts and all the main ports would be monitored. If the boat didn't dock privately as promised, Gabe would be arrested and deported back here for execution.

CHAPTER 12

To my great disappointment, Willie had slept at Brockwell's overnight. By the time she returned home at midday, the mouse had been removed by the maid. I wasn't going to let Willie get away with the childish prank, however, and confronted her in her bedroom.

"Your little joke failed," I said. "It didn't frighten me."

She lifted her chin to undo her neckerchief and regarded me in the reflection of the dressing table mirror. "What joke?"

"The mouse under my pillow."

She screwed up her nose. "I didn't put a mouse under your pillow."

"There's no point denying it. I know it was you."

She turned around. "It wasn't me. Why would I play a joke like that on you when I ain't there to see the look on your face?"

She had a point. But how did the mouse get under my pillow if she hadn't put it there? It had clearly been dead more than a day and the maid would have noticed it when she made the bed in the morning if it had burrowed under the pillow when I wasn't there. Aside from Willie, no one else would be inclined to do something so juvenile.

"I wouldn't touch a mouse anyway," she went on. "I hate 'em. Rats, too. I was once stuck down a mine shaft in the dark

160

and the ground was covered with the revolting critters. They crawled over my feet and tried to get up my legs. I had to pick 'em off, one by one. And the noise!" She shivered. "That squeak, multiplied by hundreds, is worse than nails down a chalkboard." She stuck out her tongue and made a vomiting noise.

I left her to change, feeling a little queasier than when I'd gone in.

I met Peter on the stairwell, on his way up to fetch me. "Lord Farnsworth is here, madam. Mr. Glass is with him now in the drawing room."

"Thank you, Fossett."

It was early for Lord Farnsworth to be out making calls, but he looked bright-eyed and rosy-cheeked as he sprang to his feet upon my entry. He greeted me in the Continental style with a kiss on each cheek while Matt watched on, somewhat impatiently.

Lord Farnsworth bounced on his heels and looked as though he was about to burst if he didn't tell me the reason for his visit soon. "I just informed your husband that I believe I've found your magical silversmith."

"Marianne Folgate?"

He removed a handkerchief from his inside jacket pocket and handed it to me. I unfolded it to reveal an engraved silver gentleman's ring, but I didn't have to remove the silk to know it was magical. I'd felt the warmth through the fabric.

"Well?" he prompted. "Is it hers?"

"It was made by a silversmith magician, I know that much."

He clapped his hands. "I knew it! There is no maker's mark, but the decoration is the same as my opera glasses." He pointed to the twined vine detail with his little finger. "I was out playing cards last night with Helen, and the moment I saw it on my opponent's finger, I suspected it was a Folgate creation, just like my opera glasses. I won it in a particularly tense game of poker."

"How will this lead us to her?"

He plucked the ring off the handkerchief and slipped it on his fourth finger, joining two others on the right hand. "The gentleman told me where he purchased it, and it's not from Goldman or Mallard and Son. He bought it two weeks ago from a jewelry shop on Oxford Street where the proprietor says this was newly made by the silversmith."

If it was only delivered two weeks ago then the jeweler would have a more recent address for Marianne Folgate than the outdated one given to us by Mr. Mallard. "What is the name of the shop?" I asked.

"Cuthbert's Fine Jewelry."

I turned to Matt. "I know it may lead nowhere, but we should speak to her. If she can provide convincing testimony linking Coyle to Goldman, the police might reopen the murder investigation. We should go to the shop now and ask for her address."

"No need," Lord Farnsworth said before Matt could respond. "I have it here." He whipped out a piece of paper from his pocket with a flourish and passed it to me, completing the process with an elaborate bow. "For you, dearest India."

I rolled my eyes but smiled. "Thank you, Davide. You have been an enormous help."

"I have, haven't I? Who would have suspected?"

Matt cleared his throat, clearly holding himself back from commenting.

"I shall depart and leave you two to investigate the silversmith. *Adieu!*"

* * *

Marianne Folgate would most likely prove to be a dead-end, but with nothing better to do, and the hours until Gabe's departure ticking by so slowly, calling on her was a welcome distraction. According to the jeweler on Oxford Street who'd sold the ring to Lord Farnsworth's poker opponent, Marianne Folgate now lived in Wimbledon. The cream brick townhouse with the white bay window may be small, but for someone who'd previously lived in a boarding house, it was a considerable step up. Indeed, it was a home more suited to a family.

Miss Folgate was a petite woman with large gray eyes that darted this way and that when she opened the door before finally settling on Matt, standing behind me. She was pretty with delicate features framed by tendrils of almond-colored hair. Although her friend Miss Calendar had told us Miss Folgate was young, I was surprised at how young she looked. Perhaps her size made her seem younger than she was, but she couldn't have been much older than eighteen or nineteen.

I smiled at her in what I hoped was a friendly manner. We had decided I would do most of the talking in the belief she might feel more comfortable with a woman and magician, but Matt was prepared to step in with his ever-reliable charm if I floundered. From the skittish look on her face, I wasn't sure either of us would be very successful in soothing her nerves.

"My name is India Glass," I began after she confirmed she was indeed Marianne Folgate. "This is my husband, Matthew. I'm a timepiece magician."

Her gaze finally settled on me and she seemed to see me properly for the first time. "India Glass?"

"Have you heard of me?"

She nodded. I waited for her to tell me where she'd heard my name, but she simply stared at me with those big, anxious eyes.

"I have some questions to ask you about your work," I said. "May we come inside?"

She shook her head.

"Please, Miss Folgate. We won't be long."

She hesitated. It wasn't an outright refusal.

"We can ask you the questions out here if you prefer."

After another glance up and down the street, she opened the door and ushered us inside. No well-brought up woman would allow guests to stand on the porch in the chilly spring wind with dark clouds threatening to relinquish their load at any moment.

She led us into the front sitting room that was as bland as the house's façade. There were no personal adornments one would expect to see in a young woman's home. No photographs or paintings, no vases, statues or knickknacks, and not a silver item in sight. All the furniture was new but not of the highest quality. It was mass-produced, the kind made in a factory not a craftsman's workshop. I didn't need to touch a single piece to know they didn't contain magical heat.

I sat on the sofa beside Matt. "You have a lovely home, Miss Folgate."

"Call me Marianne. Thank you," she added as an afterthought. "We haven't lived here long."

"Oh? You live here with a friend? Or family?"

She fingered the cuff of the simple gray woolen dress similar to what I used to wear before I met Matt. It was a practical cut, made of plain cotton. It was the kind of dress that a woman with very little money wore. Or one who preferred to go unnoticed.

"What is it you wanted to speak to me about?" she asked in a quiet, lilting voice that suited her.

"Some of your silverware was sold in the shop belonging to Mr. Goldman."

She looked down at her cuff and gave a small nod. "He's dead."

"That's what we came to speak to you about." I glanced at Matt for some reassurance and he nodded for me to go on. "We believe the police arrested the wrong man for his murder."

Her head snapped up. "How awful. Are you trying to find the real killer and you think I know something?" She was intelligent, I'd give her that. Intelligent and more forthright than I first thought too.

"We believe a man known as Lord Coyle had something to do with his death." I steeled myself for her reaction. We were taking a gamble by mentioning Coyle. If she worked for him, or considered him a friend or ally, we would get nowhere.

But her reaction was precisely as I'd hoped and as Matt had expected. She winced and a look of distaste passed over her.

Feeling buoyed, I pushed on. "You know him. He came to your former lodgings to speak to you."

She arched her brows. "What else do you know?"

"That you could be the link we need to connect Mr. Goldman to Lord Coyle. At the moment, we can't do that. We only have theories and suppositions. But if you can testify that you've seen them together—"

"I won't testify against anyone," she blurted out. "Particularly Coyle." As soon as she'd said her piece, she lost all of her bluster and returned to being the small, anxious creature fidgeting with her cuff and glancing toward the door.

"You don't have to testify," Matt said, speaking for the first time.

At his quietly earnest tone, she lifted her gaze to his. She was willing to listen, at least.

"All you have to do is give us the answers we need. We'll make sure Coyle faces justice, and you never have to worry about him again."

His words had a profound effect. Tears sprang to her eyes and she suddenly squeezed them shut in an effort to hold them in. After a few deep breaths, she opened them again. "What do you need to know?"

I couldn't believe our luck and launched my first question. "Did you ever see the two of them together?"

She nodded. "Mr. Goldman introduced me to Lord Coyle after he realized I was a magician."

"How did he realize?"

"He could feel the magic warmth in my silverware."

So Mr. Goldman *was* a magician, as we suspected. But as with Mr. McArdle, it was likely Mr. Goldman didn't know any gold spells although he could feel magic warmth well enough. "Did you ever see them together after the initial meeting? Did Lord Coyle visit Mr. Goldman at the shop?"

"I don't know. I only saw them together that one time. I

did get the impression I wasn't the first magician Mr. Goldman had introduced to Lord Coyle." Again, the mention of Coyle's name produced a wince from Marianne.

"You don't like him, do you?" I asked. "Every time his name is mentioned, you recoil."

Her gaze flicked from me to Matt and back again. She quickly shook her head, refusing to answer, and stared down at her cuff again.

She was going to need some encouragement. "I loathe him," I said. "Not only do I believe he killed Mr. Goldman, but he is framing our friend for the murder."

My shocking words garnered no reaction from her. Did she already know what Coyle was capable of? Did she have firsthand knowledge?

"But I hated him even before that," I went on. "He wants power. Magical and political power, and is prepared to do almost anything to get it."

Her gaze lifted slowly, slowly, until it finally met mine. It was clear, and filled with anger. She only required a little more incentive to talk, I was sure of it.

"I learned never to ask him for help. The one time I did, he made sure I owed him a favor for it."

Her breath hitched. She bit on her lower lip and blinked furiously at me.

"Is that what happened with you?" I pressed. "Did he help you in some way, then demand you do something for him in return?"

She swallowed heavily and glanced toward the door. Who was she expecting to walk in? "Lord Coyle assisted me with a…a problem when I first moved to London a year ago. After, he said I owed him."

"And has he called in the debt?"

She nodded. "Our account is settled."

I wanted to ask more, but it wasn't fair to push her. She clearly didn't want to talk about it and it was none of my business. It didn't matter to our investigation. Unless…

"Where were you on the night of the fifth?"

"Here. Why?"

"Alone?"

"No." She gasped. "Do you think I killed Mr. Goldman?"

I put up my hands. "I'm sorry. It occurred to me that Lord Coyle asked you to do it on his behalf, and you saw no way out of it. I am sorry for asking, but I had to. Our friend's life depends on it."

She relaxed a little, her shoulders hunching. "I understand, but I assure you, it wasn't me. I repaid my debt a week before the fifth. Anyway, I think you're barking up the wrong tree. As much as I'd like to see Coyle arrested for murder, I don't think he did it. He has no reason to want Goldman dead. Goldman found him magicians. Coyle needed him."

"Perhaps Goldman wanted something more in return," Matt said. "Perhaps a price Coyle wasn't willing to pay and Goldman refused to back down."

"I suppose." Marianne glanced at the door again. "Do you have any more questions? It's just that I think it's time you left. I am sorry." She bit her lip again and cast me an apologetic look

"Are you in trouble?" Matt asked.

She pressed her lips together and shook her head quickly. She rose, forcing Matt and me to stand too. If she was in any difficulty, she wouldn't admit it to us today.

We thanked her and left. With a final glance along the street, she shut the door behind us.

"Do you think she owed Coyle for the house she now lives in?" I asked Matt as we drove off. "Is that the problem he fixed for her?"

"I don't think so. She said he fixed her problem when she first moved to London, but she has only moved to the house recently. So it can't be an accommodation issue."

"How do you think she repaid him?"

"Whatever it was, it's not as simple as giving him some magical silverware. Coyle would want more. Whatever the debt, she has repaid it and we may never find out what it was. But Marianne's tale got me thinking. I now have another theory as to why Coyle set Gabe up for Goldman's murder, and it has nothing to do with me."

I turned to face him fully. "What do you think it is?"

"Marianne's account confirms that Coyle likes collecting favors from people, especially magicians. Before, I didn't realize the extent of it, but I think she and you are the tip of the iceberg. I think he's been helping magicians with whatever problems they have for years, and then calling in those debts to enhance his power. Gabe is just the latest."

"I don't understand. He made sure Gabe was arrested for the murder. That's the opposite of helping him."

"Not if he gets Gabe *off*. What if Coyle planned to influence his powerful friends and see that Gabe was acquitted? Then Gabe, a medical magician, would owe him. Imagine what Coyle could do with that debt."

"He could force Gabe to extend a life," I said on a breath. "Perhaps his own life." But he needed a watch magician for that, too.

He needed me.

Matt must have followed my thoughts because he knew precisely how to comfort me at that moment. He put his arm around me and kissed the top of my head. "Don't worry. We've ruined his plan by helping Gabe escape. He can't force Gabe to do anything now. Nor can he force you."

He had a point.

But Gabe hadn't left the country yet.

Once ensconced in the carriage, I checked the time. Eight more hours until Gabe departed London. It felt interminable.

I tucked my watch back into my reticule and slid along the seat, closer to Matt. He took my hand and kissed the back of it.

"I have an important question to ask you," he said.

His eyes danced with good humor and I couldn't help smiling back. Despite Gabe's predicament, Matt's mood had been buoyant ever since learning I might be with child. While I was still hesitant to let my hopes rise, I was becoming more and more certain. Not only had my courses still not arrived, but little things made my stomach churn when usually they wouldn't. Like now, with the gentle rocking motion of the carriage as we drove home.

"What is it?" I asked.

"Who has to move out of their room to accommodate the baby?"

I chuckled. "We do have one spare bedroom. Nobody has to move out."

"That room is small."

"Babies are small."

He pursed his lips in thought. "Do you think Willie would move into it and give up her larger room?"

"Not without a lot of whining. I want to be there when you ask her. I owe her for putting a dead mouse under my pillow."

He pulled back to see me better. "Why would she do that?"

"I have no idea. She denied it, but I can't think who else could have put it there."

"She hates mice."

"So she told me. Was she really trapped down a mine shaft with hundreds of rodents?"

"She was down a mine shaft, but she wasn't trapped and it was only for a minute or two. She got out of there sharpish when *one* rat crawled over her boot. She would have shot it if she could see, but she was afraid of shooting off her own foot."

I laughed. "A rare moment of restraint on her part."

We turned into Park Street and the carriage slowed even further. "Sir!" Woodall cried. "Sir, take a look!"

We peered through the front window of the brougham, past Woodall sitting on his perch. Up ahead, a large black carriage pulled by four horses was parked outside our house. A uniformed policeman sat on the driver's seat, and another stepped up to sit beside him. The driver flicked the reins and the horses set off. As the carriage passed, I saw it was loaded with another six policemen inside, all squashed side by side. I didn't recognize any of them.

Both Bristow and Duke greeted us on the doorstep, their faces grave.

Matt alighted from the carriage before it had come to a complete stop. "What did the police want?"

"They were looking for Gabe," Duke said with a shake of his head. "They turned the place upside down. The house is a real mess. Floorboards lifted, furniture moved…" He swore under his breath.

"My aunt?"

"Went for a walk with her maid and Willie before they arrived and hasn't returned yet."

Bristow cleared his throat. He stood ramrod straight, his hands at his back. "If I may, sir?"

"Go ahead," Matt said.

"The house will be put to rights before Miss Glass returns. Mrs. Bristow and the maid have already begun, and I'll help in a moment and Fossett too, when he returns."

"He's not here?" I asked.

"No, madam. I sent him to Scotland Yard to find out from Detective Inspector Brockwell who authorized the search. You see, I have my suspicions about those men."

Matt had been peering past Duke and Bristow into the house, but he now gave the butler his full attention. "You don't think they were police?"

"No, sir. For starters, the constable who remained behind today instead of following you looked confused."

Bristow nodded at the tall young man who'd been watching our house. The one who'd followed us in a hansom now joined him. They were in deep discussion and I agreed with Bristow's sentiment that they looked confused. Clearly they hadn't been informed about the raid.

"Secondly, there was not a senior officer among them and when I asked for paperwork authorizing the search, they couldn't produce any. Nor did they seem to care. They were incredibly rude and dismissive. Considering your relationship with Scotland Yard in the past, sir, I thought it very unusual they'd treat your household in such a fashion."

"Aye," Duke added. "They also waited until you'd gone, and Willie too, before they came. I reckon that ain't a coincidence."

"So if they weren't the police," I said. "Who were they?"

CHAPTER 13

*M*att clapped Duke on the shoulder. "Are you both all right?"

Duke nodded and Bristow said, "Yes, sir. The female staff are a little shaken but have calmed down now."

I went to check on them first and found them putting the drawing room to rights. Bristow's description hadn't quite done the scene justice. The police—if that's who they were— had moved every piece of furniture. Some of the vases had fallen off tables and lay broken on the floor, the floral arrangements scattered. The rug had been rolled up and four floor boards extracted to check for hiding spaces beneath. Paintings had been taken off the walls, the hearth cleaned out and the chimney inspected. Soot-blackened handprints had been left on the mantelpiece and ash was scattered about.

Matt entered the drawing room and surveyed the damage. "Damn it. If this is the work of the police, the commissioner will be getting a piece of my mind soon enough, and then the home secretary."

"And if it's not them?" I asked quietly.

He merely shook his head then joined in with the cleaning up efforts.

"Is it like this in every room?" I asked.

Mrs. Bristow nodded. "They searched everywhere,

including the service rooms and coach house. It's going to take some time to put to rights."

"Do Miss Glass's bedroom next and leave the other bedrooms to last. Make sure this room and the sitting room are put to rights as quickly as possible. I want the rooms Miss Glass is most likely to use back to normal before she comes home."

Mrs. Bristow bobbed a curtsy and left to fix Aunt Letitia's bedroom with the help of her husband, leaving Matt and the maid to work in the drawing room. I found Duke in the sitting room, hammering down a floor board while the two constables who were supposed to be watching the house righted the sofa. I set to work picking up the broken pieces of a vase and straightening all the paintings that had been set askew.

The footman returned a mere five minutes later with Brockwell in tow. He confirmed what we already suspected— that no one at Scotland Yard had authorized the search. We didn't continue that line of thought as we all worked together to put the house back the way it was as quickly as possible.

The main reception rooms and Aunt Letitia's bedroom were fixed by the time she arrived home, some forty-five minutes later. Willie instantly knew something was amiss, but thankfully Aunt Letitia was oblivious to the tension and assumed Brockwell had come to call on Willie. When she left us to change, Willie demanded to know what had happened.

"The police came looking for Gabe," Duke told her. "They made a mess of the house. Only we don't think it was the police."

Thankfully she merely muttered her string of expletives, although I was sure she would have liked to shout them.

Matt ushered us all to the library and closed the door. The library was in a worse condition than the other rooms, with books strewn across the floor. Some had landed open, face down, their spines cracked. We set to work putting them back, although they were out of order. I'd rearrange them another time.

"It's got to be Coyle," Duke said as he slotted two red leather-bound books side by side on a middle shelf. "Who else employs that many men and has police uniforms on hand to use as disguises?"

"Who else wants to desperately find Gabe?" Matt explained the theory he'd formed after speaking to Marianne.

They all agreed it made quite a lot of sense and explained why Coyle wanted Gabe blamed for the murder, although not why Goldman was the victim. Brockwell was the only one not completely convinced.

He refused to believe the justice system was so corrupt that Coyle could buy off a judge and have Gabe's conviction overturned.

"He doesn't have to buy anyone," Matt said. "He could have his witnesses retract their statements. There'd be a re-trial and without enough evidence, Gabe would be acquitted."

"The investigation would be re-opened," Brockwell said. "It's a high-profile case now, and everyone will want to see justice done. My colleagues at the Yard won't give up so easily."

"Good," Willie said with an emphatic nod. "Hopefully they'll focus on Coyle. Now, help me push these shelves back into place."

* * *

WITH SO MANY of us working together, the house was soon put to rights and Aunt Letitia was none the wiser. Except for a few loose floorboards, everything was as it should be in time for a late luncheon. If she thought it odd that Brockwell and the two constables were joining us in the dining room for hastily assembled sandwiches, she didn't say. She chatted amiably, asking them about their work.

The rest of us sat in silence. I was quite sure the others were considering our next move too. Lord Coyle couldn't be allowed to get away with his schemes anymore. I was angry at having my home violated, frustrated at getting nowhere, and tired of seeing him win at every turn. How much longer would we have to put up with his greed and plots to grab more power? How much longer would we have to live in fear of him?

We may have thwarted his plan by helping Gabe escape, but at what cost? Gabe shouldn't have to flee the country and live under an assumed name, away from his home for the rest of his life. And we shouldn't have to choose between giving up our lives and following him for the sake of Matt's health, or staying put and watching Matt's health fade in the years to come.

The more I thought about it, the more I wanted to *do* something. I wanted to right the wrongs done to us, Gabe, and every other magician who'd ever suffered at the hands of Lord Coyle. I wanted him to regret abusing his power to ensure magicians owed him favors, and I wanted him to go away and leave us alone.

But what could I do? We were insignificant by comparison. Matt might be wealthy, but not on the same scale as Lord Coyle. He might be the heir to a barony, but Coyle was an earl. People of all levels of society, including magicians, owed him favors and he could call in those favors whenever he wished to defeat us.

All we had was a handful of residents at number sixteen Park Street and a few friends. I might have earned the ear of the home secretary and his spy master, but they weren't prepared to move against Coyle. Even they knew they couldn't do anything without evidence and getting that evidence was proving impossible.

So what *could* we do?

By the time lunch finished and the dishes were cleared away, Aunt Letitia needed a rest. She retired to her room for a nap and the two constables returned to their post outside. Willie and Duke remained seated, their arms crossed, matching morose frowns on their faces. It was most unlike them to be silent this long.

As soon as the door closed behind the constables, Willie came to life. "Something's got to be done about Coyle. He can't get away with it no more. It ain't fair."

"Aye, but what?" Duke muttered.

Matt sat forward, leaning both elbows on the table. Without Aunt Letitia to scold him, he didn't care. He opened his mouth to speak but closed it again and scrubbed a hand over his face and jaw. He expelled a deep sigh.

"What is it?" I asked. "What are you thinking?"

He flattened his hands on the table as if that were the only way to keep them still. "I'm not thinking anything. That's the problem. I have no solutions. Coyle will never confess to having Goldman murdered, and he won't give up Abercrombie when Abercrombie can give evidence against him."

"If Abercrombie is even still alive," Brockwell added.

"Indeed. Without him, we can't prove Coyle paid the rioters."

Willie clicked her fingers. "So we make up evidence."

Duke tapped the table with his fist. "Good idea."

Brockwell groaned. "I'll pretend I didn't hear that. Glass. I urge you not to sink to Coyle's level. This must be done the right way, the legal way, or not at all."

Willie shook her head. "It ain't the time to have a moral compass, Jasper. We've got to fight dirty, like Coyle, or we'll never beat him."

"Maybe you should leave the room," Duke said to Brockwell with a measure of sympathy in his voice. "We don't want to compromise your integrity."

"Nobody needs to leave the room," Matt said. "I agree with Brockwell. We can't make up evidence."

So what could a motley group of artless and one magician do against a powerful man like Coyle? It was maddening and unfair to see such a horrid person get away with bullying, cruelty and murder. Almost everyone he'd ever met loathed him, yet none could stop him taking advantage of them.

Unless…

I did some quick calculations in my head and came up

with a surprising number. A large number, in fact. It might just be enough.

"I have an idea," I said. "It won't help Gabe or send Coyle to prison, but it might diminish his influence in the future. What is happening to Gabe can't be allowed to happen to anyone else, magician or artless."

I had their complete attention now and Matt urged me to go on.

"I'm not suggesting we do anything illegal. We simply use the only weapon we have—people loathe Coyle. Like Mari-anne Folgate and countless other magicians we've met over the course of our investigations, Coyle has used them and demanded favors be repaid. Often, the repayment is something the magician doesn't want to do. I propose we contact every magician who hates him and ask that they demand the magical artefacts he bought from them be returned because they were obtained under false pretenses. We ensure he's banned from the Collectors' Club and ask all magicians to never sell him anything again. None of that will have any real effect on his power, but it will rattle him. It will make him see that magicians hate him. Then, once that has got through to him, we have them all tell him they'll never repay the favor they owe him. If magicians can band together on this, and present a united force, he won't have any choice. He can't fight us all. He'll see he's on his own now and that no magician will bow to him anymore."

I looked at each of their faces to gauge their thoughts. Brockwell looked unmoved as he scratched his sideburns, but he was notoriously difficult to read anyway. Duke and Willie both nodded along as they considered my idea. At least neither scoffed.

Matt's reaction was quite different. He smiled. It started out small, a mere twitch of his lips, but it quickly grew. It wasn't a smile of happiness. It was something else. Pride.

It made my heart swell and gave me courage. "It's time to take back magic from those who would control it and keep control of it ourselves."

Matt clasped my face in both his hands and kissed me thoroughly on the lips. "You're beautiful when you're fierce."

"Fierce?" I scoffed. "It's a silly idea, really. It's not enough to make any real impact on Coyle." The more I thought about it, the more it sank in how ineffective my idea was.

Duke was the first to get to his feet. "It's something, India, and right now, it's all we have. Besides, I need to act."

Willie stood too. "I agree. Let's get started now. Duke, fetch paper and ink."

Brockwell had to return to work, but the rest of us set about writing letters in the library and dispatching them all over the city. We used the list of magicians' names I'd been collecting and wrote asking them to demand their artefacts be returned and to tell Coyle they would not repay a debt if they had one. We knew some of the magicians hated Coyle; we couldn't be certain how others felt but we wrote anyway. I even sent a letter to Fabian.

An hour passed in a flash and we managed to get the letters off in the mid-afternoon, using errand boys to hand deliver them. It only remained to be seen how the magicians reacted and if Coyle even cared.

We had our first inkling that the idea wasn't a terrible one when Chronos arrived a short time after the letters were delivered. My grandfather stepped out of the cab and asked me to pay the fare.

"I'm a little short at the moment," he said as he limped up the stairs, using the railing to steady himself.

"What about the rent money from the shop?" I asked as I paid the driver.

"It's hardly enough to cover day to day expenses." He waited for me to join him then took my hand and patted it. "Don't worry about such things, India. Let your husband concern himself with financial matters."

I snatched my hand away. "I'm perfectly capable of under-standing the fact you've spent more than you earn without a man explaining it to me, thank you." I watched as he headed up the steps, his gait awkward with his limp. "What happened to your leg?"

"So you noticed." He rubbed his thigh. "Just an old ache paying a visit."

"Do you need to see a doctor?"

He narrowed his gaze at me. "Seaford is unavailable."

"There are other doctors in London."

"Not for me."

I rolled my eyes then had a rather worrying thought. We were almost on the porch, level with Bristow standing by the open door. I caught Chronos's arm to stop him and lowered my voice. "You're not planning on asking Gabe to extend your life, are you?"

"I'm not planning on it because I've already asked him."

I gasped. "What possessed you to do such a thing?"

"Old age." The creases on his face merged in a wince as he set off again.

"He won't do it."

"I know," he tossed over his shoulder. "He made it quite clear he won't use his magic on anyone else." He grunted. "Waste of a good talent, if you ask me."

I picked up my skirts and marched after him into the house. "Nobody is asking you, and it's his right to refuse."

"Doesn't mean I have to like it."

I led the way into the drawing room and asked Bristow to bring a fresh pot of tea and something for Chronos to eat. My grandfather's eyes lit up at the prospect of tasting Mrs. Potter's baked goods. He lowered himself into an armchair by the fire and asked me to stoke it back to life.

"Or is that the task of your footman? Your aristocratic protocols are lost on me."

I poked the fire iron into the glowing embers and heaped more coal on top. Matt entered as I closed the brass scuttle's lid.

"Ah, Glass, there you are. Come in, come in." My grandfather seemed to want to play host and Matt humored him.

He shook Chronos's hand before taking a seat on the sofa. "You look well."

"I'm old and have more aches and pains than hairs on my head." Chronos smoothed the white fluff of hair that drifted back and forth with the drafts, but it wouldn't stay down. "Speaking of the elderly, how is Miss Glass?"

"Very well, thank you," Matt said.

"And she would not appreciate being called elderly," I added.

Chronos merely shrugged. "And your other aunt and uncle? Is Lord Rycroft well?"

"Quite well, I think," Matt said. "I don't see them often."

Chronos tapped his finger thoughtfully on the chair arm. "I see."

"What are you getting at?" I asked. "Why the sudden interest in Matt's family?"

"It's not sudden, India. I've always been interested, ever since I learned you would one day be Baroness Rycroft."

I couldn't believe what I was hearing. "Is that all you care about? Being the grandfather of a baroness? Nothing will change for you when it happens, you know."

He pouted. "Can I not come and live with you in the big house?"

"No, you may not."

"We'll see when the time comes," Matt said, with far more patience than me. "But I think it's a long way off."

Chronos grunted. "I may not be alive to *be* the grandfather of a baroness."

I was about to admonish him for his self-pity but bit my tongue. From the look of him, his ailments were bothering him and he was feeling his age keenly. If it cheered him to think of one day coming to live with us at Rycroft Hall, then it would cost me nothing to indulge him. After all, Matt's uncle was unlikely to keel over any time soon.

"There will be a place for you with us if that's what you wish," I said gently.

Chronos's creases concertinaed with his smile.

Bristow entered and set down the tray. I poured the tea while Matt passed a plate with a slice of cake to Chronos. Chronos wolfed it down, catching some of the crumbs that didn't make it to his plate on his chest. He brushed them off onto the floor.

I sighed. For someone with his liberal-minded attitude, he wasn't very considerate of the maid. "Is there a reason for this visit, Chronos?"

"There is, as it happens. Two things. One, I understand Seaford is alive and well."

Neither Matt nor I answered, since he hadn't posed it as a question.

Chronos watched us both carefully for a reaction then continued on. "And two, I wanted to let you know that your campaign is off to a good start. Don't look so surprised. Of course I know all about it. I'm well connected in the magician community."

"It's not that," I said. "I'm simply surprised you know about it already. We sent the letters only an hour ago."

"I happened to be visiting a friend, a copper-working magician."

"I didn't send any letters to a copper magician. You've never mentioned him before."

He waved his hand in dismissal. "He didn't receive a letter, another friend of his did. A mapmaker by the name of Gibbons whom he met at a meeting for the Society for the Welfare of Magicians."

"I've never heard of this society," I said.

"It's a newly formed group where the members support each other as we reveal our magic to the world. It's a deeply concerning time for some magicians, particularly older folk who've hidden their magic for so long and are now feeling somewhat exposed and vulnerable with the recent publicity. My friend formed it and asked me to speak to its members. I met Mr. Gibbons there. He was rather anxious, and I like to think I helped him see there was nothing to fear. Anyway, he came to speak to my friend as soon as he received your letter."

Mr. Gibbons was the magician mapmaker whose grandson had been kidnapped and then murdered out of jealousy by a rival mapmaker apprentice. The fate of poor Daniel Gibbons was an extreme example of what happened when the artless feared their magician rivals. It was a sober reminder of how far some would go to protect their livelihoods. It was a reminder to me of how important it was for the government to push through their new policies as soon as possible.

"And what did the three of you conclude?" Matt asked.

Chronos finished his tea and put down his cup. "That it's a good start. We all agree that something must be done about Coyle. He has grown too powerful and too greedy on the backs of magicians for too long. We are behind you one hundred percent, India. Indeed, I came to tell you that my two friends left immediately to gather more magicians to march on Coyle's house."

"When?" Matt asked.

"Now, of course. No time like the present. Strike while the iron's hot and all that."

I rubbed my forehead where a headache was blooming. It had been a long day. "While it's exactly what I hoped would happen, is it wise to confront Coyle now with just two elderly men?"

"Three, if you count me." He pushed to his feet. "I only came past to let you know. Anyway, there will be more of us, you'll see. I'd wager there'll be quite a force soon. You should be commended, India. It's time magicians let the world know we will not be taken advantage of. We are not to be taken lightly!" He pounded the air with his fist and marched for the door. He seemed ten years younger.

"You were limping before," I pointed out.

He slowed and limped the rest of the way to the door, adding a stoop for good measure. "It comes and goes." He even had the gall to add a moan.

I should have known he'd been lying in an attempt to get me to sympathize with him and ask him to live with us at Rycroft Hall when the time came. But I found I couldn't be angry with him. I was too worried.

"Chronos, wait. I don't think you should go to Coyle's house. It could be dangerous."

He patted my arm. "Thank you for your concern, but I'll be fine."

"India's right," Matt said. "Stay here. I'll go."

I rounded on him, hands on hips. "No!"

"I won't get involved, I'll merely observe. I want to know how many magicians turn up and what impact they have. Nothing terrible will happen."

"You don't know that. It's Coyle. Terrible things happen when he's involved."

He kissed my forehead, grasped my arms, and gently moved me aside so he could leave. He was gone before my frustrated sigh had completely passed my lips.

At least Chronos agreed to stay, but I suspected that had more to do with the leftover cake than anything else. However, he refused a second slice when I offered it and shifted uncomfortably in the chair. With a wince, he pressed a hand to his stomach.

"Are you all right?" I asked.

"It's nothing."

We were soon joined by Willie and Duke. I decided not to inform them of Matt's whereabouts, mostly because I was worried Willie would charge into an already inflamed situation and make it worse by brandishing her gun. When Duke asked me where Matt was, I lied and said he was upstairs in his study.

Chronos arched an eyebrow but didn't correct me. He knew his supply of food depended on remaining in my good books.

Aunt Letitia joined us too and offered to pour me another cup of tea, but the teapot was empty. "I'll fetch you another," she said, picking up my cup.

"Just ask Bristow to bring in a fresh pot."

"There's no need for the entire teapot if you're the only one having it, and there's no need to bother Bristow with such a trifle. I can ask Mrs. Bristow to make it."

Well, that was the oddest thing I'd ever heard her say. Aunt Letitia never deviated from the ritual of afternoon tea. It was always done the same way, from the housekeeper making it and the butler bringing it into us, to the pouring and drinking. What had got into her?

"Ring for Bristow," I said again. "He'll see to it if you want more."

"I don't want more; you do."

"No, I don't," I said. "Chronos?"

He shook his head.

"That's settled then," I said. "Come and sit with me and tell me about the book you're reading."

She huffed out a breath. "Are you sure you don't want a nice, refreshing tea?"

"I'm quite all right, thank you." I patted the sofa beside me. "Come and sit."

She cast a rather annoyed look at the teapot and finally sat. I leaned forward to inspect the silver to see if Peter had done a poor job of cleaning it, but the teapot reflected my face perfectly. There wasn't a single spot or smudge on it. Whatever she was annoyed at, it wasn't that.

At dusk, Cyclops walked in and asked after Matt.

Duke rose. "He's in his study. I'll fetch him."

"Send Fossett," Aunt Letitia said.

But Cyclops couldn't wait for the footman and strode past Duke. "I need to speak to him."

I sprang up to follow him and tell the truth before my little white lie unraveled in a very public way.

My grandfather didn't care about that and called out, "He's not here. He's gone to Coyle's."

Willie frowned at me. "India?"

I bit my lip and winced.

Cyclops stopped dead and spun around to face us.

"There's a disturbance at Coyle's. That's what I wanted to tell Matt about. I thought he'd want to see if Hope was all right."

"What kind of disturbance?" Willie asked, rising.

"I don't know. Reports came in as my shift ended and I came straight here to see if y'all knew."

Chronos thumped a fist on his knee. "Excellent news! I hope they give Coyle what for. The blighter deserves it."

"What's going on?" Cyclops asked carefully. "Should we be worried?"

"No, of course not," I said over the alarm bells ringing in my head. "It's a result of our letter writing campaign this afternoon." I told Cyclops and Aunt Letitia about the messages, but not the raid that had prompted it. It was still best if Matt's aunt didn't know her home had been violated. It was just the sort of thing to set her off.

"So he's gone as an observer only?" Duke asked.

I nodded. "He told me he'd stay well away and be careful."

Willie, Duke and Cyclops exchanged glances, then strode out of the drawing room.

I raced after them. "Cyclops, how bad is it?"

"I don't know," he said over his shoulder. "But it can't hurt to have a constable on show to keep the crowd calm."

Crowd? Good lord, I'd expected only a handful of magicians. I'd not sent many letters. "I'll come with you."

Cyclops moved to block my path. Despite only having one good eye, he managed a piercing glare that pinned me to the spot. He was very rarely forceful, but now he ordered me to stay without needing to utter a word.

I obeyed, partly because I wouldn't risk walking into danger if I was with child, and partly because Aunt Letitia might need me. Knowing Matt was involved in a disturbance might set off her memory lapse.

Being left behind with Aunt Letitia and Chronos left me frustrated, however. I couldn't sit still as I watched the clock on the mantel. I considered sending a message to Lord Farnsworth asking him to dine with us just for some frivolous company, but he would take an age to change into evening-wear and would probably arrive after the others returned home anyway.

I thought time ticked slowly by when we were waiting for the hour in which Gabe would depart, but it became positively snail-paced as we waited for Matt and the others. The one good thing was that the distraction would hopefully stop Coyle searching for Gabe. It gave Gabe some freedom to get to the dock unhindered.

As long as the police weren't there waiting for him.

I glanced at the clock again as it ticked over to seven PM. Gabe's boat was due to leave in an hour.

It was time for Aunt Letitia to dress for dinner. Even if it was just the three of us, she would change into something more elegant, complete with jewels.

Chronos suggested we play cards while we waited and I was just shuffling them when the glass in one of the windows shattered. I instinctively shielded my face, but not before a shard nicked my cheek.

"What the devil?" Chronos shouted.

He picked up an object from the floor. It must have struck the glass and landed on the rug. But it was such an odd thing to see. How could a paper projectile, elegantly folded into a winged shape, break a hole in the glass? It was a child's toy and feather-light at that.

Oh no.

"Put it down!" I snatched it off him and quickly shoved it under the leg of the occasional table. The weight of the table stopped it from flying away, despite the paper's attempts to relaunch.

"Paper magic," Chronos said on a breath. "That means Hendry is here."

I scanned the room. "Get rid of all the loose paper! And remove the books!"

The last time I'd seen Mr. Hendry, he'd tried to kill Willie and me by using a spell to cut us to ribbons with thousands of pieces of flying paper. He was deranged and should have gone to prison for a very long time for his crime.

But Lord Coyle had used his influence to get him acquitted. Mr. Hendry owed Coyle his freedom and possibly his life. The debt to repay was a considerable one, and it would seem getting married to a woman of Coyle's choosing wasn't enough.

Because he was here, armed with his flying spell and probably as much paper as he could carry.

CHAPTER 14

$\mathcal{T}$he paper wing stopped fluttering. It lay limply on the floor, the table leg squashing it. But I was in no doubt that Mr. Hendry had not given up. Not yet. That folded paper was a warning. He would be back.

In fact, he did not leave.

A loud banging on the front door had me running into the entrance hall as Bristow opened it. He must have thought it was Matt returning.

But it was not Matt who barged in, nor was it Mr. Hendry. Mr. Abercrombie pushed past Bristow and bestowed one of his sneers on me. The usually dapper middle-aged man looked like himself and yet not. His gray hair was disheveled, his tie askew, and his moustache was in need of oiling and a trim. The wildness in his eyes was new too. Usually they were cold, but madness gave them a liveliness that hadn't been there before. He was himself, and yet he wasn't, like a twin who'd not had the same advantages in life.

Mr. Hendry, entering the house with other men, looked worse. The fine-boned paper magician had grown a beard but not kept it neat. His long hair half-shielded his eyes and there were sores on the back of one of his hands. The fingernails of the other were dark with dried blood.

"Fossett!" Bristow shouted.

THE GOLDSMITH'S CONSPIRACY

One of the men who'd followed Mr. Abercrombie inside pulled out a gun from his jacket pocket and smashed it into Bristow's temple. The butler's eyes rolled up into his head and he collapsed to the floor in a heap.

I ran to him, but Abercrombie grabbed my arm, wrenching it almost out of the socket. I gasped as pain flared in my shoulder, white-hot. I didn't want to cry out. I didn't want to frighten Aunt Letitia, two stories above in her bedroom.

"Let her go," Chronos growled.

"Or you'll do what, old man?" Mr. Abercrombie chuckled. "Fix my watch?"

My watch. If only I had it on me. But I rarely carried it with me around the house. It was on my dressing table in my reticule. Would it work to save me from all the way up there? Could it know that my life was in danger and was at this moment chiming madly, trying to leap out of the reticule?

"What do you want?" I hissed.

Mr. Abercrombie nodded at the four men who'd followed Hendry and him inside. They all knew their orders and the men headed into different rooms or up the stairs without further instruction. They were looking for something. Or, more likely, someone.

"How dare you!" Chronos snapped. "You can't barge in here like this."

Mr. Abercrombie brandished his gun. "You'll find this gives me access wherever I want to go." He aimed the gun at my face. "You'll also find I'll shoot her if anyone attempts to do something drastic or flee. That includes the servants."

Chronos grunted. "You won't shoot her. She's too valuable to Coyle."

"She was, once, but not anymore."

Chronos shoved me behind him, earning a chuckle from Abercrombie.

"You're an old man, Steele. You can't protect her." Mr. Abercrombie glanced up the stairs and adjusted his grip on the gun. "But that watch of hers can, so…" He pointed the gun at Bristow, now groaning on the floor as he regained consciousness. "Servants are disposable, in my opinion. Do *you* consider them disposable?" When neither of us moved, his smile stretched. "I didn't think so."

Upstairs, a door slammed.

"You won't find Dr. Seaford here," I said, stepping out from my grandfather's shadow.

"Oh, I know."

I frowned. Then what was he looking for?

I didn't have to wait long to find out. One of the men descended the stairs, my watch dangling by its chain from his fingers. He tossed it to Abercrombie.

Abercrombie clutched the watch in his fist. It was silent, dormant. My life wasn't threatened so its magic didn't awaken. It didn't care about Bristow's life, or anyone else's. As long as I wasn't under direct threat, it would not chime a warning or strike Abercrombie or his men. I wasn't sure if Abercrombie had guessed this after our encounter in Harrods and that's why he didn't threaten me directly now, or he had been ordered not to harm me by Coyle.

If we could get him to admit to the police that he worked for Coyle, then perhaps this could all end in our favor. If only I could reason with him.

But from the look of him, he'd gone past the point where reason meant something. Mr. Hendry too, standing mute and angry beside Abercrombie.

Even so, I had to try. "You can still work out a deal with Scotland Yard. They want Coyle, not you. If you tell them what he's done, that you've been acting under orders, afraid for your life, they'll be lenient on you."

Mr. Abercrombie scoffed. "No one who crosses Coyle is safe. Not out here and not in prison. So forgive me when I say I won't help you. I *can't* help you. Not if I value living."

"You think you're safe now? You're a liability to him. You know too much."

He cocked the gun. The click was deafening in the other-

THE GOLDSMITH'S CONSPIRACY

wise silent hall. "You think I'm no longer useful? Think again."

"Please, don't shoot! You've got what you came for." I nodded at the watch in his fist. "Take it and go."

Beside me, Chronos straightened. "You heard my grand-daughter. Get out of her house."

Abercrombie held up the watch. "You think I want to take this talisman with me?" He dropped it on the ground. The cover sprang open but it didn't break.

He ground his heel into the watch face, smashing the glass. The *crack* and *snap* of enamel and the metal hinge breaking sent a violent shiver through me. Silver scraped on the tiles as he kicked the pieces away. They skittered across the floor and came to rest beneath the hall table. It couldn't save me now.

Mr. Abercrombie aimed the gun at me.

His tongue darted out, licking his top lip. He was relishing this.

Chronos stretched his arm out, attempting to protect me. "You can't kill her! Coyle would be furious."

"It's *his* order that she not leave this house alive."

My heart plunged to my stomach. Bile surged to my throat, burning. I felt sick. A distant part of me wondered how Abercrombie would react if I threw up on his expensive shoes.

Despite the fear gripping my body, my mind worked faster than ever. So that was why he wanted my watch—to destroy it so it couldn't save my life. His sole purpose for coming here was to kill me.

It would seem he was the only one aware of the plan, however. The shock on Mr. Hendry's face was clear, but his features quickly settled into a sneer that matched Abercrom-bie's. Of the four other men who'd all returned after searching the house, only three seemed concerned by this turn of events. The fourth looked as though he was eager to see my brains splattered around the entrance hall.

"This ain't why we came here," one of the three men said

to Abercrombie. "You said nothing about murdering a woman in cold blood."

Mr. Abercrombie continued to stare at me, his eyes now gleaming with the prospect of ending my life. "Go. You don't have to be a party to this. In fact, all of you may go. You too, Hendry. Steele, it's up to you."

"I'll remain here," Chronos growled.

Abercrombie shrugged. "Suit yourself."

"I'll stay too," Mr. Hendry said. "Coyle wanted me to bear witness, and I owe him."

"So this is your way of repaying your debt?" I cried. "By becoming embroiled in murder?" But it was hopeless to appeal to his good nature. He didn't have one. Hendry had murdered before.

"My debt's now repaid," said one of the men to Abercrombie. "You make sure Coyle knows I only left because you said so."

Abercrombie waved the gun at the door. "Yes, yes, your debt is paid, scum."

The man pressed his lips together but left without another word.

"He was a magician, wasn't he?" I asked. "He owed Coyle a debt and now he considers it paid by coming here. And you?" I asked the three remaining men. "Do you all owe Coyle?"

Two nodded while the third, the one who hadn't flinched when he realized I was to be murdered, shook his head. "I get paid," he simply said. "And I don't mind seeing a bit o' magic blood spilled. I ain't got no love for magicians. My pa lost his business when a carpenter magician opened a shop next to his. So you can all go to hell, as far as I'm concerned." He spat at the feet of the two other remaining men.

I turned to them both. "This is madness. Please, you can stop him. This has nothing to do with me being a magician and everything to do with human decency."

One man turned white as a sheet then ran out the front door. The second, the one who'd challenged Abercrombie, now stepped up to him. "There are too many witnesses, sir. You won't get away with murdering Mrs. Glass."

"I told you to go," Abercrombie snarled. "Now get out!"

But the man persisted. "It's not why I thought we were coming here or I'd never have agreed. Come now, be reasonable. She's just a woman—"

"She's a woman who can destroy *everything*! She can ruin men like me. Decent, hard-working men. As leader of the magicians, she is dangerous."

"I am the leader of nothing and no one," I said. "And this is madness. If you murder me, you will hang."

Abercrombie wiped a bead of sweat sliding down his face with his shoulder. "Coyle will protect me."

"He will only protect himself. He'll throw you to the wolves the moment it suits him."

"Listen to her!" the man urged. "She is not our leader, merely a figurehead. Murdering her won't change the magic movement. It won't send us scurrying back into hiding. Don't do this. Whatever you owe Coyle, find another way to repay him. Or join the protestors outside his house and demand he release you from your agreement. That's what I'm going to do now. I thought coming here would absolve my debt but I see now that I was wrong. The price Coyle wants from me is too high. I'll do as the others have chosen and call for him to leave us alone. If we stand together, he can't win. We're too many." He grasped Abercrombie's shoulder. "It won't matter that you're not a magician, sir. Come. Join me."

Mr. Abercrombie shook him off. "I won't stand on the same side as filth like you. Witches and demons, the lot of you." He swung his arm and angled the gun at the man's chest.

He fired.

I screamed and fell to the ground. Somewhere in the depths of the service area came more screams. Bristow covered his head with his arms.

Chronos crouched on one knee, shaking me. "India? India?"

"I'm all right," I murmured.

I glanced at the body of the dead man who'd appealed for my life. Blood poured from the gaping wound in his torso onto the tiles. His eyes stared up at the ceiling, empty. He'd not even had time to register shock. He was alive one moment and dead the next. It was utterly surreal. This could not be happening. Not here in my home in the genteel area of Mayfair. It was impossible.

And yet it was utterly, sickeningly, real.

Abercrombie was merciless. He looked down on the dead body with satisfaction. "Now there is one less witness."

"One less magician," said the man who'd searched the house. He was the only one left, along with Abercrombie and Hendry.

Mr. Hendry didn't look satisfied as he stared at the dead body. His face was blank. The cold-blooded killing hadn't affected him. The man had gone mad in the months since I'd last seen him. There would be no getting through to him, no appealing to his better nature. His better nature was lost, if he ever had one.

"We should go," the thug said. "The servants would have left through the back door to fetch Glass by now. Get on with it and let's get out of here."

All three turned to me. Once again, the gun was pointed at my head.

My heart thundered in my chest and my blood pumped, urging me to flee. But fleeing was impossible. I would not get more than one step before Abercrombie pulled the trigger. He meant to kill me. I was certain of it. It was only a matter of whether I died with dignity, staring down my killer, or with a bullet in my back.

"You can't do this!" Chronos cried. "She's a woman! She's with child, for God's sake!"

I blinked at him. How did he know? Or was it merely a ruse to get the men to re-think their crime?

Either way, it had the desired effect. Not on Abercrombie or Hendry, but on the third man, the artless thug. His lips parted with his silent gasp. He started to shake his head at Abercrombie, but Abercrombie merely straightened his arm. He pulled back the trigger.

"Another magician?" He sneered. "No, thank you."

The thug lunged at Abercrombie's outstretched arm. It dropped, but not completely and not before Abercrombie fired off a shot.

I screamed again as pain exploded in my upper thigh. I'd never known pain like it. It felt like my leg was on fire and being crushed at the same time.

I don't recall falling but I was on the ground, clutching my leg, trying to stop the bleeding and pain. But it was no use. Blood was everywhere. My skirts were soon soaked with it, and my hands.

A gushing sound filled my head, like the sound of an overflowing dam. Even louder was the sound of another gunshot and shouting voices. Lots of voices. I couldn't discern them. Male, female, old or young…there were many. Some shouts were in anger, others fear.

And then one became crystal clear, like a powerful lamp emerging from a dense fog. "India! India! Can you hear me?"

Matt.

I felt his face near mine, his ragged breath on my damp cheek. Was I crying, or him?

"My love, wake up. For God's sake, say something!"

I opened my eyes—I hadn't realized they were closed—and stared into the face of a terrified man. He'd never looked so pale, so haggard. His hair fell forward as he leaned over me, tears swam in his eyes and his mouth was twisted with fear.

His breath quickened as he realized I was alive and he drew me to his chest in a hug that was both fierce and gentle. "You're all right, India. You're going to be fine. You're all right." He said it over and over, perhaps hoping to convince himself.

But I wouldn't be all right. I was losing a lot of blood. My body knew it and I started to shake.

The voices had calmed. There was only one now, and it was Mrs. Bristow ordering my skirts to be torn and my wound bound tight to stem the blood flow. The tearing of material made me wince and then I felt my skirts being pushed all the way up.

Someone emitted a small cry of despair. It was a woman's cry, but not Willie. Aunt Letitia, then, or the maids. Not Mrs. Bristow. She was binding my leg, tying the material so tight that the blood wouldn't get through. If it didn't get through, it would keep my heart beating long enough while we waited for a doctor.

But I would lose my leg if the blood was cut off from it for too long. A cry of pain burst from my throat and Matt was holding me again. My head was in his lap, his hands on either side of my face, stroking.

"Has the doctor been sent for?" he choked out.

"Yes, sir," came Bristow's trembling voice.

"He's not the doctor we need," Chronos snapped. "She's lost too much blood already. You know where he is, don't you?"

Matt didn't hesitate. "Fetch Gabe," he ordered.

"No," I managed to whisper even though my tongue felt too big for my mouth. "Too dangerous... They'll capture him."

Matt stroked my hair from my forehead. "He's the only one who can heal you, India. We have to get him. Duke!"

"I'll go." Willie's voice was ominous. Her face appeared above me, as grave as Matt's but dry-eyed. She held up her gun for all to see then thrust it into her belt. The second gunshot must have come from her. I wondered if she'd managed to kill Abercrombie or Hendry.

I reached out to stop her, but she was gone and my hand was as heavy as a brick and moved too slowly. "Not fair," I murmured.

They were exchanging my life for Gabe's. It wasn't right.

"Go!" Matt shouted at her. "Intercept him at the dock. And if he refuses, tell him she's with child."

I closed my eyes, tried to shake my head. I wasn't sure if I'd managed it or not. We couldn't put this dilemma on Gabe. He shouldn't have to make this choice. I didn't want him to have to make it.

But it wasn't just my life anymore. If I were with child… I had to live. I *wanted* to live.

"The boat leaves in ten minutes." Duke's voice was filled with panic. "And it's a twenty minute drive to the dock."

"Then she better damn well hurry."

Even in my pain-filled, barely conscious state, I knew Willie wouldn't get to Gabe on time. And even if she did manage it, they then had another twenty-minute journey back.

Time. There wasn't enough of it.

I would die here in the arms of the man who loved me before they returned. Not too many women could ask for an end like that. Many would consider me fortunate to be so cherished, so loved and cared for.

But all I felt was an overwhelming, desperate sadness. Not for me, but for the man I'd leave behind and our child who'd never be born.

CHAPTER 15

*I*f he was true to his word, Gabe would refuse to come. He had been clear that he would not use his magic to save another life again. He certainly wouldn't jeopardize his freedom and his future by coming here.

But that was why Willie had gone, I realized. She and her gun would see that he had no choice.

My hopes rose, even as I fought against the pain and the overwhelming despair that she wouldn't reach him before he departed, and if she did, he might refuse to come. He *should* refuse, and I shouldn't *want* him to use his magic.

But I wanted this baby to live and, in that moment, nothing else mattered.

"They got away," came Cyclops's voice in between his labored breaths.

"We'll deal with them later." Matt sounded dismissive.

"How is she?"

Nobody answered.

Cyclops swore under his breath.

"Harry?" came Aunt Letitia's thin voice. "Harry, what's wrong with Veronica?"

Matt heaved a sigh and I felt his body deflate. But it wasn't he who answered. Duke and Cyclops soothed Aunt Letitia, their voices slowly, slowly fading as they steered her away. I didn't know where her maid was. Perhaps fainted from all the blood.

There must be so much blood. It was draining from me at a slower rate now, thanks to the tourniquet, but it still drained. I grew weaker, colder, with each passing minute.

Minutes. My watch.

I fought to open my eyes. Matt's face filled my vision. He seemed to take heart that I was still conscious. His chest swelled with a deep, shuddery breath.

My watch. I tried to tell him it was broken, that Gabe's magic wouldn't work without it, but my words were slurred and barely audible. I couldn't raise my voice. I lifted a finger, pointing.

He followed my gaze, then groaned and lowered his head.

"Abercrombie broke it," Chronos told him. "He knew it would save her if her life was in danger." He pressed something into my hand. I knew the shape well. "My gift to you, my dear granddaughter. The watch is now yours."

Gifting me his watch made it mine, and if it were mine it could save my life when medical and time magic were combined in it. It was how we'd saved Matt's life after his watch had broken.

I gazed up at my grandfather. He looked exhausted, his eyes sunken amid two deep shadows. He seemed to be holding himself together, as if he were in pain too and trying not to let me see it. He folded my fingers over his watch—*my watch now*—and enclosed my fist in both his hands. He held on tight, clutching me as if he would drift away if he let go.

My eyelids felt heavy but I fought to keep them open, to hold Matt's gaze with my own even though what I saw there frightened me.

But fighting became harder and harder until it was no longer possible. I let my eyelids drift closed.

"No, India!" His voice was commanding, angry. He never spoke to me in that way. Never. "I forbid you to… I forbid it."

It was an almost impossible task but I opened them again. It felt as though I'd won a battle but it had cost me energy I didn't have to spare. Matt was right, however. I had to stay awake until Gabe arrived. When he was here and he used his magic, I could give in to it.

If he came.

I concentrated on the pain. It still burned but not as sharply. It was more of a throb now.

And I kept my gaze on Matt. I knew every inch of his face, but I studied him again in minute detail. The straight nose and high cheekbones, the expressive mouth so quick to form a smile. But not now. Now it was set hard as he battled to hold in his emotions. His jaw was firm too. Bristles were already beginning to shadow it. Tiny creases fanned from the corners of his eyes and scored his forehead. Worry lines. I wanted to tell him not to worry, that all would be well, but my voice didn't work and he would know I was lying anyway.

And finally, I focused on his eyes. They were deep pools, the color swirling and changing with the lamplight and his emotions. They were two fathomless orbs of blue-black, holding entire oceans and the midnight sky, and more love than I'd ever dreamed possible. Women went their whole life never feeling love from a man like Matt. A man of physical and mental strength, so charming and handsome, caring and capable. I was lucky.

I was happy.

His face faded.

"India." My body shook and Matt's voice rose in pitch. "India! Stay awake. Stay with me. India!"

* * *

VOICES SURROUNDED ME. Angry, loud voices shouting over the top of one another. It was enough to wake the dead. The thought amused me. Perhaps I was dead.

But this was not Heaven.

"Do it!" Willie shouted. "Do it now!"

"Don't ask this of me!" Gabe. That was Gabe!

I tried to open my eyes but they wouldn't widen further than mere slits. It felt like boulders weighed down my eyelids.

"She's awake." The relief in Matt's voice caught everyone's attention.

Several faces leaned in, a mixture of relief and worry clear in each of them. Willie had wet hair. How odd when the evening had been so clear.

I still lay on the floor in the entrance hall, my head resting on Matt's lap, his hands stroking my hair, my cheek, my forehead. I could hardly feel my leg at all now. The pain was a dull ache.

I blinked at Gabe and tried to smile. "Please." I don't know if he heard my whisper but he read my lips well enough.

He closed his eyes momentarily then reopened them. "India… Please understand what you're asking of me."

I tried to nod. I wanted him to know that I knew, but was asking anyway. Pleading, in fact. "Not for me." I had to get my message across. Had to make him understand. My breathing was labored and it took enormous effort, but I managed more words. "The baby."

There was no surprise in his face, only deep sorrow and regret. "They told me. But that's the problem. What affect will the magic have on the baby? The early weeks are crucial to its development. Combining two magics in your body…what will it do to the fetus?"

Suddenly he was jerked back out of my line of sight and Willie was growling in a voice choked with emotion. "If you don't do this, I *will* kill you."

"You owe us," Duke said. "We helped you escape."

"As a doctor, I can't be responsible for experimenting on a fetus! You're all out of your minds."

"Maybe we are." That was Cyclops, his deep resonant tones bringing a measure of calm. "But you are a doctor and doctors save lives. It's madness for you *not* to try. You'll regret it if you don't. You know you will."

"I can't experiment on her when she's with child. Not with something as unknown as healing magic."

"I know it could be dangerous," Matt said, urgent now. "I know it might—" He cut himself off. "But it *will* save India's life. And one is better than none."

"You don't understand. It might kill the baby, it's true. But what concerns me more is if it lives and...the effect. It might..."

"Might what?"

"Might be born monstrous."

A dense silence fell around me, as dark and bleak as a winter's night. My heart shuddered in my chest and I closed my eyes again. The energy I'd used to regain consciousness was taking its toll and I felt my life force leaking away and the world fading.

Matt's thumb stroked my cheek, achingly gentle. When he spoke, he sounded so close, as if his words were coming from my own lips. "I will love him or her anyway."

Gabe swore softly. He was weakening, but he had not yet agreed.

I expected Willie to force him at gunpoint, but it was Chronos who spoke next. "That's the thing with experiments. Sometimes they fail. Sometimes they work but the effects are not what you expected. And sometimes they work precisely as you hope, or better."

Gabe said nothing. That was a good sign.

"Now get on her other side." Chronos's age-roughened hands touched mine, making sure I was clasping the watch. "You operate and speak your spell. I'll speak mine."

Gabe settled on my left. "Cyclops, you have the other doctor's bag? I'll remove the bullet first then sew up the wound. Chronos, start your spell."

Chronos began to chant, the words familiar to me. Gabe's spell joined his and I felt my leg being poked and prodded near the wound. I expected to feel magical heat in the watch but there was none. It was lifeless in my hands, the metal cool.

Something was wrong.

Chronos stopped. "It's not working!"

"What do you mean?" Matt asked. "Why isn't it working?"

"I don't know!"

"Is it the watch?"

"I—I don't think so."

"Are you doing it wrong?" Willie asked. "The words needs to be specific, the accent perfect."

"I know that. I think my magic has weakened."

"Why would it weaken?"

I knew why, but I could do no more than whisper.

Chronos answered. "I'm dying. I asked Seaford not to tell you." Chronos glanced across me at Gabe. Gabe swallowed and looked to Matt.

Matt grabbed Chronos's shirt front. "Try harder."

Chronos's face crumpled. "I can't," he sobbed.

"She is your only family! Try!"

"My magic is too weak."

Through the pain and the fog, I had a thought. Perhaps mine was strong enough. But I knew in my heart it wasn't. They knew it too. If Chronos's magic was too weak, then mine would be worse. I was closer to death than he.

So very close now. I could feel myself slipping away, like I was set adrift on a boat sailing across a smooth lake. I felt calm, too. My heartbeat slowed and a sense of peace washed over me. The outcome was inevitable now. There was no point fighting it.

Best to give in and let oblivion take me.

"Maybe it's the watch." Matt moved. My head still lay on his lap, but he was doing something. "Here. Try this one. It already has India's magic in it, and won't require more. Just your magic, Gabe. I'm sure of it."

He was giving them his watch.

No!

Had I spoken it aloud? Had they heard me?

I couldn't use his watch. He couldn't gift it to me. If he

did, it would no longer be his. It could no longer be used to save him. The healing magic would be all mine.

He would die without it.

I gathered every last ounce of strength. I called on every piece of energy I had left, and opened my eyes wider. He needed to see the plea in them in case my voice didn't work.

"No." The word was a mere whisper. "Don't."

I needn't have spoken. Everyone knew what Matt gifting me his watch meant. Especially him.

Someone sobbed quietly. I didn't need to see to know it was Willie.

Chronos's face appeared above me. "Accept the gift, India. Then when you are healed, he buys another one and you and Gabe put your magic into that for him."

In the foggy recess of my mind that was still capable of coherent thought, I realized how neat his solution could be. But it was too risky with so much unknown about how the healing magic worked. We didn't know if Matt would start to fade immediately he gave away the watch. It wouldn't be broken like last time. This was different. I tried telling Chronos that, but I was too exhausted to speak.

Cyclops gently moved Chronos out of the way. "You have to accept the watch, India. For the baby."

Tears slid from the corners of my eyes. The choice was an impossible one. Save the baby I wasn't sure I was carrying or my husband.

Matt stroked my tears away with the pad of his thumb. "It's all right, India." He spoke smoothly, the rich, modular timbre of his voice surrounding me, infusing me as my magic did when I called on it. "It's all right, my love. I've always known it wouldn't last, that my time on earth was borrowed. Now it's time you accepted it too."

I could never accept such a thing. Never. I closed my eyes, no longer able to look upon the pain in his.

"You must live." He moved our joined hands lower to cover my belly. "For our family."

A sob tore from my chest, leaving behind a gaping hole.

An ache settled there, more searingly painful than any wound caused by the bullet.

I turned my hand over, palm up, and accepted the watch he placed on it.

"I gift you my watch, my love. Now live."

CHAPTER 16

he magic in the watch recognized me, its creator, and instantly flared to life. The glow lightened the backs of my eyelids. It wasn't enough to heal me on its own. Gabe still needed to speak his healing spell.

With Matt so close, I felt him flagging before the others noticed. The moment the watch no longer belonged to him, the magic in it transferred to me. His energy drained, his life force faded just as the blood had drained from me. But no tourniquet could slow it. Only a watch—*his* watch—with two magics twined together within it.

Even if someone gifted him their watch now, neither I nor Chronos was strong enough to infuse our magic into it.

But perhaps together, we were.

I fought through the fog and willed my eyes to open, my voice to work. An idea took root, and I tried so hard to think it through, but I didn't have the energy. I had to operate on pure instinct now.

And instinct told me to give Matt his watch back.

"Chronos," I whispered.

His face appeared above me, deathly gray. The attempts to use his magic had taken its toll.

"My watch."

Tears slid down his cheeks. "It's broken."

"My watch," I said again, instilling as much command into it as I could muster.

The effort made me cough, and that in turn roused Matt. He sucked in a deep breath and looked around at the desperate faces surrounding us.

Willie, Duke and Cyclops moved closer. Cyclops supported Matt, helping him to sit upright. Willie sobbed into Duke's shoulder. The misery in his eyes said more than words.

Chronos reappeared and placed my watch in my hand. I'd worked on it so many times I knew every part by feel. The glass was smashed, the enamel face cracked and minute hand bent. None of that mattered. It was the mechanisms that concerned me. I fingered the silver case. It was dented but not broken.

My heart lifted. This might work. If I could stay conscious long enough, and Chronos could muster all his strength…

He removed the back cover for me and placed the watch in my hand. I traced the outline of the parts. The smooth brass of the top plate with the serial number etched into it. The wheels edged with teeth and the tiny screws holding the balance in place. They were all where they should be, but damaged. The dents wouldn't be visible to the naked eye, so small were they, but they were enough to make the watch stop.

I couldn't sit up let alone concentrate on the fine work needed to fix it. But Chronos could. He didn't need to speak a spell for this, he could use the innate skill of his seventy-plus years as a watchmaker magician. All he needed were tools.

He knew what I intended and pulled out the small traveling kit of tools he kept on him. He bent to work over the watch but clicked his tongue. "I need spare parts."

"India has some upstairs." Duke raced off, his footsteps pounding.

Chronos bent over the watch again. I pictured the watch's mechanisms as he worked, saw his tweezers removing broken parts in my mind's eye. It was delicate work and required concentration. Concentration I wasn't sure he possessed.

"India." Matt whispered my name, pleading with me to hurry with his last ounce of strength.

I wanted to reassure him, but couldn't. It wasn't up to me anymore. My life was in Chronos's hands. Both our lives were.

Duke returned and fell to his knees beside Chronos. He opened my tool kit where I kept a small but well stocked selection of spare parts. "What do you need?"

Chronos wiped his forehead with the back of his hand. "Uh, let me think."

"There's no time to think!" Willie cried.

Cyclops scolded her. "Give him space."

Willie's idea of giving space was to pace across the floor.

Chronos scrunched up his face as he bent to work. Time was already going so slowly, but it seemed to take him forever to fix the watch. And with every passing second, I could feel myself grow weaker.

Matt too. His hands no longer gripped, they merely lay with mine, limp. He would have collapsed if it weren't for Cyclops supporting him. I needed to gift his watch back to him, but I didn't have the strength to speak. I slipped his watch beneath his hand but the magic didn't work. The watch still belonged to me.

"There. Done." Chronos sat back on his haunches and looked at me with a hopeful shine in his eyes. It was a bright spot amid his otherwise gaunt face. "Your watch, India." He placed it in my hand but didn't let go. "I'll try again. Gabe, speak your spell."

I placed my other hand over his. "Together," I murmured.

Tears pooled in his eyes. He nodded and attempted a smile, but it fell flat.

Gabe's chant filled the hall, and I thought I'd never heard a more beautiful sound. Chronos's chant joined his in a harmonious duet. The watch glowed but quickly faded again. Chronos's magic wasn't strong enough.

I tried to speak the words to match his, but they were barely more than a whisper. It didn't matter. I could *think* my spells now. There was no surge of magic through me, however, no explosion into the watch. It was a trickle, a glowing coal rather than a raging fire.

Matt's breathing became shallower, fainter. He was clinging to life, but only just.

I closed my eyes and called to my magic. I summoned it from the depths of my soul, from the place where desperation lurked and heartache threatened to dwell. I shut out everything, my own pain, even my hopes, and focused on the magic. It was mine to call on as I wished. It was part of me, in my bones and blood, my muscle and sinew.

It was bright and beautiful, but weaker.

It began with a swell then grew until it filled me. It swirled inside me, gathering strength as I continued to focus on it. I pushed hard at it, then cajoled and teased it to work alone, then pushed again.

Then finally it merged with Chronos's. It was as if it found its way, as if Chronos's magic guided it from me and into the watch. His magic was a beacon, not strong enough to go the distance alone, but able to direct and act as a conduit.

Together, our two weakened magics made a whole one, and met Gabe's at full strength.

The burst of healing light from the watch lit up the room like a flare. I felt Gabe's magic rush through me like a torrent. It sped up my veins, throwing out healing properties, mending my wound, renewing the damaged flesh and muscle of my leg, and restoring lost blood.

Someone untied the tourniquet.

I sat bolt upright, gasping in huge gulps of air, filling my lungs. The fog of my barely-conscious state receded like a speeding train, taking pain with it. I was healed. Better than healed. I was enhanced. I felt as though I could climb a mountain or run a marathon.

I pressed a hand to my breast to make sure. My heart beat strongly.

Then I touched my belly.

"Matt!" Willie's cry had me spinning around.

Matt's eyes were closed, his face white. I touched his cheek. Cold. He'd stopped breathing. Without knowing what I was doing, I pressed my mouth to his, intending to breathe life back into him in a desperate last act.

I didn't need to. His feather-light breath whispered across my lips. "Hurry!"

Duke pressed Matt's watch back into his hand, but nothing happened. The lid was open, it was ready. But it didn't work.

"You have to gift it back to him, India," Chronos said, his voice weak.

I closed Matt's hand around the watch. "I gift it back to you. It's yours again."

A bright purple light burst from it and I had to shield my eyes. When I looked again, Matt's veins were glowing with the magic racing up them, all the way to his face. The magic knew what to do. It was still there from the last time Gabe and I had spoken our spells into it. The magic was still strong enough to heal him whenever his body needed to call on it. Now that the watch once again belonged to him, so did the magic. We magicians were not required to speak our spells again.

Matt opened his eyes and drew in a deep breath. It was the most beautiful sight in the world.

I threw my arms around him and burst into tears.

Willie threw her arms around us both, sobbing. Cyclops, supporting Matt, folded us all in a big, hearty embrace.

"India," Matt murmured.

"Yes. I'm all right. We're all right." It was difficult to speak with my throat tight with tears, but I needed him to know all was well.

He drew back and cupped my face between his hands, studying me, searching for signs of health and vitality. I did the same and smiled when I saw he was back to being himself. He tried to smile too, but it was crooked with emotion. He pressed his forehead to mine.

"Thank God," he whispered.

Behind me, Gabe swore. "Mr. Steele!"

I'd forgotten about Chronos in my relief. He lay on the floor, covered in some of my blood, his face ashen, his breathing unsteady.

Gabe loosened Chronos's collar then bent to listen to his heart. "It's weak."

The effort of summoning his magic had cost Chronos all the strength he had left.

I scooted to his side and took his hand in mine. It was cool, clammy. "Can you do something?"

Gabe shook his head. "Just make him comfortable."

Oh God.

Cyclops lifted Chronos and carried him into the drawing room where he lay him on the sofa. My grandfather seemed so small and fragile. The vibrant man had been drained of energy, leaving behind a shell.

"Gabe—"

"No," he said. "Not this time. I won't play God again."

I thought I had no tears left to shed, but it seemed I did. I knelt by the sofa and took Chronos's hand. I willed him to get better. But without magic, it wouldn't happen tonight, if at all.

Matt drew me into his arms and held me. My blood throbbed in response, my heartbeat quickened in anticipation. The magic within me responded to the magic in him. It was comforting, and that had to be enough now.

"Come upstairs," Matt said. "You need to clean up and change."

I looked down at my dress, splattered from the waist down with blood.

"Duke, Willie, see that Gabe gets safely back to the hotel, and quickly."

The boat wouldn't have waited for him, and would now

be long gone. Matt would have to find another secure passage out of England.

I let him lead me by the hand back into the entrance hall. There were two bodies there, and it took me a moment to realize one was the magician who'd argued with Abercrombie and the other was the artless thug who'd changed his mind about killing me when he learned I was with child. He saved my life by forcing Abercrombie to lower the gun.

Abercrombie must have shot him.

The front door suddenly burst open. In the commotion, no one had locked it. Constables poured in, led by the detective investigating Mr. Goldman's murder.

He pointed at Gabe. "Arrest him."

There was nowhere to flee now, not with so many constables in the house.

Gabe didn't try to escape. He put his hands up in surrender. "I came here asking for their assistance and was refused. The Glasses had nothing to do with my escape from prison."

The detective wasn't interested in his explanation, however. He'd turned his attention to the bodies on the tiles. "Does someone want to explain what happened here?"

"They attacked my wife," Matt said.

"Actually they tried to stop my attacker from shooting me," I said. "He killed them in retaliation."

The detective lowered his gaze to my skirt. "Are you all right, Mrs. Glass?"

"A bullet grazed my thigh, but I'm fine, thank you."

"That's a lot of blood for just a graze."

"Some of it's theirs. They thought they were coming here to search for my magical watch." I opened my hand to show it to him before closing it again. "But it turned out that the man they'd come with wanted me dead."

"And who is this man?"

"You'd better step into the library," Matt said. "This could take some time and the servants want to clean up out here before my aunt comes down."

The detective scrubbed his sideburns in much the same

THE GOLDSMITH'S CONSPIRACY

way as Brockwell did. After a moment's thought he nodded. "See that the scene is recorded and the bodies taken to the morgue," he instructed two of his constables. "The rest of you, escort Dr. Seaford to Scotland Yard." He paused as something caught his eye. "Isn't that your medical bag?"

"No," Gabe said. "It belongs to the Glass's regular doctor. He came here and left that for me to use to tend to Mrs. Glass's wound. He's not involved in any of this."

"Why couldn't he tend Mrs. Glass himself?"

"Gabe's a better doctor," Matt said. "And since he was here, we thought we'd make good use of him."

"But if her wound was merely a graze, why wasn't your regular doctor good enough?"

He was clever, I'd give him that. Explaining just enough to satisfy him was going to be difficult without telling him about Gabe's medical magic.

To my immense relief, Brockwell arrived brandishing orders. He was out of breath, but his rapid breathing seemed to stop altogether when he took in the bodies and the blood. His gaze quickly flew about until he found Willie.

She offered him a weak smile and he nodded back in return. His relief was plain to see.

"I'm taking over this investigation," he told the first detective.

"Why? It's linked to the Goldman case. Seaford was hiding out here—"

"He wasn't," Matt said. "He just told you. He came here seeking our help after his escape."

The detective grunted. He didn't believe us.

"This is a separate incident and I've been assigned to it." Brockwell showed him the orders. "If you don't like it, take it up with Commissioner Munro."

The detective pressed his lips together and folded up the paper. He handed it back to Brockwell. "I've got a prisoner to process anyway." He nodded at the constables escorting Gabe and they headed out the door.

"No!" I cried. "He's innocent. He's a good man."

"You know it, Detective," Matt added.

The detective hesitated then touched the brim of his hat. "Good evening, Mrs. Glass, Mr. Glass. I'll call on you tomorrow if I have any questions for you."

We waited for him to go then I turned into Matt's chest. He held me, but I didn't cry. I was all out of tears. But my heart ached.

"It's not yet lost," Matt said gently. "While he is alive, there is hope." But not even Matt could keep the doubt out of his voice.

"Are those orders fraudulent?" Cyclops asked.

I pulled away from Matt to see Brockwell looking indignant. "Of course not. They're entirely legitimate. The moment your footman arrived at Scotland Yard and alerted me to a disturbance here, I spoke to the commissioner. I convinced him this was separate to the Goldman investigation and was a magical matter. He assigned me without hesitation." He glanced at the door. "I don't think he's too impressed with my colleague anyway after he couldn't relocate Dr. Seaford."

"That will change now," Matt muttered darkly.

I hugged myself, warding off a chill. We were right back where we started with Gabe arrested. The prison would double their security this time. We'd never be able to rescue him again.

Bristow emerged from the shadows near the door to the service area. "I'll bring refreshments to the library while…" He lifted his chin, studiously avoiding looking at the bodies and the bloody floor. It would need to be scrubbed to see it returned to its gleaming state.

"Thank you, Bristow," Matt said. "And tell Fossett I'll speak to him in the morning to thank him for fetching Detective Inspector Brockwell."

We filed into the library and each found a chair. I wasn't physically tired. I felt healthier than ever. But I was drained nevertheless. My nerves were stretched to breaking point. I needed this to be over. I needed it all to end so I could be with my husband.

Between us, we pieced together the events for Brockwell as well as each other. I learned that Peter had fetched Matt and the others from outside Coyle's house when Abercrombie came. I learned that Willie had shot at Abercrombie as he and Hendry fled through the back entrance. She'd missed, much to her frustration, and the bullet was still lodged in the narrow corridor near the kitchen. I also learned that Willie had ridden one of the horses to the private dock to intercept Gabe before the boat departed, as the carriage was too slow. She hadn't made it on time, however, so hired a lad to row her out in one of the moored dinghies. The lad was drunk but built like Cyclops, as she put it, and they reached the boat carrying Gabe as it steamed off along the Thames. Unfortunately, the drunk rower had stood up when they reached it to help her and they'd both fallen in.

It would have made us all laugh if we weren't so sick with worry about Gabe and Chronos, and exhausted from our ordeal.

We held nothing back from Brockwell. There was no need. He would edit out the parts about Gabe's magic in his report. It was best kept a secret. It was too special and too dangerous for others to know about it, including the government. It was dreadful enough that Coyle seemed to know, and that Le Grand suspected.

Coyle!

When he learned Gabe had been recaptured, he would set his plan in motion again. "Coyle will intervene now. He'll get what he wants—Gabe owing him a debt."

Matt reached across the gap between us and took my hand. "Coyle won't find out. Not tonight. There are angry protesters outside his house, not allowing anyone in or out. Word won't reach him."

"And I'll assign men that I trust to Gabe's cell," Brockwell added.

It didn't make me feel any better. Gabe was not free.

"Was the situation at Coyle's peaceful?" I asked.

"It was when we left," Matt said. "They were simply

demanding their artefacts be returned, and telling him in no uncertain terms that they no longer owed him anything."

It was just as I'd hoped, how I'd expressed it in my letters. The magicians had rallied. They'd joined forces. Individually, they had no influence, but together they had power and control.

Just like Chronos and me. Our magic had worked together. Separately, we'd been too weak, but our combined magic, and that of Gabe's, had saved my life. I opened my hand to stare at my watch. I traced my thumb over the crack in the dial and along the bent minute hand. I would hammer the dents out the first chance I got, but the dial needed replacing. Or perhaps I'd leave it. I'd do as Matt did and tuck it away in a secret hidden pocket close to my heart where pickpockets couldn't reach it. It was too valuable to leave in my reticule now.

That night, after the entrance hall was cleaned, Brockwell left, and Chronos was settled, Matt and I finally got to bed. He held me as my body trembled. I couldn't seem to make it stop, but I wasn't cold.

"It happens sometimes after a distressing event," he said, his arms tightening.

I lay there, listening to his heartbeat, wondering if mine sounded as strong. It certainly felt it.

My trembling subsided eventually, but I still couldn't sleep. I replayed the evening over in my head, wondering if there was something we could have done to avoid Gabe being rearrested.

I rolled onto my back with a sigh. Matt propped himself up on his elbow and looked down at me. I could just make out his silhouette in the darkness, but nothing else.

"Are you all right?" he asked.

"Just worried."

He settled back down beside me and rested his head next to mine on the pillow. He placed a hand over my left breast and felt my heart beat its new, steady rhythm. I stroked his hair and his breathing soon became even.

I thought he'd fallen asleep when he said, "We made the right decisions. It was the only way."

"I know."

"You can't worry. It's not good." Not good for the baby, he meant.

"I know that too." But telling me not to worry wouldn't stop me from worrying.

He was right, however. We had made the right decisions. It was the only way we could both survive. But now we had to wait and see the result of blasting my body with two kinds of magic. We would know in a little under nine months. Because now that I was healthier than ever, I was more aware of my body.

And I was absolutely certain I carried new life.

CHAPTER 17

*T*he servants were marvelous. By the time I awoke, the house was clean and there was no sign of the terrors that had occurred the evening before. Aunt Letitia was none the wiser, having fallen asleep in her bedroom still believing she was thirty years younger and living with her brother, not her nephew. Her lady's maid had stayed with her through the night. I gave Polly the day off as well as the housemaids. Bristow, Mrs. Bristow, Mrs. Potter and Peter Fossett all insisted on staying close by. The butler and housekeeper assured me they would take some time off the following week. Matt paid them all a generous bonus for their loyalty, hard work and discretion.

I looked in on Chronos after breakfast. He lay on the bed in the spare room, his breathing weak and shallow. I touched his hand and he murmured something incomprehensible. As I left him, I instructed Mrs. Bristow to fetch a doctor if he didn't improve.

Matt was keen to see how the situation at Lord Coyle's fared. I refused to be left out, but I didn't have to argue with him about going. He readily agreed. He was reluctant to leave me on my own with Abercrombie still out there.

Woodall drove to Belgravia but stopped some distance from Coyle's townhouse. He could proceed no further. There was quite a crowd standing on the pavement and spilling onto the street. Their angry shouts and shaking fists made the horses skittish.

Matt, Willie, Duke and I alighted but Matt insisted that he and I remain near the carriage. He was being over-protective, but I couldn't blame him. Duke and Willie joined the crowd and promised to report back. I didn't need to hear their report to know what the throng demanded. Their shouts were clear, but their wishes were not what I expected.

Instead of insisting Coyle give back their magical objects and absolve them of their debts, they demanded he come out and face justice for the attack on me and for the murder of Mr. Goldman.

"How do they even know?" I asked.

Matt simply smiled a secret little smile.

"Matt?"

He indicated a familiar figure emerging from the crowd and approaching. "I sent word to Barratt just before we went to bed."

Oscar strode up to us, Professor Nash in tow. Both greeted me warmly.

"I'm glad to see you looking well, India," Oscar said. "Your husband's message had me worried."

"He just informed me that he wrote to you. This is all your doing?"

"It was his idea. I merely put it into motion."

He turned back to the crowd, calling for justice at the top of their lungs. The dozens of constables watching on made sure they didn't get too close to the front steps.

Matt put out his hand and Oscar shook it. They exchanged knowing nods. It was the first time Matt had shown real friendship toward the journalist.

"Your suggestion was an excellent one, Glass," Professor Nash said. "To gather all these magicians and supporters is inspired. Strength in numbers and all that. You have a lot of friends in the community, Mrs. Glass."

I followed his gaze to where Duke and Willie were joining

their voices with the others. I gauged there to be over two hundred people. I recognized several. Oscar's brother, Isaac, for one. He must have been in London already to get here so quickly. Elderly Mr. Gibbons, the mapmaker magician, stood next to his daughter. Mr. Mirnov the toymaker magician was there, his brightly painted cart full of wondrous delights to entertain children parked out of the way for safekeeping. I spotted Mr. and Mrs. Delancey too, and Louisa. Abigail Pilcher the silk magician and former nun stood alongside the woodwork magician nun dressed in her habit. I had a soft spot for Sister Bernadette. If it weren't for her bravery in squirreling orphaned baby Gabe Seaford out of the convent all those years ago, Matt wouldn't be alive now.

Mr. Pyke, the wool magician, stood with his wife and the Fullers, artless rug makers he planned to enter into business with, if allowed to trade by the guild. To see them side by side, calling for Coyle to come out, was a sight that lifted my spirits. Artless and magicians could work together. Compromises could be made.

Standing tall among the people we'd helped over the last year or more was Cyclops, out of uniform. He wasn't a policeman today. He wouldn't protect Coyle if he emerged from the house as his colleagues were instructed to do. Beside him, looking small beside her fiancé, was my dearest friend Catherine. Beside her was her brother and business partner, Ronnie, youngest brother Gareth the scallywag, and oldest brother Orwell. Mr. and Mrs. Mason were there too. Once, they'd been too scared to allow Catherine to associate with me for fear of retribution from the Watchmakers' Guild. Now, they brandished their fists and called for justice alongside magicians, demanding Coyle be arrested for Mr. Goldman's murder and the attack on me.

Overwhelmed with love, I took Matt's hand. He squeezed. "He can't remain holed up in there forever," he said.

"True," Nash said. "But it remains to be seen if the police will arrest him when he comes out or if they take his side."

"They might forcibly disperse the crowd first," Oscar

added darkly. He pointed to several onlookers, standing at a distance. Some had cameras on tripods, taking photographs. "A journalist from every newspaper in the city is here. Something will have to be done soon. A disturbance as large as this won't be allowed to continue. The police will have to intervene."

If they did, and protected Coyle instead of arresting him, what would the crowd do?

The front door opened and the constables standing on the porch stepped aside to allow someone to emerge. The crowd hushed, the only sounds coming from shuffling feet as they repositioned themselves for a better look.

But it wasn't Coyle who emerged; it was Hope. From this distance, she looked vulnerable, her hair golden in the morning sunlight. She held a piece of paper in her hand. Behind her stood the companion, Mrs. Fry, scowling.

Matt strode forward and I followed him, plunging into the gathering. Now that we were closer, I could see Hope's trembling hand, her exhaustion. The gathering would have kept her up all night. That and the worry.

"My husband would like me to issue the following statement," she read.

The crowd murmured. Someone asked why Coyle wouldn't read it himself.

Hope read, "'I, the earl of Coyle, will not give into the demands of a common rabble.'"

Protests erupted, heads shook in disbelief. Someone tried to start up a chant of "Get Coyle" but it wasn't repeated. Hope was speaking again.

"I have always championed magicians and advocated for your safety. I have been a friend to you all."

This was met with scoffs and more head shakes. "You mean you wanted to control us!" someone shouted.

"I will not admit to something I didn't do,'" Hope went on. "'I will not give myself up when I have done no wrong.'"

"You killed a man!"

"You tried to kill India Glass!"

"You manipulated us!"

The crowd jeered, booing at Hope, calling for her to fetch her husband to face justice.

She pressed on, her head held high. "'I am not afraid of you. You may be magicians, but your power is weak, your spells largely useless. I have nothing to fear from any of you.'"

Despite the shouts and jeers, Hope stood erect, her chin thrust out in defiance. She looked regal, a queen born to hold court and lord it over her subjects. The only outward show of her fear was the trembling hands.

If the crowd saw that fear, they didn't care. They shook their fists at her, called her a coward and murderer. They didn't see her as separate from her husband. As far as most of them were concerned, Hope and Coyle were one and the same and they were both guilty.

Hope turned away and the butler standing by the door opened it for her.

"Hope!" Matt called out. He tried to climb the steps, but the constables blocked his path. They received angry jeers from the crowd for their efforts.

"I have nothing more to say," Hope said. "I *cannot* say more." She turned to go.

"Wait! You don't have to go back." He held out his hand to her. "Come with us. We'll protect you from him."

Mrs. Fry crossed her arms and glared at Matt. "You're not welcome here."

Hope's eyes fluttered closed before reopening. They were larger than ever and that made her look more innocent and vulnerable. For the first time, I felt sorry for her. She was taking her wedding vows seriously and standing by her husband. She wasn't asking for a way out of her marriage, nor was she asking for our pity for finding herself married to such a cruel, manipulative man. She was taking responsibility for her choice and not burdening anyone else by asking for assistance.

Her gaze leveled with mine. I gave her a single nod of

understanding, and she gave one back. It was a show of mutual respect between two women who may be of unequal birth but were now equal in every way that mattered.

"Thank you for the kind offer," she said to Matt. "But my husband needs me."

Matt stepped forward, but the constables moved too, as did Mrs. Fry, blocking him. I caught his hand and tugged him away.

"She made her choice," I said.

"It's the wrong choice," he growled.

"You can't protect someone who doesn't want to be protected."

He sighed. "I know. She's a stubborn fool."

Willie pushed through the crowd and appeared at Matt's elbow. "Hope ain't as weak as you think she is. She's got bigger nuggets than some men I know."

"Matt! India!" I heard Brockwell before I saw him. He managed to forge a path through the throng, ducking a fist pumping the air, proving he was surprisingly nimble. "Willie, are you all right?"

"Course I am." She clasped his face in both her hands and kissed him thoroughly on the mouth. "But thanks for asking."

He blinked at her, somewhat dazed, until Duke thumped him on the shoulder and growled at him to get on with it. "I've just come from your house. Your butler said I'd find you here." Brockwell winced as the crowd's shouts grew louder. "I need to tell you something, but not here. It'll only inflame the situation."

"The situation needs to be inflamed." Willie had to shout to be heard. "I reckon we can get past the constables and get in the house and drag him out, if we work together."

"That's breaking and entering!"

She crossed her arms and arched her brows at him.

He *humphed*. "You're trouble, Willie."

She grinned. "Aye, and a bad influence on you. But that's why you love me."

He stared at her. Duke nudged him with his elbow, but

Brockwell didn't respond. Willie's sentence hung between them like a baited hook waiting for a fish to bite.

She turned her back on him and joined in the chant for Coyle to be arrested.

Matt led the way through the crowd, past Mr. Pyke and the Fullers, until we were clear. "What is it you wanted to tell us?" he asked Brockwell. "Have Abercrombie and Hendry been found?"

The detective inspector had regained a measure of his professional composure, but he looked more worried than ever as he watched the magicians and their supporters surging around the front steps of Coyle's house. The constables threatened to beat them back with their truncheons. So far, they'd not needed to use force. I doubted the relative peace would last much longer.

Brockwell scrubbed his sideburns. "They've crawled back into whatever hole they came out of. I came here to give you some bad news. Dr. Seaford will be hanged as soon as possible. The hope is that his death will see an end to this."

Matt swore. "It will only make it worse."

"I tried telling them that, but no one will listen to me."

I clutched his arm. "When is it?"

"Today at two."

My God. So soon. *Too* soon.

Matt placed a hand at my back and I turned into him, trying to comprehend. How could we have got to this point? How could a good man be sentenced to death for something he didn't do? It wasn't fair.

And it was all Lord Coyle's fault.

With Matt's arm around me, I watched the crowd. They surged forward like a school of fish, only to be pushed back by the constables on the steps. They brandished their truncheons, prepared to use them. More constables had made their way to the front. There were dozens of them, a show of force, protecting a man they didn't know who didn't deserve their regard. The crowd had become an angry, seething mob, riled further by Coyle's statement. They would trample the constables to get to the door if we didn't do something soon.

"We can't allow this to happen." I looked up at Matt.

His grave face peered down at me and I knew he was at a loss. He had no solutions, no ideas for how to save Gabe.

I had one, but he wouldn't like it. "We have to find proof against Coyle. Even if we found Abercrombie, he won't admit Coyle forced him. We must look for other evidence to incriminate him." I turned to the house. "We have to find some correspondence or *something* that points to his guilt."

"All well and good except I have no authority to search the premises," Brockwell said.

"If we wait for your superiors to allow it, we'll never get inside. They won't cross Coyle. We make our own way in. Forcefully."

"There is no 'we' in that scenario," Matt said. "You're going home."

I leveled my gaze with his. "I'm needed."

Matt cursed under his breath.

Brockwell put up his hands. "I'm not hearing any of this."

"Go," I ordered. "I don't want you losing your position over this."

Brockwell eyed each of us in turn. He gave me a grim, flat smile, then walked away.

"India," Matt pressed, his tone stern, urgent.

"You're not talking me out of this. We're using magic to get in. It's the only way to ensure no one is hurt."

"You can't stay. You have to take care of yourself."

"I will. But I have to help. I'm needed." I walked off, but Matt grabbed my arm.

"India—"

"Let me go, Matt."

His grip tightened. "You're being unreasonable. There are other things we can do to get in. Willie can climb the walls."

"In broad daylight? No, Matt." When he didn't release me, I jerked free. I hurried off, putting distance between us.

"India! INDIA!" He caught up to me, but I plunged into

the crowd, searching for someone. Staying out of Matt's reach.

He must have decided to let me go because I lost sight of him. I found Mr. Pyke, however, and told him my plan.

He liked it, but wasn't completely convinced we could manage it. "It will only work if all the magicians have a piece of their craft with them. I have no carpet."

"What about a woolen suit?" I spotted a woman with a knitted shawl draped around her shoulders. "Or that?"

He touched it, feeling the weight and quality. The woman turned, brows arched. He asked her if he could borrow it. She removed the shawl and watched as he spoke his moving spell into it. The shawl lifted off his outstretched hands and shot up into the air. It did a loop and dove into the crowd.

Those nearest ducked out of the way. Everyone else gasped then cried out as it flew up again, jerking this way and that above our heads. Mr. Pyke could move it but not control it; it was why his career as a pilot of magical flying carpets had been abandoned in such spectacular fashion.

I spoke Mr. Pyke's wool moving spell too and pictured the shawl flying at a steadier pace and along the path I wanted it to take. The words came easily to me. I remembered them well. The shawl floated above one of the constables on the porch. He tipped his head back, watching it. Too late, he realized what I intended. I directed the shawl to wrap around his body, pinning his arms to his sides.

The crowd cheered.

I stopped my chant and so did Mr. Pyke. The constable untangled himself from the shawl and kicked it away.

"Can you multiply that by a hundred?" Mr. Pyke asked.

"We'll soon find out."

Mr. Pyke and I moved through the crowd, teaching the magicians among us the words to the moving spell, instructing them how to change the relevant word and insert the magical name for their own craft. I learned the words they used for their magical craft too and memorized them. Hopefully I wouldn't need them, but it couldn't hurt. It took some time, but the fast learners helped the slower ones and before long, we had objects they'd brought with them lifting into the air and flying about above our heads.

Few stayed where they should, however. A wooden crucifix smacked Duke on the cheek. A silk handkerchief drifted on the breeze like an autumn leaf. The brim of a bowler hat would have sliced a man's head off if it had been made of steel instead of felt.

The crowd watched their flying creations with a sense of wonder and excitement. The chanting of the spells blended, creating their own kind of harmony. They grew louder as each magician vied with their neighbor to be heard. The artless watched on, reverently quiet at first, then whispering as they pointed, and finally gasping in delight and applauding.

They could all see the potential of this magic, and how we could use it to get inside Coyle's house.

But the flight paths were erratic. Some magicians could control their craft better than others, but not for long. I stood in the middle of the crowd of magicians, the artless now pushed to the outer circle, and concentrated on each flying object, moving them with my mind, speaking the spell only in my head.

But it took enormous effort. If I focused too long on a wooden spoon, the scarf lost momentum. The spool of cotton thread unraveled when I had to switch my focus onto a brick that could rise no higher than ankles, and that fell onto the nearest foot when I had to stop a small silver-handled dagger from plunging into Oscar's throat.

"Sorry," Marianne Folgate said as she picked it up from the ground. "I'm so sorry, Mrs. Glass."

"It's all right. But do you have something blunter to use instead?"

She removed a silver chain from around her neck. "It won't be all that useful."

"On the contrary. Chains are quite good at wrapping themselves around wrists. Believe me, I know."

"Look out!" Matt pushed me out of the way as a small bronze statue of an Egyptian goddess flew past. So he hadn't been far away, after all.

My lapse in concentration to speak to Marianne had resulted in utter chaos. Objects I'd been controlling, in a fashion, now dove and swooped or simply fell to the ground. They couldn't fly cleanly without my intervention. I had to make sure I was giving the spells my utmost attention if this was to work.

I looked up as a handkerchief floated above me, caught by the wind. A curtain at one of the upper windows fluttered. We were being watched.

"India." Matt caught my shoulders and forced me to look at him. He was in anguish. He desperately wanted me to leave, but he knew I had to stay. "If he has a gun…"

"If he shoots, he will have to be arrested. He'll give the police no choice. He won't shoot, Matt. Trust me. I'll be fine."

He pulled me to him in a fierce embrace and pressed his lips to my forehead. I scrunched his jacket in my fists and drew the scent of him into my lungs, then let go.

"You should stand back with the other artless," I said.

"Do you not know me at all?" It was said with a heavy dose of sarcasm and softened with a crooked smile.

"If you get hit on the head with a brick, it's not my fault." I stood on my toes and gave him a swift kiss.

A sergeant on the steps called for calm. "Stand down! Do not approach. Do not use your flying…things or there *will* be arrests!"

"Arrest Coyle! He's the villain, not us! Arrest Coyle! Arrest Coyle!"

The cry was taken up by the artless. The magicians joined in with their chanted spells that saw objects of all shapes, sizes and materials rise into the air at varying speeds.

Matt lay a hand gently on the back of my neck. "Do what you must before that brick knocks someone unconscious."

I directed the brick to land on the foot of one of the constables. He yelped and hopped on his good foot, which made everyone laugh. The resulting lack of concentration from the magicians sent objects flying in all directions. I quickly focused. I splashed Oscar's ink into the face of a sergeant, and covered the eyes of another with the handkerchief. But as I gave them my full attention, a collection of brass buttons rained down on the Mason family.

I lifted all five buttons with my mind's eye and sent them shooting towards the two constables nearest the door. They saw them coming and ducked. The buttons pinged against the wall like pellets released from a slingshot.

Moving five buttons took more concentration than I realized, and several other objects now fell out of the sky or flew off in all directions. There was no way I could control everything. There were too many constables to get past by either blinding them with woolen scarves or ink, or dropping bricks on their feet. I couldn't do that and open the door too. Besides, the door was locked. Perhaps we should break a window and Willie could climb through.

"Bloody hell!" Mr. Mirnov ducked as a miniature toy horse and cart came toward him at full speed.

It hurtled to the pavement and would have smashed if it didn't suddenly come to a halt in mid-air then slowly rise and settle on Mr. Mirnov's outstretched hand.

"You can control the flying spell?" I asked.

He looked past me. "It was not me. It was him."

I turned to see Fabian Charbonneau standing there, grasping an iron bar.

Matt moved to my side, drawing up to his full height. He glared at Fabian. The much smaller man cleared his throat then suddenly dashed out of the way of a flying silver chain.

I sent the chain back the way it had come.

Fabian eyed Matt carefully. "You need help, India."

"I can do it alone."

He watched the five buttons scatter. "I can unlock that door from here, or remove the hinges. I have no liking for Coyle. I want to see him brought to justice too. Let me assist you and see it happen."

I shook my head.

Matt stepped into my line of sight, turning his back to Fabian. Fabian, with his iron bar and his powerful iron magic. Matt was either too trusting or too foolish. He was rarely either of those things and it took me by surprise. "India, let him help."

"But what if he—?"

"I won't harm you or your husband," Fabian said. "If I wanted to, I could have done so already." He held up the iron bar. "Let me help, India. Let me make amends for my actions. Or try to."

"Nothing you do will make me forgive you."

He flinched as if I'd struck him. "What I did was unforgiveable. I know you would never have me now. I know there will never be another man for you after he is gone. But…let me do this. Let me help bring Coyle to justice before I leave for France."

He was leaving? That was some good news, at least.

"Stop!" I shouted. "Everyone, stop your spells!"

Objects fell to the ground or fluttered lightly, sending magicians, artless and policemen covering their heads or ducking out of the way. The resulting silence was like the tense calm of the storm as the eye passes through. We all knew it wasn't over.

"Fabian, open the door."

Instead of fashioning a key to fit in the lock as he'd once done to escape prison, he simply twisted the iron hinges with a murmured spell until they snapped. The door swung open on the hinged side.

The sergeant swore and directed his men to block our path.

"Ready, Fabian?" I waited for his nod, then called out, "Now!"

Objects lifted off the ground and darted in the air. I quickly controlled those closest to me while Fabian tore strips off the iron rod he'd brought with him and flung them, one at a time, at the policemen. They were small and sharp enough to distract and sting, but not to do any real harm. Between his iron and the other magical objects controlled by me, we forced the policemen down the stairs and away from the door.

Matt, Duke, Willie and Cyclops stormed up the steps and disappeared inside. I followed. Magical objects dropped once more now that I no longer controlled them. I heard Oscar giving orders, telling the crowd to surround the police and stop them coming after us. It was the best way, for now, but if reinforcements arrived, it could spell danger for the protestors.

Coyle's servants were nowhere to be seen. I suspected they were cowering in the service area, out of sight. We found Hope first, sitting in the drawing room, looking like a queen about to be led to her execution. Regal, but defeated. Mrs. Fry stood behind her, one hand resting on the back of the chair. The executioner.

We headed into the library.

Lord Coyle sat in the armchair in the small room. A fire raged in the grate. The library was stifling hot. He'd burned any evidence that might incriminate him, any letters or documents that proved he was involved in Goldman's murder or other illegal activities. I wasn't surprised, but I was disappointed.

He leaned back in his chair and lit a cigar. He didn't seem worried. Ill and tired, but not concerned. Why should he be when he'd just destroyed all the evidence against him?

We'd come to a dead end again and I didn't know where to go next.

But Matt did. "Everyone is against you now. Every magician, every member of the Collectors' Club. Your magical collection is worthless. Everyone is refusing to pay back their so-called debt. No one wants your advice or opinion. No one cares about you anymore. Speak to the witnesses you paid and have them retract their statements."

Coyle puffed on the cigar. "Why would I do that? What's in it for me?"

Matt opened the door to the secret chamber that hid Coyle's magical collection. The objects inside were in the same position as the last time I'd seen them. Matt gathered an armful and tossed them onto the fire.

"No!" Coyle heaved himself out of the chair and fell to his knees on the hearth. He reached in and removed a wooden pipe before it caught alight, but dropped it suddenly as it burned his fingers. He plucked out a brass bowl, a silver candlestick and a tray. The stack of paper caught alight, however.

"We're going to remove everything in your collection and return them to their owners or destroy them. Unless you do as we ask."

The lunge had cost Coyle. He coughed violently, sending gobs of spittle into his moustache. His body shook with the effort and he doubled over, a hand pressed to his chest. The episode lasted several seconds until he finally brought it under control. He tried to haul himself to his feet, but couldn't manage it.

"You think that threat will force me to free your friend?"

"We know you want him freed too. We know you're aware of his magic and want him to owe you a favor. A magical favor."

He settled onto his backside with a grunt. "Very good. You guessed correctly." He chuckled, which resulted in more phlegmy coughing. When it finally stopped, he wiped the back of his hand across his mouth and moustache. "You thought I'd never know he saved your life? You thought you could keep secrets from me? Ha!"

Matt removed more magical objects from the storeroom, this time taking only those made of flammable material. "Tell the witnesses you paid to say they saw Gabe the night of Goldman's murder to retract their statements and your collection will be saved."

Coyle's nostrils flared. He gazed at the items in Matt's hands as if they were his pets and he would be sorry to see them go. But see them go, he would. "I need Seaford's magic. I'm unwell. I'm not dying, but I will."

"We all will," I pointed out.

"Yes, but I'm not *finished*." He coughed again. "I have so much still to do with my life. So much more to achieve. If Seaford can make someone live longer, then why not me?"

"Gabe's magic is not yours to command," Matt said.

"Isn't it? Does he not want to live?" His moustache twitched with his cruel smile, if that's what the twist of his lips could be called. "I thought so. Tell him I will have the witnesses retract their statements, but he must promise me he'll repay me by using his magic to heal me."

"Agreed," I said quickly.

Matt's gaze slid to me but he remained silent. I suspected he hadn't been ready to give in so easily.

Coyle put a hand on the armchair and tried to get up, but failed. "Make sure Seaford understands that I can also undo it all if he doesn't keep his word. I can find new witnesses to say they saw him. I can ensure the police uncover new evidence of his guilt. I can send him back to prison like that." He snapped his fingers. "He'll be hanged before you even hear about it if he fails to do as I ask."

"He'll keep his side of the bargain," I assured him.

"You, black pirate, help me to my feet."

Cyclops crossed his arms.

"Get up yourself," Willie spat.

Matt stepped closer and crouched so that he was almost level with Coyle. "And I want Abercrombie."

"Ah. Of course you do. Then let him be my gift to you both."

Matt assisted him to stand and we waited while Coyle wrote letters to the witnesses. He then scrawled an address on a piece of paper. He handed the messages to Matt who read them before pocketing them.

That was it? He truly was handing Abercrombie over to us to face justice? It was almost too good to be true.

Perhaps it was.

Willie led the way out of the library and almost bumped into Hope, standing by the door. Her hands were clasped in front of her, the fingers twisting around each other. Her knuckles were white, her face too.

Her liquid gaze flew to Matt's. "Is your friend going to be saved?"

"Yes," Matt said.

She released an unsteady breath. "I am so relieved."

"You don't care about him," Willie sneered. She pushed past Hope and headed outside.

"Wife!" Coyle shouted from the library.

Hope flinched.

"Wife, get in here! We need to talk about the long life I have to look forward to, and your role in it. Mark me, things will change. Your expenditure, for one. And your loyalty to me, for another. Get in here, NOW!"

She picked up her skirts, but Matt grasped her elbow. "This is not your only choice."

Her chin trembled but she managed to rein in her emotions and school her features. With her head held high and her shoulders thrown back, she looked like a countess with the world at her feet again.

Matt let her go and she marched into the library and closed the door.

We passed Mrs. Fry in the entrance hall, smiling in triumph.

CHAPTER 18

*I*t was fortunate that we delivered Coyle's letters of instruction to the witnesses in person. The apprentice baker was reluctant to take his changed story to Scotland Yard.

Jack Crabb tore up the note and tossed it in Matt's face. The pieces settled on the front porch of the tenement building in which he lived and blew away in the breeze. "You tell his lordship it'll cost him extra."

Matt curled his hands into fists at his sides. "We don't work for Coyle. Nor do we have time for this. Those are your instructions and you will abide by them or see yourself arrested for giving false testimony."

Mr. Crabb crossed his arms over his bulging stomach and settled his feet apart. "His lordship won't let that happen."

Behind us, the carriage door opened. "Everything all right?" Cyclops asked.

Matt put up a hand, ordering them to stay back. "India, if you'd return to the pavement, I'd be grateful."

I stepped down the three steps and joined Cyclops, Duke and Willie beside the carriage.

"I'm not asking you, I'm ordering you," Matt said tightly. "Come with us to Scotland Yard and change your statement."

"Or what?"

"Or I'll make you."

The apprentice baker snickered. "You going to get your friends to rough me up?"

"I don't need their help."

"You reckon you can do it alone? You, a toff? I'll have you know, I was bare-knuckle middleweight champion before I gave it up to become a baker."

Willie grunted. "You might have been a middleweight before you became a baker, but you ain't now."

"Congratulations," Matt said to Mr. Crabb. "Now get in the carriage."

"Make me." Mr. Crabb puffed out his chest. Despite being shorter than Matt, he was considerably larger, particularly in his mid-section. He would be very difficult to move and he knew it.

"If you want to act like a child, then I'll treat you like one. Let's settle this like schoolboys, right there on the pavement."

Mr. Crabb peered past Matt at the gathering audience of local children and passersby who'd stopped to watch the confrontation. "All right. But it's got to be a fair fight. Your friends can't help."

"Of course."

"If I lose, I go with you to Scotland Yard and change my statement. If I win, what do I get?"

Matt removed his silver watch and held it up by the chain. It was his everyday watch, not his magical one. It was quite valuable. Mr. Crabb knew it, too. He rolled up his sleeves as he moved past Matt.

Matt handed his watch, jacket and waistcoat to me and loosened his tie. He rolled up his sleeves too, revealing strong forearms. But the baker's arms were thicker, thanks to his physically demanding work.

The crowd watching on began to choose favorites. Some made wagers. At the first punch thrown, a cheer rose, despite it missing its target. Matt had neatly side-stepped Mr. Crabb's strike.

He dodged the next punch too, and the next. Matt's feet

were light, always moving, and he read Mr. Crabb's actions easily.

"Stand still!" the baker growled.

Beside me, Willie chuckled.

With another snarl, Mr. Crabb charged at Matt and swung his fist. Matt nimbly stepped out of the way again and, as he did so, landed a punch on Mr. Crabb's belly with his left and another into the soft underside where jaw met throat with his right. The baker lost his balance and fell onto his backside on the pavement, wheezing. He did not get up.

Willie stood over him. "You're lucky he pulled back or your windpipe would be smashed."

Mr. Crabb clutched at his throat, alternately swallowing and drawing in deep breaths.

Matt put out his hand. "A deal's a deal."

The baker eyed the hand then reluctantly took it. Matt hauled him to his feet.

The journey to Scotland Yard was uneventful, and we waited while both witnesses spoke to the detective in charge of the Goldman case. When he emerged from his office, he glared at us with both hands stamped on his hips and shook his head in disbelief.

"Your friend is fortunate indeed." He pulled out his watch and opened the cover. "Less than two hours."

"Then you'd better hurry," Matt growled.

"Only the commissioner can issue a stay of execution."

"So let's speak to him. Now."

The commissioner issued the order without delay and a telegram was sent to Newgate Prison, where the execution was to be held. We didn't leave until we had a response that it had been received and Gabe was safe.

We were almost bowled over by a stampede of constables as we exited the telegraph room. Brockwell brought up the rear, barking orders.

"What's going on?" Matt asked.

"According to those witnesses, the true murderer lives a

mere stone's throw from here. We're going to arrest him now."

Matt and I glanced at one another. Coyle's instructions to the witnesses had simply told them to retract their statements about Gabe, not implicate someone else. He must have given this instruction earlier, perhaps even warning them from the beginning that they would need to change their story.

Matt indicated we should follow. "I believe I know where they're going."

I knew too. The lodgings on Tudor Street where Lord Coyle claimed Mr. Abercrombie could be found.

We arrived at the building at the same time as the police, something for which I was grateful. I doubted Matt would wait if we beat them. He'd gone quiet on the short journey to Tudor Street, but his thumb was busy, tapping away at his thigh. His anger simmered as he drew closer to confronting my attacker.

Matt ordered me to stay in the carriage with Duke, while he, Willie and Cyclops entered the building behind the police. After an excruciating two minutes, I gave in and followed them. Duke didn't protest. He agreed the scene must be secured by now.

Indeed it was. It was calm. Constables filed out of the flat and walked back down the stairs, unhurried and unconcerned. I rushed through the open door and stopped dead. For one horrific moment, I thought Matt had taken revenge on Abercrombie and killed him. There was blood all over the floor, reminiscent of the previous evening when Abercrombie had shot dead one of his men before turning the gun on me.

But Abercrombie hadn't been shot, he'd been stabbed in the stomach. And he wasn't dead.

He was dying, however. There was too much blood spilled for him to survive. His face was drained of color and the hand trying to stem the blood flow began to shake uncontrollably. His *pince nez* had fallen beside him. It was bent, the glass cracked and smeared with blood. Coyle must have sent an assassin here to kill the one man who could implicate him.

But the hired killer must have been interrupted by our arrival and failed to carry out the task properly.

Abercrombie's panicked gaze searched the faces above him, settling on me. "It was him," he whispered so softly I had to lean forward to hear. "He did this."

"Who?" Matt asked.

"He ordered me…to kill you. And…start…riots."

"Say his name?" Brockwell pressed.

Abercrombie's tongue lolled in his open mouth, searching for moisture. "Coyle."

Matt sat back on his haunches and glanced up at me. He didn't smile, but I sensed his triumph.

Brockwell scribbled something in his notebook, his pencil moving faster than I'd ever seen it. "You all heard that, yes?"

"Yes," I said on a breath. I felt numb. There was no sadness in my heart for this man, no sorrow as I lay watching him fade away in a pool of his own blood. I felt nothing. I couldn't believe it was over, that our troubles with him were at an end.

Willie let out a whoop, catching everyone unawares. She threw her arms around Duke then Cyclops and finally me. "We got him. We got Coyle! Ain't that right, Jasper? You got to arrest him now."

"I do." Brockwell passed his hand over Abercrombie's face, closing the dead eyes.

He'd died as we'd celebrated. I found it difficult to feel guilty about that, but a small part of me wished we'd shown a little more respect. Abercrombie may have brought this on himself, but dying in such violent circumstances, surrounded by people who hated him, was not an ending I'd wish on anyone.

Brockwell gave orders for two constables to see that the body was taken to the morgue, and then we left. He wasn't interested in delaying any more than we were.

We piled back into our carriage and Matt ordered Woodall to follow the police vehicle. Then he sat beside me and clasped my hand. He kissed it.

"Are you all right?" he asked.

I nodded, still not quite believing it. Abercrombie, dead, after all the suffering he'd caused me. It was hard to believe that we didn't have to worry about him anymore, or about Lord Coyle. One dead, the other about to be arrested. It was simply too wondrous for me to comprehend.

"We can't celebrate yet," Cyclops said in his no-nonsense way. "You've forgotten something."

"What do you mean?" Matt asked.

"Coyle will still demand Gabe fulfil his promise and use his magic to heal him."

"Won't do him any good in prison," Duke pointed out.

"If Coyle doesn't get what he bargained for, he'll see that Gabe is arrested for Goldman's murder again. He will have given instructions to the witnesses to change their statements back, or paid for others who are now waiting for their orders to implicate Gabe."

Willie scoffed. "He can't order anyone from prison, Cyclops. And anyway, the police will accept the current statements. They won't listen to anything different now."

"Are you certain about that? Are you willing to wager Gabe's life on it?"

Willie slouched in the seat, no mean feat when she was wedged between Duke and me.

"Coyle will want his repayment," Cyclops said again.

"Then he can have it," Matt said, smiling for the first time today. "We'll tell Gabe what's at stake. I'm sure he'll realize he has no choice and will fulfil his end of the bargain."

"Have you been hit on the head?" Willie cried. "Have you lost your marbles?"

Duke shook his head. "Matt, I don't think we should tell Gabe."

Cyclops disagreed. "We have to tell him. He has to make the decision himself, knowing all the facts."

"He won't do it." Willie was adamant. "He won't save Coyle's life."

Duke wasn't so sure.

I smiled back at Matt. "Shall we put them out of their misery?"

"I was going to let them discuss it a little longer, but it might be wise to end this now." He nodded at Duke and Willie. "It's too crowded in here for a fight."

Cyclops angled himself to look at Matt properly. "What are you talking about?"

Matt indicated me. "India will tell you."

I was happy to enlighten them. "Coyle demanded Gabe use his healing magic in return for being set free."

I was greeted with three shrugs and three expectant looks.

"Just Gabe," I pointed out. "Not me as well."

Understanding dawned.

Cyclops huffed out a gruff laugh. "I forgot. Gabe's magic doesn't last. He needs to put his magic into a watch and you need to speak the extension spell too."

"And Coyle doesn't know that," Duke said. "He thinks Gabe is enough." He barked a laugh. "I can't wait to see the look on his face when we tell him."

"We won't tell him," Matt said. "He needs to believe Gabe's magic is enough. I'm not counting on prison stopping him from manipulating events again. He can always go back on his word and have Gabe re-arrested, and I won't risk Gabe's freedom by trusting Coyle to keep to his side of the bargain."

Willie whooped again. "He's gonna die in a prison cell. And soon, I reckon. The man ain't a healthy specimen."

"Are we going to divert course and tell Gabe?" I asked.

Matt shook his head. "We'll fetch Gabe soon and have him do his part. But first, we watch Coyle get arrested."

* * *

THE CROWD outside the Coyle residence had dispersed, with only a few journalists and their photographers lingering, hoping to catch Lord or Lady Coyle leaving the house. They swarmed on us as we stepped out of the carriage, and Matt had to fend them off.

"Mrs. Glass! Mrs. Glass, do you wish to say something about the events that occurred here earlier?" asked one.

Another asked what we'd said to Coyle in our earlier meeting with him.

A photographer wanted me to stand still so he could capture my image.

The constables ordered them back and Matt ushered me up the steps. The door's broken hinges had already been replaced and the butler answered our knock by opening it a mere crack. He opened it wider on Brockwell's command and let us in.

"His lordship is indisposed at the moment." The butler tried valiantly to keep to protocol, but we were having none of it.

Matt checked the library, but it was empty. We headed up the stairs to the sound of the butler's protests.

Hope met us on the landing, Mrs. Fry beside her. Hope looked as beautiful as ever, not like the stoic but frightened shell we'd witnessed earlier. Her gaze was sharp again, her cheeks flushed with color, and she greeted us amiably. She showed no sign that the mob had worried her or that she feared her husband. She looked happy.

She reached out and took Matt's hand. "My husband is in his study. I haven't seen him since he entered it and closed the door, just after you left. Come. We'll greet him together."

I let them walk ahead of me and exchanged a glance with Willie. She lifted a shoulder in a shrug.

Brockwell barged into the study without knocking but stopped in the doorway.

Lord Coyle sat in his chair, bent over with his head resting on the desk. Vomit covered some papers and clogged his mouth. The enclosed room reeked of it.

My stomach churned. I fled and managed to reach a potted palm on the landing before emptying the contents of my stomach.

Matt joined me and offered his handkerchief. He ordered a maid I'd not seen to bring me a glass of lemonade, if there was any, and water if not. He steered me toward a chair.

"He's dead, isn't he?" I asked.

He nodded.

"His illness was too far along then."

He looked up to see Hope emerging from the study, a lace handkerchief pressed to her nose. "I didn't realize you were so sensitive, India. I thought your constitution stronger."

I didn't bother to tell her about the baby. I wanted to wait a little longer to be sure before we announced it. Besides, I didn't care enough about her opinion of me to correct her.

"An autopsy will prove how he died," Matt said, as if someone had asked.

I frowned at him, but he was staring at Hope.

She lowered the handkerchief. "Only if the death is suspicious and everyone knows my husband wasn't well. The coroner won't trouble himself with an old man who'd been ill for some time."

Matt conceded the point with a nod. "He has always been an unhealthy specimen, as Willie puts it. But he's only become sicker in the last few weeks. Since your marriage, as it happens."

She stiffened. "Why, Matt! What are you implying?"

Good lord. He *was* implying she'd killed him!

Matt looked to the study. "Brockwell is incredibly thorough and is not corruptible."

"The detective inspector is excellent at his job. But he's also a stickler for the rules and following orders. Isn't that so? And if his orders are *not* to raise concerns about the manner of my husband's death then that is what he'll do. You'd be wise not to as well. After all, his death is to everyone's advantage. Particularly yours."

I didn't need to see the body again to know she'd murdered her own husband. I didn't need to know anything about poisons to realize that's how she'd killed him. The admission was written in her face, in her triumphant smile,

243

and her sheer elation. She'd not even bothered to *attempt* to play the grieving widow. She was utterly certain she'd get away with it.

And she would.

It was in everyone's best interests to let the death be recorded as a combination of age and unhealthy living. Coyle wasn't just a thorn in our side, he would prove troublesome for the government too, I had no doubt. They would not push for a coroner's inquest. Besides, no one wanted to see Hope hang for murdering such a vile man. Not even me.

"You're my cousin," Matt said. "I only ever wanted to protect you from him."

The smile she gave him was condescending. It made my stomach churn again. "That's very sweet of you, Matt, but we both know your protection was not needed. It was as unnecessary today as it was on my wedding day. I've always known what I was getting into. Always." So Matt had been right about that too. She'd been poisoning him since the day they married, perhaps feeding him a little each day, enough to make him ill but not enough to kill him. That way, when the time came, no one would be surprised by his death.

I suddenly recalled that Charity gave Matt a parcel to deliver to Hope on the night he'd checked on her. That parcel most likely contained poison to replenish Hope's depleted stock. With Mrs. Fry watching her every move, Hope hadn't been able to acquire it herself so she'd somehow got word to her sister. Charity had been eager to help. Perhaps she'd known Hope's plan all along.

Hope must have planned this since her wedding day, perhaps even before. I wouldn't put it past her to plot his demise purely so she could inherit his wealth and gain her freedom. A rich widow could do as she pleased, whereas a daughter or wife had to obey her father or husband. Hope had played the game to win from the beginning and outsmarted Lord Coyle. Now she'd claimed her prize.

A maid arrived and handed me a glass of lemonade. She

bobbed a curtsy and was about to depart when her mistress barked at her to wait.

"Tell the other servants I wish to see them in the drawing room immediately," Hope said.

The girl bobbed another curtsy then departed through a hidden door in the paneled wall.

Mrs. Fry emerged from the study, her face ashen. She bobbed a demure curtsy. "May I offer my condolences, my lady."

Hope stepped toward her companion until she was mere inches away. She may have been shorter than Mrs. Fry, but with her outthrust chin and flashing eyes, she looked superior in every way. "You have five minutes to gather your things and get out of my house. One minute more and I'll have you thrown out."

Mrs. Fry picked up her skirts and raced up the stairs to her room.

Hope moved past us, a swan gliding across a lake as calmly as she pleased. "If you'll excuse me, I have to advise the servants of the situation." She headed down the stairs, only to stop and turn. "Tell your magician friends they're welcome to collect the things he bought from them whenever they wish. I have no desire to keep them."

Matt rested his hand on my shoulder as we watched her descend the stairs. Once she was gone from sight, we both released long-held breaths.

He held out a hand to me. "Are you well enough to leave?"

"You don't want to stay and see what Brockwell thinks about the manner in which Coyle died? I can send Woodall back for you."

He shook his head. "There's no reason to stay. It's all over now."

* * *

THERE WERE no repercussions for Hope. Brockwell confirmed two days later that the coroner had decided not to hold an inquest. Coyle's death was officially recorded as 'Visitation by God', a common way to explain a death by natural causes. From the way he almost spat out the words, it was clear Brockwell was unhappy with the verdict. He knew Hope murdered her husband, but his hands were tied. The commissioner had ordered him not to raise his concerns. Just as Hope guessed, Brockwell wouldn't disobey his superior. Not over the death of someone like Coyle.

Brockwell also confirmed that Mr. Hendry had not been found, despite a thorough search of the city. It was likely Coyle had given him access to a secret property as well as money, and helped him change his name to avoid detection. Being a magician, Hendry was more important to Coyle than Abercrombie.

The following morning, I met with the prime minister and cabinet again to write down details of new policies and taxes for so-called luxury goods, which was just another name for magician-made products. The newspapers had all been apprised of how magic worked, and they'd reported that it didn't last long. It had gone some way to stem the desire for magician-made items, but not entirely. The wealthy still clamored for them.

Within a week of Coyle's death, the city was calmer. The riots had ended and tensions no longer boiled over. Sometimes an argument broke out between a magician and his nearest artless neighbor, but those never escalated. The guilds, worried about their own relevance in the future, had agreed to welcome magicians into the fold and grant them licenses to trade. A surprising side-benefit was the inclusion of women in their new bylaws.

To everyone's amazement, several artless and magicians took a leaf out of Mr. Pyke and Mr. Fuller's book and formed new partnerships. With magicians so used to hiding, terrified of attracting attention, many didn't have large-scale operations set up for manufacture, whereas some artless did. It made sense for them to add a luxury product to their catalog to expand their business. Some magicians were only too happy to make a superior product exclusively for them.

The city may have quieted, but our own household was again thrown into a spin. There had been so many deaths of late, but a mere week after Lord Coyle died, there was one more.

Gabe and Nancy called on us for afternoon tea and a private consultation. Although I'd already been thoroughly checked by a midwife, Matt insisted Gabe also make sure the baby progressed.

With the consultation over, Gabe held out his hand to me and assisted me to sit up. "I see no reason to doubt the baby is growing strongly."

I blew out a measured breath and glanced at Matt. He placed a hand on the back of my neck and gently massaged. "And the effect of the magic?" I asked, tapping my chest where my watch with the cracked face and healing magic was safely tucked away in a pocket sewn into my corset.

Gabe patted my hand. "We won't know until the baby is born, so try not to worry."

That was easier said than done. Matt sat on the bed beside me and drew me into his arms. He touched my chin as it began to wobble. "Whatever happens, no matter how the magic has affected the baby, nothing changes. We'll love him or her with all our hearts, and we'll be all the better for being a family of three."

I nodded at the door. "I believe there are several people waiting in the drawing room for us who'd disagree that baby makes three. We'll be eight, at least."

He laughed softly and pressed his forehead to mine.

Gabe cleared his throat. "Before you go, I want to thank you both properly for what you did."

"You wouldn't have been in trouble in the first place if it weren't for us," Matt pointed out. "Coyle's spy wouldn't have reported your magic if you hadn't saved my life."

"That may be true, but you put your own lives in danger

to help me escape, and you were a good friend to Nancy in my absence." He took my hand and kissed it. "I was growing used to the idea of moving to America while in that hotel, but it was simply desperation speaking. Rest assured, we've decided to stay in London. Neither of us want to leave the hospital. And, as a thank you to you both, I also want to assure you that my magic is available to you, until we are all in our dotage."

Matt shook his hand. "Thank you, Gabe. Hopefully we won't need to trouble you. The magic in our watches feels strong. I'd wager it'll be some time before it fades."

As if it had heard, I felt my watch grow warmer through the fabric of the pocket.

We returned to the drawing room where Willie was entertaining Nancy with tales of her exploits in America, and Duke was interjecting with the real version, much to Willie's annoyance and Nancy's amusement. Aunt Letitia listened in, occasionally scoffing or rolling her eyes. Being a Sunday and Cyclops's day off, he and Catherine were also present. It was the perfect time to tell them officially about the baby. Only those who'd been with me as I lay dying knew. We'd kept it from the others.

Except someone was missing. "Matt, will you see if Chronos is up to joining us?"

He left and returned a few moments later, looking grave.

I hurried to his side, suddenly feeling sick to my bones. "Where's Chronos?"

"I'm here, I'm here." My grandfather limped in with the aid of a walking stick, and waved away Matt when he offered to assist him. "Stop treating me like an old man."

"You are an old man, and a cantankerous one at that." I stopped him and hugged him. "But you're my family, and I love you dearly."

His face softened and his eyes turned misty. "I love you too, Granddaughter." He patted my cheek. "Is something amiss?"

"No, nothing. But Matt and I have an announcement to make, so go and join the others."

"I already know about that." His gaze narrowed. "Or is it something else? Has Seaford agreed to teach his future children his medical magic?"

"Good lord, he and Nancy aren't even married yet." I took his hand and placed it on my arm. "Now, let me assist you if you don't want Matt's help."

He grudgingly allowed me to guide him to the nearest chair, vacated by Cyclops. Cyclops went to stand behind Catherine and placed a hand on her shoulder. They exchanged warm smiles.

I sat too, and Matt came to stand alongside me. He didn't smile, however. The air of gravity that had come over him was at odds with his earlier good mood. "Matt? Is something the matter?"

He held out his hand to me and shrugged off his somberness. He replaced it with a genuine smile. "Before we feast on Mrs. Potter's cakes and confections, India has an announcement to make." He indicated I should continue.

I smiled at my family and friends. "Indeed I do. I'm with child."

Catherine leaped up and threw her arms around me. "Congratulations! I knew it! Didn't I say it, Nate?"

Cyclops was too busy embracing Matt to comment. Rounds of hugs and congratulations followed, even from those who already knew. Since we hadn't mentioned it to them again, they'd perhaps assumed I'd made a mistake.

Aunt Letitia held out her hands to me, grinning from ear to ear. "I knew it would work."

I frowned. "Knew what would work?"

"It's me you have to thank," she said, indicating my belly.

Willie leaned close to me and whispered. "Will you tell her that's not how babies are made or can I?"

I nudged her away with my elbow lest I start to giggle. "What do you mean, Aunt?"

"If I hadn't stepped in, who knows how long it would have taken?"

Matt came up behind me and placed a hand on my lower back. "What *are* you talking about?"

Aunt Letitia gave him a smug smile. "I went to see a woman about India's inability to conceive, and she gave me some herbal therapies. I've been placing them in her hot chocolate from time to time."

"That's why it tasted bitter." I thought back to the times she'd made me a pot of chocolate herself. If I was right with my calculations, then Aunt Letitia's remedies hadn't been of any help. I was already pregnant by then. "I hope you didn't spend much to buy them."

She waved off my concern. "I wonder if it was the herbs that did the trick or the mouse."

I gasped. "That was you! *You* put a dead mouse under my pillow! I blamed Willie for that."

"Understandable," Duke muttered.

Willie poked her tongue out at him.

"Aunt," Matt chided. "That wasn't nice."

Aunt Letitia lifted a shoulder in a dainty shrug. "But it worked, didn't it?"

He was about to set her straight but I took his arm and squeezed. "I threw the mouse away before I slept on it," I told her.

"Then it was definitely the herbs." She clapped her hands. "Oh, I am so thrilled. A little baby to dote on...how marvelous."

"A magician baby," Chronos said with wonder in his voice. "I hope he or she will be as strong as you, India. Stronger, even."

"He'll quite possibly be weaker, or artless altogether given that Matt isn't a magician," I said.

Chronos gave Matt an accusatory glare.

"And that is quite all right with us and it will be for you too unless you wish to move out of this house and not be a part of the baby's life."

He closed his mouth with an audible clack of back teeth and had the decency to look sheepish.

Aunt Letitia hadn't been listening to the exchange. Her eyes were bright as she patted my hand again. "You know, India, Letitia is an old family name."

Willie gave her a skeptical look. "Then why didn't Rycroft use it for one of his girls?"

"Because my horrid sister-in-law insisted on those ridiculous names. She has no sense of tradition."

Chronos tapped his walking stick into the floor to get our attention. "Gideon has been used in our family for generations too. Gideon Glass doesn't have the same ring to it as Gideon Steele, but it's still a fine name."

Aunt Letitia made a miffed sound through her nose. "It's not a suitable name for the Rycroft heir, I'm afraid. What about Henry, after Matthew's father?"

"I thought his name was Harry," Willie said.

"Harry is what most Henrys are called in England."

"Huh."

Matt took Aunt Letitia's hand and she instantly quieted. Her face fell. She'd seen the same earnest gravity in his eyes that I had. He steered her toward a chair and gently lowered her onto it. He crouched before her, still holding her hand.

"I'm afraid I have some bad news, Aunt."

CHAPTER 19

*M*att pulled out a letter from his pocket and unfolded it. "This just arrived from Aunt Beatrice. She wished to inform me that Uncle Richard died peacefully in his sleep last night."

Aunt Letitia's jaw went slack. I rushed to her side, worried the news would shock her into thinking she was in the past. But she merely closed her mouth and flattened her hands on her lap. Her eyes remained dry and clear as she regarded Matt.

"You're Lord Rycroft now," she said.

Shock rippled across Matt's features, bringing a small smile to his aunt's face. He had not realized the full implication of his uncle's death. It wasn't just the gaining of a title, it was the gaining of an estate and the manor house with it, as well as the tenant farms and the farmers who worked his land. It was all the responsibilities of being a nobleman within a tight-knit rural community, and the privileges that went with the title. He'd expected to learn how to be Lord Rycroft in the coming years, but his uncle's untimely death had pulled the rug out from under him. He looked utterly bewildered by the prospect.

Aunt Letitia patted his cheek. "You should consider moving to Rycroft Hall before the baby comes, particularly if

Mr. Steele is staying with us." She looked around the drawing room. "While this house is lovely, it's already bursting at the seams."

"We can't move in," Matt said. "Not while Aunt Beatrice and Charity live there. It's their home. This is ours."

She smiled at him as if indulging a child. "Rycroft Hall *is* your home now."

Matt shook his head. "It's just a house. My home is where my wife is, and where all of you are."

Later, as we lay in bed with Matt's hand resting over my stomach and his head on my chest, I stroked his hair. "Are you all right?" I asked. "The news of your uncle's death has rattled you."

His thumb caressed my still flat belly. "It was a lot to take in. There's so much to consider." He turned to look up at me. "I'm not sure I'm ready to be landed gentry."

"You don't have to get used to it all at once. The staff will keep the place going until you're ready. Address them at the funeral to ease their minds and tell them you'll visit properly at a later date. That'll buy you some time, and them too."

"I need to also speak to Aunt Beatrice about her future, and Charity's. I want her to know it's their home for as long as they live."

Rycroft Hall was a large house. So large that we could live separate lives there from his aunt and cousin, even with Aunt Letitia, my grandfather, Willie, Duke and the baby with us. Yet the idea of living under the same roof as them didn't appeal to me.

Aunt Letitia was right, however. The Mayfair house was too small for a growing family. Other arrangements would need to be made. "You have so much on your plate already. Would you like me to speak to Lady Rycroft?"

He propped himself up on his elbow and regarded me. "*Dowager* Lady Rycroft. You're Lady Rycroft now."

Good lord. So I was. I giggled, partly because it seemed so ridiculous that the daughter of a watchmaker could rise to such heights, and partly because Matt was kissing his way from my throat to my belly and his lips tickled.

* * *

I HARDLY SPOKE to Beatrice at the funeral at Rycroft Hall. She was too busy with arrangements and welcoming old friends into her home for the duration. I tried to help where I could, but I felt as though I was getting in the way. She knew every inch of that house, which member of staff should be assigned which tasks, where they all should be, the protocols and traditions. Learning it all would take some time. By the end of our visit, I was glad to return to the familiar streets of London. It might be noisy, grimy and full of scoundrels at all levels of society, but it was my home.

After the funeral, my days were occupied helping Catherine prepare for her wedding day. A welcome relief from the whirlwind came in the form of an invitation to a Collectors' Club meeting. Indeed, the fact that I did welcome it surprised me. I'd never enjoyed the events much. I'd always felt as though I were a freak at the show. But the faces were familiar to me and most of them were friendly and often pleased to see me. Even the Delanceys, who hosted the latest event, were not as irksome as usual.

There were no lectures scheduled for the evening, no meeting agenda. It was purely social, and I made sure to speak to as many people as I could. All had heard about the baby and speculated on his or her magical strength. A few cast irritated glances at Matt for potentially diluting our baby's magic, but he pretended not to notice. Indeed, he spent much of the evening talking to Professor Nash, Mr. Delancey and Oscar.

"I believe congratulations are in order, Lady Rycroft."

It took me a moment to realize Louisa spoke to me. I still wasn't used to the title. "Please continue to call me India."

She smiled. "I'm so pleased you consider me friend enough to do so."

I forced a smile in return and refrained from telling her I didn't like her and I only wished to be called India because I didn't feel like Lady Rycroft. "Have you been well, Louisa?"

It was a polite question, asked many times throughout the day of friends and acquaintances, without expecting more than a nominal response. But Louisa's face suddenly fell and her gaze grew distant, sad.

I suspected Fabian's departure was to blame. He had left London a week earlier, allowing me to finally breathe a little easier. I'd never be able to trust him again after his attempts on Matt's life and having him living in the same city as us gave me cause to worry. When he left, the last of our troubles left with him. It was like a weight had been lifted from my shoulders.

"I'm well enough," Louisa said with a dull smile that didn't reach her eyes. "I'm pleased for your happy news. I do hope the baby is a magician."

"It doesn't concern us, either way." I don't know why I bothered. She, and others like her, would never be convinced that a child without magical abilities would be loved as much as a child with powers.

"Have you heard from Fabian?" she asked suddenly.

"No. Nor do I expect to."

She sighed and her gaze fell on Oscar. She sighed again, as if coming to a conclusion she didn't particularly like. "Do you think you can put in a good word for me?"

"To Oscar?" Good lord, was she honestly considering asking him to court her again? "Of course I will. Perhaps I'll do it now." I had no interest in mentioning her to Oscar at all, but it was the easiest and politest way to remove myself from her presence.

Oscar greeted me with an arched brow. "Did she ask you to tell me she and I are a good match?"

"In a way. Have you spoken to her recently?"

"I have, and I rejected her advances."

"Again? Good lord, will she ever give up?"

He smiled slyly. "I believe she will, soon. I have a few

magician acquaintances ready to meet her. All are bachelors looking for a wife who comes with money and influence."

"And she will get the magician husband and perhaps even the magician children she always wanted. Are the men not concerned about diluting their magical lineage?"

"No." He looked at Louisa, now speaking to two ladies. He huffed out a humorless laugh. "She is certainly a prize, for some. Of course, any husband she takes will have to contend with her being in love with another." He lifted his glass of port in salute, a wicked gleam in his eye. He wasn't in the least sad about their relationship falling apart.

"And what about you?" I asked. "Will you look for a wife now and settle down? Someone less like Louisa and more like you?"

"We'll see where life takes me. I'm not going in search of a wife, but if I fall in love, then so be it. I've come to the belief that it's better to remain a bachelor than be trapped in a love-less marriage."

I took Matt's arm. "How true."

"Anyway, an intriguing prospect has presented itself. One I must take advantage of or I'll regret it."

"Oh?"

He nodded at Professor Nash, talking to Matt and Mr. Delancey about financial matters. When Matt noticed I was listening, he broke off the conversation.

"I've just agreed to donate a sum of money to Professor Nash's new project," he said. "I hope you don't mind."

Mr. Delancey pulled a face. "Don't ask your wife, man! Good lord. She'll expect you to consult her on how you wear your whiskers, next."

"Not at all," I said smoothly. "My husband already knows that I dislike moustaches and beards. He agreed not to grow them."

Mr. Delancey stared at me, his glass tilted to the side. Matt righted it so that it didn't spill on the Aubusson carpet.

"My wife has an excellent business sense," Matt said. "She owns property in her own right and ran a business and household for a number of years before we met. Besides, I believe this venture is one that will be of particular interest to her."

Mr. Delancey snorted and snuffled. "Quite right, quite right."

"What is the business venture?" I asked.

The professor beamed. "May I be the one to tell her?" At Matt's nod, he said, "I'm going to travel the world in search of books, manuscripts and other written material on the subject of magic. I'll house the purchases in a library here in London."

"How exciting for you."

"Exciting for everyone! Finally, information about magic will be stored in one place, available for anyone to research. Now that magic is no longer a secret, it makes sense to study it and try to understand it. Of course, it's going to take me quite some time to amass something worthy of even being called a library." He chuckled. "But I find I'm rather looking forward to it. Now that Mr. Glass—I mean Lord Rycroft—and Mr. Delancey have agreed to partially fund it, I'll give my notice at the college. I have some savings put aside and will use that to cover my own travel expenses."

I hadn't taken him for an adventurous spirit, but he certainly looked enthused by the idea. I suspected that learning about new places appealed to his inquisitive nature as much as the collection of books. He was rather a delicate man, however, and I couldn't imagine him continuing with an adventure the moment it became too hard. I wasn't sure he was suited to traveling around the world, visiting far off lands that were nothing like England.

"Oscar is going to help me, aren't you, Barratt?"

"I am indeed." Oscar raised his port glass. "That was the intriguing prospect I referred to earlier, India. I'm looking forward to it."

I smiled, feeling enthused now too. With a practical companion like Oscar at his side, taking care of the day to day tasks of international travel, the professor could concentrate on what he did best—research.

Mrs. Delancey stood in the middle of the drawing room and called for our attention in a voice that wouldn't have been out of place on a battlefield. "Listen to me, please! Everyone!" When the room quieted, she bestowed a smile on her guests. "Thank you all for coming tonight. It's such a pleasure to see all your lovely faces. It's particularly wonderful of you to join us, Lady Rycroft." She emphasized the title, just in case there were those present who didn't know Matt had recently inherited. "I haven't just called you all here for idle chatter, however. There are important matters to discuss. Namely, what to do now that magic isn't a secret. Do we carry on as if nothing changes? If we do change, what will be our new aim?"

Matt leaned closer to me. "Do you want to stay for this?"

"I'd rather have all my teeth pulled out."

Mrs. Delancey picked up a piece of paper and pencil from the table at her side. "Let's settle on an agenda here and now."

Neither of us wanted to wait for our hostess to be free, so we thanked her husband and saw ourselves out.

"I didn't know she was such an organizer," Matt said as we settled into the carriage. "I always thought her vapid."

"She is a society hostess. She might be vapid, but she can organize a charity event or party at a moment's notice. This isn't much different."

"Do you think the club will continue?"

I considered it a moment then couldn't help my smile. "I find I don't really care."

He smiled too, but his held a hint of wickedness. He circled me in his arms and nudged the collar of my velvet cloak aside. "Good," he murmured against my throat. "Because you look exquisite and I have you all to myself."

* * *

THE WEDDING of Cyclops to Catherine was held in high summer, a month before Gabe and Nancy married. Both occasions were joyous, filled with love and friendship, and promises of a bright future. Cyclops moved into the rooms above Catherine and Ronnie's shop with his new bride. His departure from number sixteen Park Street was another stage in our lives, neither a happy one nor sad. It was both an ending and a beginning, and it gave Matt and I the impetus to finally speak to his Aunt Beatrice about Rycroft Hall. He'd been putting it off, citing his aunt's mourning, but it could be delayed no longer.

We traveled by rail then hired a local man to drive us to the estate. The entire journey only took a few hours. Although we'd been there before, I appreciated it as the mistress this time. Situated behind a tall hedge and set back from the road, we suddenly came across the estate as we rounded the bend. The iron gates set between ancient, moss covered stone piers were thrown open in welcome. The long drive led us past a lake and a shady woodland and finally through a gatehouse and into the walled garden. The smooth lawns and symmetrical garden beds with matching plants were the sort of cultivated perfection I expected from the dowager, but the wisteria vine rambling unchecked over part of the stone wall spoke of a gardener with a free spirit.

A soft pink climbing rose was in full bloom to one side of the house's entrance, adding color to the graceful gray stone and inviting us inside. The house had been home to nobility since the seventeenth century; it had been purchased by Matt's great grandfather. Its nine bedrooms were more than enough for us, as well as Matt's Aunt Beatrice and cousin, Charity. Still, I wouldn't be able to avoid them altogether.

The dowager greeted us in the magnificent drawing room with its golden drapes and furnishings, and soft yellow walls with gilded chandelier dripping from an intricately plastered ceiling. Her three daughters sat on the sofa, reminding me of the days when I'd first met them. Hope occupied prime position on the left, however, despite being the youngest. Her marriage to Lord Coyle had boosted her into first place in her mother's eyes. Next came Charity, the middle child, and on the right was Patience, whose husband had been stripped of his title when an older half-brother stepped forward and claimed the Cox barony. Patience was just Mrs. Swinsbury now, and she looked as though she'd rather be anywhere else but sitting on the sofa alongside her sisters.

She brightened upon seeing us and hugged me fiercely. We hadn't seen her since her father's funeral, and we'd not had much of an opportunity to speak then.

"You look well, India," she said, indicating my swelling belly. "Well and happy."

"I am. And you?"

She leaned in. "I will be just as soon as I leave here."

"Patience," her mother snapped. "Sit. They're not here to see you."

Patience rolled her eyes but dutifully sat.

Matt, Aunt Letitia and I greeted each of them in turn. I was surprised at how different they all seemed. Hope had always been the prettiest but had faded during her marriage. Now, she glowed with vitality once more. Even Charity looked upon us all with a measure of amusement, as if someone had said a joke.

A butler brought in refreshments and we exchanged pleasantries until Aunt Beatrice offered to take us on a tour of the house. "You didn't see all of the rooms on your previous visits. I trust you'll be happy with them all."

"I'm sure we will be," Matt said.

"I had bathrooms installed and other modern amenities," she went on as we exited the drawing room. "But I've otherwise left it. My late husband preferred it that way."

For once, I was in agreement with Matt's uncle. I liked the old feel of the house with its paneled walls, enormous fireplaces, and decorative plasterwork on the ceilings. The furniture was mostly of the spindly, elegant style of the Georgians rather than the sturdier fashion of the moment, but that suited the house. Indeed, what I'd seen so far was in impeccable condition.

"I won't change a thing," I said as I peered up at the portrait of one of Matt's female ancestors dressed in a silvery blue Regency ball gown. She had the sort of face one could study for hours, with warm gray eyes and a smile that hinted at secrets.

"Really? Why not?" The dowager pulled a face at the next portrait hanging on the stairwell wall. It showed a commanding fellow in military uniform sporting a disapproving scowl. The painting was saved by the brown and white dog with soulful eyes at the gentleman's side.

"You must continue to feel at home here," I said as we continued up the stairs.

"Whatever for? It's your home now, India. Isn't that why you're here? To look over it and see what needs improving?"

"I can't see anything that requires improvement. Anyway, I don't want you to feel as though you don't belong."

She turned a vase on the table on the landing to show off the creamy yellow roses to their fullest advantage. "I never belonged here. It was always my husband's home. I'll be glad to put the place behind me."

Matt's pace quickened. "You're not going to continue to live here?"

"Good lord, no. Why would I do that when the house in London is available? London is where my friends are. It's so dull here, away from everyone and everything. Entertainment here consists of having the local vicar and his wife to tea once a week, and believe me, you'll regret extending the invitation to them the moment you meet them."

We had met them at the funeral. They both seemed lovely. I suspected Beatrice and I had quite different views on what made a conversation dull.

"So you and Charity won't be staying on once we move in?" I needed to make absolutely certain before I allowed my heart to sing.

"My dear, we're only here to welcome you officially, then it's back to London on the first train tomorrow morning."

Aunt Letitia's hands clasped my arm. "My prayers have been answered."

"We have to be home in time to get ready for the opera," Beatrice went on. "We've been invited to sit in Lord and Lady Haversmith's box. It's going to be quite the evening. I purchased a new gown for the occasion and Hope will lend me her emeralds, won't you, dearest?"

"Actually I'm wearing the emeralds myself tomorrow night," Hope said. "I'm also attending the opera."

Her mother's smile slipped. "What about the Coyle diamonds?"

"Being cleaned."

Her mother's lips pinched. I suspected she knew her daughter was purposely thwarting her attempts to borrow jewelry. Hope smiled serenely, as if she were still the dutiful daughter. But her eyes held a hard gleam to them that hadn't been there in the months before her marriage. I shivered. Beneath the perfect façade lurked the heart of a cold-blooded killer.

Patience clicked her tongue. "Listen to you both. Does it not occur to you that you're still in full mourning for your husbands? If you must go to the opera, you shouldn't be wearing any jewelry at all, let alone emeralds or diamonds."

"I'll wear a black gown," Hope said. "Even though it doesn't go well with my complexion."

"But it matches your soul," Charity sneered.

Hope bristled. Her nostrils flared like a bull about to charge. "Mother, the Haversmiths have a son, don't they?"

"Three," Beatrice said.

"The third one is single, is he not? You should inquire if he's going to the opera too. Make a point of it, in fact."

"The lad is of marriageable age, it's true, but he's the *third* son." Beatrice wrinkled her nose. "He's also lame and half blind, so the army is out of the question. I'm afraid it'll be an ecclesiastical career for him."

"Beggars can't be choosers." Hope bestowed a twisted smile on her middle sister.

Charity looked as though she wanted to choke her with her bare hands. So much for the sisterly affection she'd shown Hope when she snuck the poison in to her room.

We continued with the tour, and I mentally assigned bedrooms to everyone. Aunt Letitia already had a large suite assigned to her, but I suspected Chronos would appreciate the only one positioned on the ground floor. It wasn't large, but it was close to the kitchen and he could use the adjoining sitting room as a work room. He'd be happy to spend his days tinkering and making new friends in the village. He'd never quite recovered after using his magic to save me. I doubted his health would improve now. It was the one tragedy to come out of that entire time, and it was not one I could fix. What was done was done. All we could do was be there for Chronos when he needed us and make him as comfortable as possible. Thankfully his mind was as sharp as ever.

Although I wasn't yet sure if Duke and Willie were moving to the country with us, I was quite sure I knew which rooms they would choose. They were two of the largest and had beautiful views of the rolling hills and the vast sky. They were also next to each other. As much as they bickered, they were like brother and sister, and liked one another's company but loathed admitting it.

We finished the tour in the garden, having not been shown any of the service area or the outbuildings. According to Beatrice, they weren't important. She'd rarely visited them in all her years. I would make a point of seeing them before we left, as well as meet the below stairs servants and the gardeners.

The tour was over, but I wasn't yet ready to go inside. The day was warm and the garden smelled so lovely. For someone used to the endless gray of London, the colors were a revelation. I didn't know grass could be so green as to hurt the eyes, or the sky so blue you wanted to reach out and touch it to see if it was real.

"Would you like to stay out here for another turn around the garden?" Matt asked, reading my mind.

I hooked my arm through his. "Yes, please." I wanted to be alone with him, but propriety dictated I ask the others to join us.

Aunt Letitia excused herself, while Hope refused too. I suspected she didn't want to be alone with us these days. It was hard to look her in the eye, knowing what we knew. Patience must have sensed that we wished to be alone and also made her excuses.

"Come with me, Mother, Charity," she said. "I have a few moments to talk before I go to the station to meet Byron and the children."

Her mother didn't respond but she did leave with her, with Charity walking a few feet behind, as usual. At the lavender bush, Beatrice stopped and waited for her middle daughter to catch up. "I've been thinking about the Haversmith boy, and I believe Hope is right. He'd make an excellent husband for you."

"No!" Charity stamped her foot. "I don't *want* to marry a lame, blind vicar. I'd rather *die*!"

"Pipe down, Child. It would be a good match. His father is a marquess, for goodness' sake! He may not be entitled to much, but you never know, his older brothers could die before they have sons."

"I will *not* marry him!"

Her mother grabbed her arm and dragged her away. "You will flirt with him at the opera and that's that. He may not be of the caliber that Lord Coyle was, and no one would expect you to do better than Hope, but it would certainly be a better match than the one Patience made."

Patience stopped mid-step. She was facing away from us so I couldn't see her expression, but her shoulders sagged, her head lowered.

I glanced at Matt and indicated I would go to her. But then Patience closed her fists at her sides and stormed after her mother and sister. She blocked their path, rounding on them.

"You're wrong, Mother. I made the best marriage of all, and I include yours in that. Ours is a love match. We want to be together, all the time, not tear one another apart with snide comments or the silent treatment. But I don't expect you to agree that I have the best marriage, because you are incapable of knowing love when you see it. All three of you are. I pity you. I wouldn't give up the man who cherishes me for all the jewels or titles in the world. Now, if you'll excuse me, I have to collect my family from the station. And if I so much as hear one cruel word from any of you tonight, we will never see you again."

She strode back toward Matt and me, apologized, and strode off toward the stables and coach house.

I watched her mother leave with Charity and wondered if Beatrice cared a whit about Patience's threat. From her stiff back, I suspected it had hit home, but I doubted it would change her opinion of her eldest daughter and son-in-law. Patience was right. Beatrice was incapable of love. Simply realizing that meant sweet, sensitive Patience could stop trying to please her and move on with her life. She would be the happier for it, and I couldn't be more gratified to see her finally stand up to the dragon.

Matt took my hand and steered me out of the walled garden toward the woods and lake. The chirp of insects and croak of frogs filled the air with their song, and the sun streaming between the tree canopies warmed my skin. He picked a frilly pink Dianthus and tucked it into my hair then led me to the stone bridge crossing the narrowest part of the lake. We stopped half way to survey our new home. The scene was like a painting with the gabled rooftop of the house framed by the trees and spires of purple Lythrum in the foreground fringing the crystal waters of the lake. A duck paddled past, unhurried, proving we hadn't fallen inside a masterpiece after all.

Matt stood behind me and circled me in his arms. He rested his chin on the top of my head and settled a hand on my belly. "Will you miss London?" he asked.

"Yes. But it's only a few hours away by train, and I can visit when I get the urge." I folded my arms over his. "Besides, this is where I want to bring up our child. This is where I want to make my new home. It's perfect, Matt. Just perfect."

He turned me around and settled his hands on my hips. His gaze softened and that familiar intense look that I cherished drank me in. No words were necessary, and he simply kissed me with a tenderness that filled my heart and soul.

EPILOGUE

"*Y*ou're not doing it properly!" Willie put down her side of the trunk and rounded it to join Duke who set his end down. "Hold it here." She indicated where she'd placed her hands. "And lift with your legs." She performed a little squat to show him.

He nudged her aside. "*You* lift with your legs, I'll lift with my arms. That's where my strength is."

"And your brain."

"What brain?" Cyclops waved them both off and picked up the trunk. He carried it outside to the cart without assistance.

Catherine admired his efforts with a little smile, her gaze heated.

She followed me into the drawing room and lowered herself onto the sofa, her hand supporting her pregnant belly. Her baby was due in a month and she was under strict instructions not to help with the packing and moving. There was little to pack anyway, just some personal items, as the furniture was staying at Rycroft Hall and we wanted to keep the Park Street house furnished for our city visits.

We'd decided to wait until after the baby was born in February to move. Matt and I both felt more at ease if Gabe attended the birth, just in case there was a magical medical emergency. All had gone smoothly, however.

Cyclops returned, bringing Duke, Willie and Brockwell with him. The detective inspector looked awkward, as if he wished to be anywhere but here. I made a point of going up to him and asking him what the matter was.

He scratched his sideburns. "I don't like goodbyes."

"This isn't goodbye. Matt and I will visit London frequently."

His gaze shifted to Willie, now talking with Catherine and Cyclops.

"She will visit even more than us, I'm sure of it."

"It's not that. I asked her to move in with me."

"Oh. I take it she refused."

"Not outright. She said she needed to think about it. She says moving in together is as good as being married, and she doesn't want to be married."

The Romany woman's prediction of Willie having two marriages sprang to mind, but I kept my mouth shut. I didn't think it would cheer Brockwell to hear it again in light of what he'd just told me. Besides, I wasn't even sure I believed in fortune telling.

"I don't care about that," he went on. "She can live wherever she wants. I just wish she didn't choose to live so far away."

"You're more than welcome to visit her at Rycroft Hall whenever you can take leave." I grasped his arm and squeezed. "Anyway, I give it a month before she decides the countryside is not for her. She needs to be constantly amused, and there isn't a single gambling den for miles about."

He nodded thoughtfully, and a look of contentment slowly lifted his features. "You're probably right."

"I'm definitely right. She'll miss you. You'll see, she'll be here more than she's there. Duke too, although perhaps not quite so much now that he found a new friend on the estate."

Brockwell raised his eyebrows in question.

"One of the farmer's daughters has been paying him a lot of attention on our visits."

Matt entered the room, a precious bundle in his arms and Aunt Letitia beside him. "He's changed and ready to travel." He was about to pass the bundle to me, but Catherine asked if she could hold him.

She pulled faces at little Gabriel in an attempt to get him to smile, but he simply blinked his blue eyes at her and gurgled. He wasn't quite at the smiling stage yet, although Matt was convinced he had once, right before Gabriel broke wind.

"You're going to be a wonderful mother," I told her.

"Right now, I'm more worried about the birth. Please tell me it's not that bad."

"It's not that bad."

She cocked her head to the side and regarded me. "You could at least try to instill some sincerity into it."

"Very well, I'll tell you the truth. It's horrible and frightening, but at the end, you have a beautiful angel to hold in your arms." I stroked my finger over Gabriel's soft cheek. Nothing was as smooth as a baby's skin. "It'll all be worth it. You'll see."

"I'm not looking forward to it."

"As soon as you go into labor, you must send word to Rycroft Hall. I'll come as quickly as I can."

She leaned closer to me. "Thank you, India. You are a true friend. Just like our little ones will be. And if I have a girl, perhaps they'll be closer than friends."

I grinned. "I do hope so. That will save me worrying about what sort of family Gabriel marries into."

Catherine's baby kicked and she asked me to take Gabriel from her while she rubbed her belly.

"Would you like to hold him, Willie?" I asked, offering her the bundle.

She pulled a face. "I'll spend time with him when he can walk and talk."

"You will *not* teach him to swear," Aunt Letitia said snippily.

"Only in American. I'm going to teach him to shoot, too."

"I'll teach him to ride," Duke added. "And how to play poker."

Cyclops rested his hand on Catherine's shoulder. "And I'll teach him to ignore everything you two say."

Chronos limped in, leaning heavily on his walking stick, and brought Lord Farnsworth with him. "Found him lurking in the entrance hall."

"I wasn't lurking," Farnsworth said with a sniff. "The front door was open and there wasn't a servant in sight. I wasn't sure what to do with my hat or coat." He indicated the hat in his left hand and the coat slung over his arm. "I'll just place them here, shall I?" He set them down on one of the tables and sniffed again.

"Are you crying?" Willie asked.

"This is a sad day."

Oh dear. It looked as though I was going to have to have the same conversation with him that I'd had with Brockwell. But it was Brockwell who stepped into the role of consoler. He placed his arm around Lord Farnsworth's shoulders and gave him a manly hug.

"Want to go out drinking tonight and drown our sorrows?"

Lord Farnsworth brightened. "I say, what a grand idea! Imagine the sort of trouble I can get away with having a Scotland Yard detective at my side."

Brockwell chuckled, not looking the least shocked. He'd changed since we'd first met him. While he still employed an abundance of caution in his work, he was no longer as rigid in his private life.

"Isn't Lady Helen returning to London soon?" Duke asked.

Lord Farnsworth lifted a shoulder in a casual shrug. "If she is, it's nothing to do with me. She told me I was too ridiculous for her and she wants a husband she can be proud of. She did say we can still have fun together, but I don't think I'm all that inclined to associate with someone who thinks I'm a joke."

Matt and I exchanged small smiles.

"You'd do well to stay clear of her," Aunt Letitia said. "Her aunt, Lady Sloane, confided in me that she suspects the girl has been kissed *thoroughly*."

Willie feigned shock. "Diabolical!"

Aunt Letitia nodded knowingly. "If word gets out, she'll be ruined, so do keep it between us. I wouldn't want to be the instrument of her downfall. The girl is very sweet and quite reserved, and we shouldn't let one mistake put an end to what could be a bright future."

Duke snorted. "Reserved?"

Willie stood on his foot.

"Anyway." Lord Farnsworth flourished his hand in the air, as if conjuring a magic trick. "I have decided to remain a bachelor a while longer. I'll spend my evenings with my good friend, Jasper." He slapped Brockwell on the shoulder. "We'll drink, gamble, and get up to all sorts of mischief."

Willie pouted and I half expected her to change her mind then and there and not leave with us.

Matt left to tell the servants we were ready to depart. While we waited, Chronos asked if he could hold the baby so I placed Gabriel in his arms. A little hand emerged from the blanket and I tucked it back inside, but not before I touched each one of his tiny fingers. He was perfect in every way.

"I never held your father like this when he was a babe," Chronos said as he gazed down at his great grandson. "Your grandmother never let me. She said babies were women's business. It's a shame, that."

I stroked Gabriel's forehead with my thumb. "A very great shame indeed. But you can hold him whenever you wish. I hope you'll teach him all about timepieces when he's older."

"Just as soon as his fingers can hold a pair of tweezers,

we'll be taking apart his watch." Chronos had given Gabriel a set of his own tools as a Christening gift. Matt and I had given him a watch engraved with his initials inside the Rycroft family crest. I'd wanted Marianne Folgate to create the silver cover and do the etching, but Matt said he couldn't find her. She'd moved from her Wimbledon residence and left no forwarding address.

"I wonder how his magic will manifest itself," Chronos said. He meant it innocently enough, but whenever I thought about the magic my body absorbed while in the early stages of pregnancy, panic set in.

But it eased just as quickly. Gabriel was healthy, his development where it ought to be at six weeks of age. The magic had not affected him in any obvious way.

"I think he'll be more powerful than you, India. I can tell from his eyes. He has Steele eyes."

"Nonsense. He has Matt's eyes."

Chronos sighed. "Let's just hope he doesn't have your husband's lack of magic too." He passed Gabriel back to me. "But if he doesn't possess magic, I'll still teach him to fix a watch in under five minutes."

Matt returned and announced we were set. Chronos pushed to his feet with the aid of his walking stick and followed the others out of the drawing room. Matt offered me his hand and assisted me to stand.

"Ready?" he asked.

I looked around the room and felt somewhat unsteady as nostalgia washed over me. So much had happened in this house. We'd shared our first kiss, fallen in love, laughed, cried and almost died, and welcomed our son into the world. The house was a part of us and our history together. But it was just a house. Our *home* was wherever the other lived, and baby Gabriel. Mostly that would be at Rycroft Hall, but sometimes it would be here.

And sometimes it would be all over the country when we decided to travel, or even overseas. Our health was good, the magic in our watches strong, and I saw no reason not to visit other continents, although I would feel better if Gabe Seaford came with us. We'd not seen much of him and Nancy since his namesake's birth. They'd been busy at the hospital, and we had a baby to occupy us and a move to organize.

Matt placed his arm around me and drew me into a hug. With a contented sigh, I kissed the spot on his throat where the blood flowed powerfully through his veins, pumped by a heart so big it needed magic to help it. Gabe's magic.

My magic.

We were the same now, Matt and me. Sometimes, when I placed my palm over his chest, our heartbeats synchronized. The rhythm was always steady, always strong. We needed our watches to survive, and we'd both come to terms with that.

We needed each other too, and our son.

With Gabriel falling asleep in my arms, we took one last wistful look around the drawing room then together we stepped into the next phase of our lives.

Author's Note:

This is the end of the Glass and Steele series. Thank you for coming on this journey with me. I have loved writing about India, Matt and their friends. From the moment Matt threw India over his shoulder and stormed out of her shop, I knew they were special. This may be the end of their story, but it's not the end for all the characters. There is a spin-off series featuring their son, Gabriel, and a librarian with a secret past. Set twenty-eight years after THE GOLDSMITH'S CONSPIRACY ends, The Glass Library series has all the adventure, magic, mystery and romance of Glass and Steele. You'll also see what some of your favorite characters got up to in the intervening years. To decide if the new series is something you'll enjoy, read an excerpt of THE LIBRARIAN OF CROOKED LANE, book one of The Glass Library series, on my website at CJARCHER.COM.

Available from 6th September 2022:
THE LIBRARIAN OF CROOKED LANE
The 1st book in The Glass Library series

Turn the page to read an excerpt.

EXCERPT: THE LIBRARIAN OF CROOKED LANE

THE GLASS LIBRARY BOOK 1

About this Book

A librarian with a mysterious past, a war hero with a secret, and the heist of a magic painting. THE LIBRARIAN OF CROOKED LANE is an intriguing new fantasy from C.J. Archer, the USA Today bestselling author of the Glass and Steele series.

Librarian Sylvia Ashe knows nothing about her past, having grown up without a father and a mother who refused to discuss him. When she stumbles upon a diary that suggests she's descended from magicians, she's skeptical. After all, magicians are special, and she's just an ordinary woman who loves books. She seeks answers from a member of the most prominent family of magicians, but she quickly learns that finding the truth won't be easy, especially when he turns out to be as artless as her, and more compelling and dangerous than books.

War hero Gabe is gifted with wealth, a loving family, and an incredible amount of luck that saw him survive four harrowing years of a brutal war without injury. But not all injuries are visible. Burying himself in his work as a consultant for Scotland Yard, Gabe is going through the motions as he investigates the theft of a magician-made painting. But his life changes when he unwittingly gets Sylvia dismissed from her job and places her in danger.

After securing her new employment in a library housing the world's greatest collection of books about magic, Gabe and Sylvia's lives become intwined as they work together to find both the painting and the truth about Sylvia's past before powerful people can stop them.

But sometimes the past is better left buried…

Chapter 1

London, Spring 1920

The woman crouching under the desk near my feet expelled an unladylike snort of derision.

I stilled. I didn't dare urge her to keep quiet with a nudge of my boot for fear that Mr. Parmiter, the head librarian, would notice. At the sound of the snort, he'd turned back and scrutinized me yet again. He had a way of making me feel like a speck under a microscope. Moments ago, he'd pressed both palms on the desk, leaned in until his face was close to mine, and inspected me with all the rigor of a detective searching for evidence at a crime scene.

Indeed, Mr. Parmiter's initial scrutiny had come about because he did suspect me of a crime. The crime of wearing makeup. According to the library charter, which I'd never seen, female staff were forbidden from adding so much as a smudge of color to their cheeks. Although I was sure the rule never existed since I was the first female employee, I didn't question him. I simply informed him I was not wearing makeup. He'd sniffed, as if trying to smell a lie, then turned away.

Until Daisy had gone and snorted like a bull at a red rag.

Mr. Parmiter scrutinized me again, but this time he stood a foot back from the desk. "Are you unwell, Miss Ashe?"

"No," I said. "I was just clearing my throat."

Those beady eyes of his narrowed further. He moistened his lips with a lizard-like flicker of his tongue, dampening the overhanging gray moustache. I wouldn't have been surprised if he reached across the desk to touch my forehead, checking for a fever, but the fear of getting too close held him back. I couldn't blame him for that. The Spanish flu had recently wreaked devastation and we all worried it would return.

"You should go home if you feel unwell," he said.

"I feel fine."

He waved a hand at my face. "And remove that vile stuff. This is a respectable institution where gentlemen of learning come for quiet study. Attractive women are a distraction. If it were up to me, I wouldn't have employed someone like you, but needs must." This last sentence he muttered as he walked off.

Thankfully Daisy didn't emit another snort. She was probably too shocked and angry to speak. I was just as angry but not shocked. In the two months since I'd taken the position of assistant librarian at the London Philosophical Society's library, I'd been exposed to Mr. Parmiter's misogyny on a regular basis. He blamed young women for just about every ill that had ever befallen him—or the world in general. I'm sure he could find a way to blame us for the war if he put his mind to it.

"It's safe," I whispered.

Daisy crawled out from the desk's footwell and cast a disdainful look in the direction in which Mr. Parmiter had departed. She hadn't seen him leave; it was the only exit from the reading nook. I was using the empty desk to inspect some old books for signs of disrepair. Tucked away on the first floor, between the stacks, it was the perfect place for quiet research—or hiding from one's manager while chatting to a friend who shouldn't be in the library at all. Daisy was not a member of the London Philosophical Society. She wasn't at all philosophical, not even after drinking too many cocktails. A drunk Daisy was a giggling Daisy, not terribly unlike a sober Daisy.

But she wasn't giggling now as she perched herself on the edge of the desk and regarded me with a frown. "What did he mean when he said he wouldn't have employed 'someone like you, but needs must?'"

I balanced the book on pragmatism on both my hands then closed it with a satisfying *thunk* of its thick pages and heavy leather cover. The smell of old paper wafted up, causing Daisy to cover her nose. I breathed the scent deeply into my lungs. "There were no other suitable applicants for the position of assistant librarian," I told her. "He had to resort to hiring a *female*." I rolled my eyes and gave a wry laugh.

"Really? Even with all the returned soldiers looking for work?"

"There were other applicants, but according to Mr. Parmiter, none were *suitable*. There were three others, in fact, all returned from the war. One was blind in one eye, another was missing a leg, and the third had shattered nerves that saw him jump at any loud noise. Mr. Parmiter claimed he couldn't employ them because they are a distressing reminder of the war and will put off the Society's members."

"He truly said that?"

I nodded.

"After everything those poor souls have been through, and now they have to endure the sneers of people like Priggy Parmiter. And to imply you're only attractive when you're wearing makeup! The nerve of him." The heat with which she said it was on par with her defense of the returned soldiers. To Daisy, the two wrongs were equally abhorrent. "You're pretty, Sylvia, and don't let a dusty old bore like him tell you otherwise."

I thanked her for the compliment, but to be quite honest, I was no beauty. Not like Daisy, with her blue eyes and strawberry-blonde hair cut into a wavy bob that framed her face. The style was very modern, but in the few short months I'd known her, I'd come to realize Daisy followed trends like winter follows autumn—inevitably. She never settled for very long before moving on to the next thing that caught her eye. Her desire to try new things was understandable. I didn't blame her for shrugging off the heavy blanket that had shrouded the nation after four years of war and another one and a half of the flu. Sometimes the bleakness had seemed as though it would never end. But despite their personal losses, some people were ready to move on. Daisy *needed* to move forward with her life.

I hadn't quite reached that point yet.

"Speaking of dusty…" Daisy wrinkled her nose as she pushed away the book I'd been about to inspect for damage. One of the pages had come loose and the corners of several others had been turned over to act as a bookmark. The thin layer of dust on it bothered Daisy more.

It had been on the desk for some time, waiting for a librarian to tend to it. Years ago, someone had collected all the books in the library that looked as though they might need to be sent away for repairs and piled them up on this desk in the remotest reading nook in the building. Then war had broken out, the assistant librarian had died on the battlefields of France, and no one had been employed in his stead until I started work in March. Filling a dead man's shoes wasn't easy, particularly when Mr. Parmiter made it clear my gender meant my work was inferior to my predecessor's, but I enjoyed it when he wasn't bothering me.

It was quiet. Few members came into the library and when they did, they preferred to speak to Mr. Parmiter rather than me. The job didn't pay particularly well, but I could walk to work, saving myself the cost of transport. I also got to chat to Daisy, when she wasn't in her flat painting—which seemed to be most afternoons—and when she wasn't hiding from Mr. Parmiter who came upstairs to check on me from time to time.

Daisy watched me as I gently opened the book she'd pushed away. "If you must work in a library, why not work in a modern one with novels?"

"With all the returning soldiers resuming their previous employment, there are few jobs for women. I was fortunate to get this one."

She sighed. "It's a pity you have to work at all, really."

I looked up, frowning. She looked back at me with sympathy. "Don't *you* have to?" I asked.

"Oh yes, but we artists don't have a schedule like regular people. We work when the muse strikes. Besides, I was left a little money by my grandparents. It keeps me going."

It was the first time she'd mentioned an inheritance. Daisy's parents lived in Wiltshire and didn't approve of their middle child moving to London. She had an older sister who'd lost her husband in the war and a younger brother who'd signed up upon turning eighteen in 1918. Thankfully he survived.

"I actually like working," I said, and I meant it.

Whether Daisy believed me or not, I never found out. She became distracted by a newspaper discarded on a small table beside the armchair. She flounced into the chair and began to read.

I sat too and made notes on the damage to the books, sorting them into different piles according to the type of repairs required. For the many pages with dog-eared corners,

I smoothed out the creases with my thumb. It was easy and relaxing work. Although the topics didn't particularly interest me, it was satisfying to know these books would once again be read and valued by the society's members thanks to my efforts today.

"He is the prime article," Daisy murmured from the armchair. She folded the newspaper in half and turned it to show me what she'd been reading. I couldn't make out much from this distance, however, just a dark-haired man standing on the deck of a yacht. "Handsome, rich, the heir to a title *and* a war hero. So many virtues in one man."

"None of those are virtues, Daisy, except for perhaps being a war hero. He could be selfish and vain for all we know."

"You're so unromantic, Sylvia."

I picked up the book on pragmatism and waved it at her. "Perhaps I've worked here too long." I smiled but she took me seriously.

"I'm glad you finally agree."

"I was referring to this title. I've only been here two months."

"Long enough." She glanced around, worried our conversation was being overheard. "If it weren't for me, your days would drag."

I laughed. Daisy's unfailing self-confidence had won me over when we met. If I could bottle it, I would take a sip whenever I felt my own confidence waning.

She studied the newspaper article again. "I wonder if he's married."

"If not, he soon will be. A paragon like that won't be single for long. The unmarried women of England won't allow it." One of the saddest outcomes of war was that it took young men. Now that we were emerging from the fog, women my age were bemoaning the lack of eligible bachelors.

I was not among them. I was still shrouded by the fog. I'd not only lost my brother in the war, but my mother succumbed to the flu pandemic that had struck down so many in the war's aftermath. They'd been my only family. I'd also left behind friends when I moved to London. Not that I had many friends to lose. We'd moved too often to put down deep roots anywhere.

But I was determined to make a go of it in London. In the two and a half months since my arrival, I'd made a friend in Daisy and found gainful employment. It was a foundation I could build on to help me climb out of the fog, in time.

"What has the paragon done to warrant an article written about him?" I asked.

"He attempted to rescue a fisherman and his teenage son while out sailing off the coast of the Isle of Wight. Apparently he saw their boat capsize and didn't hesitate to dive in and risk his life to save them. They were tangled up in their net under water and he had to cut it to free them. The son survived but the father didn't."

"How awful."

"The article says it was a miracle Mr. Glass didn't drown too. It then goes on to list all the medals he won in the war. Good lord."

I peered over her shoulder. "What is it?"

"He joined up at the start of the war and survived the entire four years on the front lines. He was there for every major battle, and he didn't once get seriously injured."

"Then he couldn't have been in *every* major battle for the entire duration. Besides, the heir to a title would be given something safe to do well away from the enemy."

"Not according to this. Gallipoli, the Somme, Ypres, Amiens…he fought in them all. His parents must have been beside themselves with worry. It says here he is the only child of Lord and Lady Rycroft."

I read over her shoulder. "'Mr. Gabriel Glass, Baron and Baroness of Rycroft. Lady Rycroft is the famed magician, India Glass, nee Steele.'"

"Where can a girl meet such a man?"

"The Isle of Wight, apparently." I returned to the desk but instead of picking up a book, I stared out of the window. The view wasn't interesting, just the dark gray buildings opposite and a thin layer of cloudy sky above the roofline. I hardly registered any of it. My mind was elsewhere. "Daisy, does the name India Glass mean anything to you?"

She shook her head. "No, but I'm not a magician, nor can I afford to buy magical objects. I'm trying to make the inheritance last, and I'm yet to sell a painting."

"Does the article say anything else about her?"

"Just that she gave up practicing watchmaking magic to marry Lord Rycroft and has been an advisor to the government on magician policies for years. Why? Have you heard of her?"

"The name rings a bell." I just couldn't remember why. The memory was there in my mind, just out of reach, buried in the fog.

***

I lay on my back on the narrow bed in the room I rented at the lodging house and stared at the water stain on the ceiling. I felt tired but pushed against it, wading through the fog as I searched for the name.

India Glass.

Where had I seen it? I knew I'd *seen* it, not heard it. That meant it had appeared in a letter or an article, but I rarely read the newspaper, so it must be private correspondence. There was only one person who ever wrote to me. One person whose letters I'd kept.

I pushed the chair up against the wardrobe and stood on it, rising onto my toes to reach, cursing my short stature. Fortunately, the suitcase was light. I managed to grasp it without pulling the entire thing down on my head. It was a child's suitcase made of tan leather, small enough for a young girl to drag around the country. And drag it I had. Frequent moves accounted for the scratches and patchwork of dents. I opened it on the bed and stared at the remaining contents of my mother's and brother's lives.

I'd kept her favorite shawl, made of emerald green silk with Japanese motifs embroidered throughout, as well as a plain silver ring, two enamel hair combs and some old photographs of James and me as children. James's belongings were just as meager. I'd not seen any point bringing his old clothes with me so I'd sold them before leaving for London. I'd needed the money. I set aside his pocket watch, war medal, and notebook. I plucked out the two packets of letters, both tied with string. One packet was thick and contained dozens of letters written by my mother and me to James. He'd kept them all, and they'd been returned to us after his death. The other packet contained letters he'd sent to us. I untied the string around them and lightly caressed the topmost envelope.

The sight of his neat, precise handwriting brought a fierce ache to my chest.

I read each letter but didn't find any reference to India Glass. Perhaps I'd misremembered or I'd seen the name elsewhere.

I retied the string and, with a heavy sigh, placed the letters back into the suitcase, wedged between the notebook and the back.

I removed the notebook and flipped it open. It had been with James a long time. The leather cover was scratched and faded from its original forest green to the color of a muddy puddle. The pages were crinkled from being damp and drying out, making the whole book fatter than it would have been when new. My brother's dirty fingerprints appeared on almost every page, and the once white paper was now brown from the mud of the Western Front. I'd read the notebook cover to cover after it was returned to us before storing it in the suitcase with his other belongings. With Mother becoming ill and dying, then contracting the flu myself, I'd forgotten about it and not looked at it since. Reading James's words had been painful then, so soon after losing him. It was still painful now, but the initial sharp ache dulled to a throb as I became lost in my search for the name.

India Glass.

I scanned the pages, not wanting to read every word. That would only make the ache in my chest swell again. The pages were filled with James's thoughts, some forming complete sentences, others merely fragments of ideas in the form of single words or a sketch. He'd been a good artist.

I found the name near the end. It was on a line of its own and didn't form part of a sentence. It was just those two words, India Glass, which I'd thought meant glass from India when I first read it, perhaps referring to a vase or trinket. I'd not wondered why my brother would be making notes on glassware from a country he'd never been to, but back then, I'd been too grief stricken to think clearly about anything.

Knowing the words were in fact a name gave the notes above and below it new meaning. When I'd first read them, I'd been shocked to learn my brother thought he was a silversmith magician, simply because he liked silver things. Who didn't like silver things? I was partial to jewelry set in silver, but I preferred gold. I owned neither, unless I counted the silver band of my mother's. Magic couldn't possibly run in our blood. We were unremarkable. Mother had been a seamstress, James a teacher, and I'd written articles for several local newspapers and journals before that work dried up when the soldiers returned in large numbers. Female journalists were once again relegated to the sections on cookery, housekeeping and fashion, none being topics in which I could claim any expertise or flair. The Ashes weren't craftspeople. We were just a family with dissimilar interests.

I fought back tears as I removed Mother's ring from the suitcase and slipped it on my finger. It fit my middle one. It was simple, plain and thin, not a special item at all. I felt nothing as I touched it. Wasn't I supposed to feel something if it had silver magic in it? Or did only other magicians feel magic?

I didn't know how it worked. I couldn't afford magician-made things, so I'd never bothered to learn about magic.

I returned to the notebook. According to James's notes, he'd asked Mother about silver magic, and she'd told him he was mistaken and to not bring it up again.

Below the name India Glass he'd written the word

"Answers" followed by a question mark. Answers to what? To the question of whether the Ashe family could perform silver magic?

I closed the book and returned it and the suitcase to the space above the wardrobe. I fell asleep and thought no more about India Glass, silver magic, or my brother until the following morning when I returned to the reading nook on the first floor of the library and spotted the newspaper Daisy had been reading.

"War hero saves boy in miraculous underwater rescue" the attention-grabbing headline read.

The image of the brave rescuer stared back at the camera. Gabriel Glass looked a little annoyed by the attention, as if he wanted to shout at the journalists to leave him alone. As a former journalist, I'd been told to go away many times. I'd lacked the confidence to insist where my colleagues had persisted. It was probably why I was one of the first women to lose their jobs when the journalists-turned-soldiers returned from the war.

I placed the newspaper in the desk drawer and worked until Daisy snuck into the library. When she flopped into the armchair with a dramatic sigh of boredom, I handed it to her.

She frowned. "Are you trying to tell me something?"

"I want to meet his mother, India Glass—Lady Rycroft."

She sat up straight. "If you think the way to a man is through his mother, you know even less about men than I thought you did."

I bristled. "I know as much about men as you, Daisy."

She battled with a smile. "Dear, sweet Sylvia, have you exchanged more than a 'good afternoon' with a single man since arriving in London?" I opened my mouth to answer her, but she put up a finger to stop me. "Priggy Parmiter doesn't count."

I snatched the newspaper from her. "I'm not interested in meeting Gabriel Glass. I'm interested in his mother."

"Lady Rycroft? Why?"

Footsteps on the staircase cut off my answer. "Blast. Hide, Daisy, quickly."

She dove into the cavity under the desk, tucking her legs into her body. I stood behind the desk, blocking the view to the cavity as best as I could in case Mr. Parmiter decided to come around to my side.

I smiled and pretended to listen as the head librarian complained about a particular member who hadn't returned a book that was now well overdue. I was actually thinking about my brother's claim that he might be a silver magician and our mother's denial. Although I agreed with my mother, I felt as though I owed it to James's memory to find out, once and for all. If he believed India Glass could provide answers then I would do everything I could to speak with her.

But first I had to find her.

*You can read a longer excerpt on CJ's website:
CJARCHER.COM

Available from 6th September 2022:
THE LIBRARIAN OF CROOKED LANE
The 1st book in The Glass Library series

GET A FREE SHORT STORY

I wrote a short story for the Glass and Steele series that is set before THE WATCHMAKER'S DAUGHTER. Titled THE TRAITOR'S GAMBLE it features Matt and his friends in the Wild West town of Broken Creek. It contains spoilers from THE WATCHMAKER'S DAUGHTER, so you must read that first. The best part is, the short story is FREE, but only to my newsletter subscribers. So subscribe now via my website CJARCHER.COM if you haven't already.

A MESSAGE FROM THE AUTHOR

I hope you enjoyed reading THE GOLDSMITH'S CONSPIRACY as much as I enjoyed writing it. As an independent author, getting the word out about my book is vital to its success, so if you liked this book please consider telling your friends and writing a review at the store where you purchased it. If you would like to be contacted when I release a new book, subscribe to my newsletter at http://cjarcher.com/contact-cj/newsletter/. You will only be contacted when I have a new book out.

ABOUT THE AUTHOR

C.J. Archer has loved history and books for as long as she can remember and feels fortunate that she found a way to combine the two. She spent her early childhood in the dramatic beauty of outback Queensland, Australia, but now lives in suburban Melbourne with her husband, two children and a mischievous black & white cat named Coco.

facebook.com/CJArcherAuthorPage
twitter.com/cj_archer
instagram.com/authorcjarcher
bookbub.com/authors/c-j-archer

Printed in Great Britain
by Amazon